Fledgling Space Pilots in
a Battle for Earth's Destiny . . .

"I'm here because I've been in a knife fight with 'em," McQueen said, ". . . and survived. Now listen up. They come at you in groups, so check your six. They have a low angle of attack, so keep your nose level. That could be tough since the flyers you've been issued have an upgripe in the retro thrusters. And one more thing . . ."

The grizzled vet lowered his voice so that the cadets had to lean forward to listen.

"It's okay to be afraid."

Books by Peter Telep

Space: Above and Beyond

Squire
Squire's Blood
Squire's Honor*

*coming soon

SPACE:
ABOVE AND BEYOND

PETER TELEP

HarperPrism
An Imprint of HarperPaperbacks

HarperPaperbacks   *A Division of* HarperCollins*Publishers*
10 East 53rd Street, New York, N.Y. 10022

Back cover photo: Jason Boland and Paul Broben

First printing: October 1995

Printed in the United States of America

HarperPrism is an imprint of HarperPaperbacks. HarperPaperbacks, HarperPrism, and colophon are trademarks of HarperCollins*Publishers.*

❖ 10 9 8 7 6 5 4 3 2 1

This novel is dedicated to:
Nicholas Zahn, Corporal, Retired, United States
Marine Corps, 13th Defense Battalion

*Because he soldiered his way through my
teenage years and kept me squared away.*

ACKNOWLEDGMENTS

Glen Morgan and James Wong have written for and produced such shows as *21 Jump Street* and *The Commish*. Barbara Kantrowitz and Adam Rogers of *Newsweek* said they wrote "some of the most compelling episodes" of *The X-Files*. Their teleplay, on which this novel is based, was another example of their exciting and inventive work. I am pleased to be able to thank them for it here.

Lise Vansen at the production office answered my many questions and provided me with the photographs and artwork I needed to keep this novel as accurate as possible.

I'm indebted to the folks at HarperPrism: John Silbersack, Christopher Schelling, and Caitlin Blasdell for choosing me for this project. Their trust and faith is deeply appreciated.

My agent, Robert Drake, did what he does best and did it quickly. I describe this as "bing-a-da-bang-a-da-boom" contract negotiations.

Mr. Ken Nuckols served as my first reader. He went through the text line by line and any errors you may find are his. Seriously, Mr. Nuckols spent many hours helping me to polish the manuscript which was written under a tight deadline. I hope to return the favor on his novel.

My wife, Nancy, was a trooper. She suffered through dinners listening to me tell her how many pages I wrote each day and what challenges faced me the next. I admire her patience. I know it's hard living with a man whose body is present but whose mind is somewhere in the Epsilon Eridani star system.

SPACE:
ABOVE AND
BEYOND

prologue

Possibilities.

Lovell knew about possibilities, about losing them and about finding them. He had once defined his life as a bet that had not paid off. One too many relationships and ten times too many manual-labor jobs had siphoned away his will. He had grown tired, tired of searching for something that would make him happy. And for a time he had existed. Nothing more.

But one night his car had broken down, and he and his blond mutt had been forced to walk five kilometers down a stretch of lonely, dark farm road. It had been then that he realized—finally realized—that he couldn't live without being happy. He had looked forward and had looked back, and there had been only darkness.

Then he had looked to the sky. And they had been there. And he had seen them as if for the first time. Stars, a perfect celestial field, neither fettered by clouds nor choked by light pollution. Lovell had laughed out loud, realizing how ridiculous he looked standing in the middle of the road, staring slack-jawed into space. But when his laughter had subsided, and he had turned and continued his walk, he had come to know for the first time in many years that a possibility had been before him.

Now, twenty-one months later, he and his dog stood on alien soil. He wiped his sweaty palms on the hips of his rust-colored flight overalls, then resumed holding hands with Jax and the woman to his right. As the wind picked up, hinting of the scent of jasmine and causing the hair on the back of his neck to stand, Lovell let his gaze play over the 250 men, women, and children of the Vesta Colony Mission who had gathered to listen to Colonial Governor Borman. He glanced past the crowd to the thick jungle that stretched to horizon. Above the trees, where orange and mauve should have been, was a strange violet twilight superimposed by brilliant planetary rings that arced across the sky. A single full moon, ice-blue and not exactly round, hung low but followed an ecliptic that took it much higher in the sky than Earth's satellite. For Lovell, Vesta was a place of eerie beauty, and it already felt like home.

"Incredible, isn't it?" Jax observed.

"Yes," he answered without looking at her. "Actually, I was seeing another night in my mind. I guess it's moments like this that make a person reminisce."

"Judging from what you told me back on the cutter, coming here is the smartest thing you've done in a long time."

He gazed on her and smiled. "Are you calling me stupid?"

She returned a grin of her own, a *very* nice one. "You know what I mean. We've all made mistakes."

"And what mistakes have you made?" he asked, then squeezed her hand.

She squeezed back. "True, I haven't said much. But we'll have time later." She gestured with her head. "Here comes the governor."

Lovell watched as Governor Borman strode to a position in the front of the group, turned to face everyone, then cleared his throat. If Borman was a day over forty he didn't look it, and there was a glimmer in his eyes that spoke volumes of his determination. Lovell averted his gaze at the sound of a whimper from his dog.

"What's the matter, Captain Krunch?"

"Captain Krunch?" Jax asked incredulously. "What kind of a name is that for—"

Lovell cut her off with a sigh. "It's a long story." He

released his grip on Jax's hand then patted the dog. The mutt wagged his tail and kept his attention focused on the sky. Jax took Lovell's hand in her own.

"Tonight we stand beneath a new heaven," Borman began. "After one hundred and fifty years of calling out, the silence of the universe assures us that life on Earth is unique. We are . . . alone."

There was something, well, *lonely* about Borman's words. Lovell wanted to believe that there was another race out there, a race that knew the secret to discovering and maintaining happiness and could teach that incredible knowledge to humans. Admittedly, it was hard to argue against one hundred and fifty years of silence, but that silence would not douse Lovell's hope.

The governor shifted his weight, then cleared his throat once again. "You and I are among the first to bring life to the stars, to this planet, the farthest any humans have ever ventured."

Captain Krunch let out a bark. Many of the colonists looked to the mutt, and a few half-grinned. Lovell felt his face warm with embarrassment.

"He's barking because Borman forgot to mention him," Jax said softly.

Lovell nudged the dog with his foot. The mutt turned around and sat on his hind legs, facing Lovell. "Good. Now you stay there and be quiet." He looked up—into Borman's gaze. He mouthed "I'm sorry."

Borman nodded slightly, then closed his eyes. "The light that shines from this new sun will not touch our old home for another sixteen years." The governor opened his eyes, then paused.

Lovell considered Borman's words. He was *sixteen light-years* from home, standing on a planet in the Epsilon Eridani star system. Though the governor had just reminded him of that fact, it was still well-nigh impossible to comprehend the distance.

"Unlike that light . . . we cannot go back. We can only move forward." The governor swallowed, then blinked hard several times, fighting back what had to be a surge of emotions. "I know there are those back home who say we're only here as a status symbol. Others call us fortune hunters or say that we're running away. But I know we're here because of faith, a faith in each other, in a better world."

Out of the corner of his eye, Lovell caught a tear sliding down Jax's cheek. Instead of turning to her, he allowed her the moment and kept his gaze on Borman; as he did so, he felt his own eyes grow moist.

Borman continued. "The rocket fuel that brought us here can be burned away, but the belief in ourselves, in one another—in the future—never can be. Never will be."

A man Lovell recognized as the pilot of the cutter stepped up to Borman and handed him a flagpole. The pilot resumed his position in the crowd. Borman paused a moment before lifting the flag, studying it with reverence. Then the governor stabbed the flagpole into the soil. A white flag with a blue Earth in it unfurled in the Vestan wind.

The colonists around Lovell took the flag's presence as their cue to let out a cheer. The woman to Lovell's left, a slim brunette who was probably in her twenties, pulled him toward her. Lovell released Jax's hand and found himself in an embrace with the girl. She hugged him hard, then thrust him backward, keeping her hands on his shoulders. Lovell saw that the name patch on her flight overalls read: TISHA, JOAN.

"Oh, what a rush!" she said, then looked at his name patch. "Lovell. Does that mean you have a will to love?"

Immediately Lovell knew that she was *not* one of the engineers responsible for designing the ship that had carried them to Vesta. "Uh, I'm not sure."

"Oh," she said, her cheeks flushing. She let her hands slide off his shoulders. "Well, I bet you do. It's nice to meet you."

Lovell detected the weight of a hand at the base of

his neck. He turned to see Jax move in next to him. She took his arm in hers, and suddenly Lovell felt nervous.

"It's nice to meet you, too, Tisha," Jax said. "Now if you'll excuse us." Jax pulled Lovell away from the young woman and steered him through the dissipating crowd. Captain Krunch fell in at Lovell's side.

"I didn't know we were an 'us,'" Lovell said.

Jax tossed her head to remove some golden locks that had strayed into one of her eyes, then lifted her brow. "You didn't?"

He shook his head no. "Does that mean we are?"

"Maybe," she said, then started away. "Come on, let's get something to eat."

Lovell groaned. "I hate it when they're coy." He regarded Captain Krunch. "Don't you, boy?"

The mutt wagged his tail fiercely, licked his chops, then barked.

For two Vestan months, the equivalent of two and a half Earth months, Lovell helped build the settlement. The cutter's fuselage, an enormous structure which lay on its side in the clearing of the lush tropical rain forest they had chosen for their home, was utilized as a storage warehouse. Though in the years to come they would build permanent dwellings, for now they lived out of prefab Quonset huts arrayed about the cutter like tin cans lying on their sides, half-buried in the soil. Lovell participated in the raising of the satellite dish, a project that should have been accomplished in one day, but one that had taken the team of five nearly a week.

Of the sixteen rovers that had been packed for the journey, all but one was functional. There was something wrong with the transmission on the vehicle, a defect that had been present before loading. Lovell suggested they cannibalize the rover for spare parts. Borman agreed.

Lovell shared nearly every meal with Jax. Though she

was busy with her geological studies, she always found time for him. He knew they were destined to become lovers, but thus far *he* was the one holding back. What scared him was the fact that if their relationship didn't work out, there was nowhere to run. One planet. One settlement. And he knew he would hate the awkwardness of having to occasionally be in her presence.

But her wanted her. Badly.

After one particularly long day of serving on a construction team, Lovell skipped dinner, went back to his hut and collapsed on his cot. He shared the hut with fifteen other colonists, all of whom were, thankfully, away. He knew Jax would be upset with him, but he would make her understand. He dug his back deeper into the cot and closed his eyes. Then he felt Captain Krunch leap onto the bed. The dog used his muzzle to drive Lovell's legs to one side of the bed.

"Oh, come on, dog, can't you sleep on the floor?"

But the Captain would do no such thing. He found a spot and settled down, resting his chin on one of Lovell's ankles.

Sometime during the night Lovell was awakened by a snarl from his mutt. He opened his eyes and focused on the clock at his bedside; it was 2:00 A.M.—early—even on a planet with thirty-hour days. Lovell cocked and lifted his head a little, then squinted at the window. A wedge of blue moonlight shone into the room and split the floor in two. The window's curtain, an old T-shirt hanging half-off, billowed in the wind. Something rose behind the curtain, something like steam or fog, but Lovell dismissed the image as a trick of his sleepy eyes. Captain Krunch rose shakily on the bed, then hopped off onto firm ground.

Lovell sat up and rubbed his eyes on the heels of his hands. "What now, Captain?"

The dog paused before the window; then uttered a

steady, foreboding growl that rose slightly in pitch but dramatically in volume.

Reluctantly, Lovell threw off his covers, scratched at his belly button, then got out of bed. He crossed gingerly to the window, swearing under his breath that he didn't have a pair of slippers to insulate his feet from the icy floor of the hut. "This had better be important," he told the dog.

Lovell rested an arm on the windowsill, looked right, then left, and saw no one outside the hut. He wasn't sure why, but he felt the impulse to look skyward. The tableau was peaceful . . . but then he saw something, and he felt his mouth open. Three horizontal slits of light, in formation, approached the settlement.

First thought: *We don't need any help. Why the hell did they send another team here? What the hell were they thinking?*

Second thought: *They wouldn't send another team. . . .*

Then he heard the thrusters of jets. It was a sound with attitude, an angry, malevolent sound that swelled and struck fear in Lovell. He detected something new in the air, a smell the likes of which he had never encountered. The closest thing he could compare it to was that of burning leaves.

He studied the slits of light, probing deeper into his memory, trying to draw angles from them, insignia, something. And in his next heartbeat they were visible: a squadron of black, triangular warplanes in a diamond attack formation. Lovell toyed with the idea that the planes were part of some top-secret military project, but at the same time that he tried to rationalize their presence, his heart told him they were not from Earth. The military would not spend that much money to put fighters this far out. The only people in the system were the colonists.

From somewhere outside came a thunderous approach of footsteps. As he turned away from the window, Lovell's mouth went dry and a knot formed in his stomach.

Jax!

Screams rose from the Quonset hut beside his. Lovell craned his neck, shot a look through window and saw colonists fleeing from the rear exit of the shelter. Above, a warplane swooped down, its engine howling, and let loose with a volley of laser fire that tore the hut into gleaming, sizzling ribbons of corrugated steel. Lovell's dog howled back at the roar of destruction.

By now, the other colonists were bolting from their cots, and Andrea, a biotech, rushed up to Lovell, her face a mask of fear and concern. "What's going on?"

"We're under attack," he said, the words sounding more like a question than a statement.

"Ohmygod . . . "

Lovell spun away from Andrea and started for the door. Jax's hut was only two down from his. He could make it.

A sound came from behind the door, a hissing, and Lovell froze.

The door blasted off its hinges and slammed onto the floor. Through an acrid-smelling cloud of smoke, an immense silhouette appeared and advanced into the threshold. Other silhouettes became visible behind it.

Then Lovell caught a glimpse of the thing. It was a flat, black and green creature, and because of the straight-lined patterns all over its body, Lovell assumed it was armored. *Somewhat* humanoid, it clenched in what could be called its hand the cylindrical device it had used on the door.

Lovell's dog bounded for the alien shock trooper.

Amid the screams of the colonists outside and inside the hut, Lovell heard his name. He looked over his shoulder and saw Jax standing in the rear doorway of the hut.

He shot a glance forward and saw his dog prepare to leap onto the shock trooper. The alien raised its weapon.

Lovell turned and ran toward the rear exit, but the other colonists clogged his path.

The last things he heard were a yelp from his dog and the *Shhhhhaaaa!* of the alien's weapon igniting.

Jax was hurtled five meters away from the rear doorway by the shock trooper's weapon. She collapsed onto her side, felt a fire in her hip, brushed it off, then rolled and stood. "Lovell," she said, her voice cracked and tremulous. Jax backed away from the hut, then in one fluid motion, turned and sprinted away.

She heard the demonic cry of an alien warplane, then laser fire paralleled both sides of her path. Dirt and stones shot into her legs from the barrage. She was between Quonset huts, and up ahead lay the relative safety of the jungle. A tremendous explosion sounded in the west. She looked right, just as the giant satellite dish exploded and toppled to the ground. Above it, alien warplanes swooped like metallic ravens over the treetops, flying in flocking formation, hunting. . . .

From within the hut to her right came the hysterical voice of a colonist. "Mayday! Mayday! This is the—"

A salvo of alien laser fire ended the man's message.

Jax rounded the corner of the hut, and there, in the distance, she caught sight of the Earth flag, flapping defiantly against a wall of flames. A shock trooper ran by the flag, then swung around, aimed its weapon and torched the emblem. *Bastards!* Jax felt a rush of air from behind her and came to a jarring halt. She looked over her shoulder and saw an alien warplane diving to zero in on her. The urge to duck passed instantly, for she knew that no matter what she did the alien would not miss. Every nerve in her body thundered. For a moment there was only the deafening thump of her heartbeat. Then the world became a place of intense heat and light.

one

"We are T-minus thirty seconds and counting . . . "
Nathan West was strapped tightly into his launch seat. He listened to the steady, feminine voice of the mission commander through his helmet's comlink. It didn't matter that Nathan had heard her run through the checklist over a dozen times in the past; each and every time her voice made his adrenaline pump.

"H_2 tank pressurization . . . "
Though wearing his flight suit, Nathan tried to scratch away the gooseflesh fanning across his left breast. He passed gloved fingers over the Tellus Colony Mission emblem on the suit, but wasn't getting anywhere near his icy chest.

"We are GO!" the EFT commander announced.
"T-minus twenty . . . Auxiliary Power Unit start . . . "
"GO!" the APU commander replied.
"T-minus fifteen seconds . . . Tellus, you have a GO for auto sequence start. Lock your visors and initiate O_2 flow . . . ten . . . "
Nathan pulled his clear helmet visor over his eyes. He engaged a knob on the helmet, allowing a gentle hiss of oxygen to flow. His heart raced, and he swore that if he were fifty-five instead of twenty-two his runaway pulse would be the end of him. He drew in a long, slow breath, then counted to himself along with the mission commander.

"Nine . . . eight . . . seven . . . "
He turned his head slightly right and looked across the other colonists seated next to him. Their flight suits

were, like his, centered with Earth flag patches, and, to someone making a cursory glance, the colonists looked alike, that is unless one focused on the faces. Among those faces Nathan found Kylen. She beamed at him from behind her visor, then gave him a subtle "thumbs up."

Kylen Celina. She was twenty-one and *the* one for Nathan. Period. Nathan's mother had always told him: "You'll know when you know."

Nathan knew. And as he looked into the light in Kylen's eyes, a light that her visor could not contain, Nathan knew even more.

"Six . . . five . . . four . . . three . . . "

He smiled and nodded to Kylen—

An alarm buzzed.

"Countdown HOLD! T-minus three seconds."

There are some things Nathan would rather have not heard while sitting atop a forty-five-story launch vehicle encircled by ten solid rocket boosters. An emergency buzzer was number one on his list.

But this one had been planned. He reached up and flipped down the double-trio of toggles, and the cabin fell silent.

"Tellus colony . . . this is Mission Comm . . . simulated launch sequence complete . . . all systems are nominal. Reset countdown for nine hours, four minutes and twelve seconds . . . you are GO for launch."

Yes!

Nathan's comlink reverberated with a cheer from the colonists. He shot a glance at Kylen. She flipped up her visor and blew him a kiss.

As he and the rest of the colonists unstrapped themselves, Nathan knew that by now the techs already had the launch tower access arm in place and were in the white room unsealing the vehicle's hatch. Nathan fell in behind Drake, a doctor, and Kylen. Drake crawled into the tunnel of the hatch, then took the hand of a tech standing on the other side. As he passed out of view, the mission commander's voice echoed from a speaker:

"Tellus colonists shall report to the launch vehicle by 2140 hours."

Kylen moved into the tunnel. Nathan smacked her butt.

"Hey!"

"Get in there, girl."

While he waited for Kylen to exit, Nathan overheard a conversation in the white room.

"Vesta colony never went this smoothly," Drake said.

"They're still having problems. We lost communication with Vesta this morning," a tech or engineer answered.

"Probably just solar flare interference again," another one chipped in.

Kylen passed through the hatch, then Nathan saw her turn and wait for him. He wiggled into the tube, and when he reached its end, he waved off a tech offering to help and made it alone through the hatch. He emerged into the white room, exhilarated.

"Man, if I'm this pumped by a test launch I won't need a rocket."

Kylen grinned, then her attention was directed to a wall clock digitally running off the countdown. Nathan noted that Kylen's usually roseate cheeks had faded as completely as her grin. "Final countdown," she said, sounding a little scared.

Nathan studied her a moment further, then nodded. "I know. Just think, most people don't know if their dreams will ever come true. Our dream is definitely eight hours and fifty-nine minutes away."

With that, Kylen's gaze ignited, and suddenly there was a trace of color back in her cheeks. Nathan moved in to kiss her, but the rims of their helmets kept them inches apart. Nathan laughed. He and Kylen had sacrificed a lot more than kisses to get where they were.

"Attention colonists Ausbury, Brown, Nuckols, Gonzales, Palladino, Heim, Larlee, Manesis, Vitaris, West, and Celina . . . "

Nathan pulled back from Kylen. She looked as immediately concerned as he felt.

The mission commander continued, "Report to Governor Overmeyer's office immediately.

"Oh God, we're too close for something to go wrong now," Kylen said, then sighed disgustedly.

Though Nathan felt his stomach twisting and his heart jetting back to its runaway pace, he did his best to conceal his anxiety from her. "Gotta be a last-minute pep talk. That's all it is."

Kylen squinted into a thought. "I don't see what we all have in common. The names seem random. It's not like we're all in the same sub-team or anything."

"Stop worrying. Let's go."

Nathan stood in Governor Overmeyer's sparsely furnished office, staring out the window at the Tellus colony launch tower, a mighty scepter thrust into the dusk. A single metropolis of clouds floated over the tower, its underbelly stained a burning orange. Farther above the clouds, the stars were beginning to flicker on.

Behind him, he listened to Kylen pace. Twice he had asked her to sit down.

"We're told to report *immediately*," she blurted into the silent room. "And then they make us wait two hours. The others didn't have to wait."

Nathan sighed long and hard. The first five minutes had been tense. After an hour he had classified the wait as excruciating. By ninety minutes he had searched the room for some sort of weapon to use on whomever had subjected them to the torture. But now that the two-hour mark had been breached, there was only a sickening numbness.

"What do you think could be —"

Kylen's question was cut short by the opening of the door. Nathan turned from the window to see Colonial Governor Jonathan Overmeyer enter the room. He had grown to respect Overmeyer, a respect the governor had earned from every colonist. The man was strong and inspirational, and Overmeyer knew the three keys to successful leadership: to have a vision, to share it with others, and to execute it. The governor reminded Nathan of his father.

Yet now Overmeyer did not look strong. He crossed to his large glass desk, and as he did so, his gaze never met Nathan's.

"Good evening, sir. The launch simulation went perfectly," Nathan said.

Overmeyer nodded absently.

Nathan swallowed. "We are still a 'GO'?"

Without answering, Overmeyer slid his chair out from under his desk and sat. He set his elbows on the glass surface and steepled his fingers. Then—finally—he looked at both of them. "I know you are aware of the growing rights movement for In Vitroes, those conceived and born in artificial gestation tanks, uh, artificial gestation *chambers* . . . "

Nathan subtly glanced at Kylen. Back in the white room she had looked as concerned as he felt. Now she appeared as stiff.

"Is this regarding the rally we attended?" Nathan asked.

Overmeyer pursed his lips then said, "In a way . . . the rally has brought about . . . a problem."

Nathan took a step toward the governor's desk. "Sir, we have every right to support In Vitroes. We stand by what we did."

The governor closed his eyes and paused.

To Nathan, Overmeyer's silence meant the man was irritated, and Nathan felt his guard go up.

Kylen took a step forward to join him. "They are human beings, sir. Just like us, only conceived from parents who never lived. Farmed by the government as slaves to fight in the A.I. War after too many of us were killed. It's not their fault it didn't succeed. They are equal."

"If anything, we owe them," Nathan added.

A handful of heartbeats passed, and then Overmeyer opened his eyes and lowered his hands to the desk. "Last evening the Tellus Board of Governors was issued a directive from the United States Senate. The launch will be scratched unless ten In Vitroes are aboard."

Nathan's stomach found a new home between his ankles. "What?"

"Given the restrictions on weight, rations, and personnel capacity—"

"Are you saying we're being replaced?" Kylen asked.

Overmeyer averted his gaze. "It is my *sincere* regret to inform you . . . that . . . one . . . of you will not be on board."

"Jesus!" Nathan tore away from the governor's desk. It was only now that the irony fully hit him. "I don't believe this!" He faced Overmeyer. "*One* of us?"

The governor raised his voice. "Nine colonists have been released. Deciding factors include age, experience—"

"Postpone the mission."

"If we don't go in six hours the forecasted wormhole passage to Tellus won't open for another twelve years."

Nathan beat his fist into his palm. "They're not even trained—send them on the next—"

"The next colonial expedition won't be ready for five years. There are members of Congress who need to look good—now."

"We'll both resign," Kylen said, her tone suggesting that tears would follow.

"Not going is *not* an option. You have a commitment to execute vital assignments on the mission, duties which one of you could cover, but for which no one else is trained. Not to mention the severe legal consequences of breaking your contract."

Nathan looked at Kylen; she looked as if there was a sea of glass in her eyes. *They* had made the commitment. How could only *one* of them keep it?

"I know both of you . . ." Overmeyer groped for words. "It's your dream to go to space."

Kylen sniffled and still fought desperately against her tears. "The dream was to go together."

Overmeyer nodded slightly, and his expression grew sympathetic. "I know of the intense feelings you have for each other. The fact you entered the program—together—with the intent of colonizing—together—and ultimately both being accepted over ten thousand applicants . . . is a testament to your devotion . . ." The governor raked fingers through his hair, then rubbed his nape. "The world was so much simpler twenty years ago. I'm on record as saying this directive stinks. I fought it all the way . . . and lost."

I'll bet you would've fought it a little harder if your own ass was on the line. . . .

"Off the record," Overmeyer added, "because of your situation . . . rather than issuing an order . . . I'm allowing the two of you to decide who will remain."

Meeting Kylen's gaze was never more painful. Her lower lip trembled slightly; what was left of her composure hung on by unraveling threads. Nathan lowered his head and rubbed his eyelids.

"There is an alternative," Overmeyer said.

Nathan looked up.

"Your Colonial certificates are immediately transferable for entrance into the Marine Corps Air and Space Cavalry."

Kylen snickered in disbelief. "The military?"

Nathan added his own question to hers. "You call that an alternative? Maybe you haven't heard, but there's no longer a need for the military. We're beyond war."

"Yes, but there's a possibility the Marine Corps Space Cavalry may be assigned duty as Colonial sentries."

Kylen snickered again. "'Possibility?' You want us to bet our lives on a 'possibility'?"

Nathan wanted to know the answer to just one

question: What do you do when the whole world drops out from under you, when everything you've worked for, everything that held time and place in your life, is ripped from your guts and thrown to the ground and stomped on as if all of it really meant nothing, as if all of it was only a paper airplane in the rain?

If there was an answer, Nathan considered strangling it out of Overmeyer. He lifted an index finger and took aim at the governor. "We did it the way you wanted! We followed the rules! These . . . In Vitroes didn't train. These . . . senators haven't sacrificed. Why should we pay for a mistake they made before we were even born? You're letting them throw away our lives! We believed in you!"

Overmeyer did not go on the defensive. He looked saddened by Nathan's outburst, and his expression woke a pang of guilt in Nathan. "I'm sorry you feel that way," the governor said. "All you can believe in now . . . is each other."

Kylen turned away from Overmeyer, crossed to the window and bowed her head, still in control of her tears. As Nathan turned to go to her, Overmeyer stood. "Please arrive at your decision by 2130—today," the governor said, then headed for the door.

Though Nathan was sure Overmeyer hadn't meant to do it, it sounded as if the governor had slammed the door behind him.

Nathan put a hand on Kylen's shoulder. The room was a hollow, empty box, and he wanted to fill it with words, words that would mean something. He searched for something to say. Then he realized the search would take a lifetime. He slid in front of Kylen, closed his eyes and embraced her. He felt a life-and-death intensity about the hug.

After a moment, he opened his eyes and looked out at the rocket. Lights on the launch tower now twinkled like stars, and soon great spotlights would come on and bathe the vehicle so intensely in light that it would take on the sheen of a diamond. The billboard-sized digital clock posted near the observation stand read:

LAUNCH COUNTDOWN
06:02:29

He glanced at the rocket and began to lose his breath as he wondered which of them would be aboard in six hours. He would fight for Kylen to go, and she would, of course, try to convince him that he was much more passionate about colonizing than she. They could lie to each other as long as they liked. Nothing, nothing would change.

two

The billboard depicted the architectural concept of a sleek, 145-story skyscraper, beneath which were the words:

PHILADELPHIA CENTER. COMPLETION:
SPRING 2106.
CELEBRATING 425 YEARS OF BROTHERLY LOVE!

In the lower-right corner was the well-known Aero-Tech construction company rocket logo.

Cooper Hawkes looked away from the sign and moved into the sun-soaked construction yard. The building, presently a seven-story skeleton of polymeric graphite girders encompassed by scaffolding, would take up, with its environs, two or three city blocks. At least a hundred laborers in powersuits shifted I-bars, girders, and struts around as if the materials weighed only ounces instead of hundreds of kilos. Two anti-grav cranes hung motionless over the structure. Then one hummed to life and floated two girders down to a pair of men standing on the seventh floor, one of whom gave hand signals to the crane's operator.

"Hey, you the new guy?"

Hawkes stopped and turned around. The man before him was in his twenties, about Hawkes's age, and had obviously spent too much time on construction sites or in the gym. There were no curves about him, only sharp angles. "Yeah, I guess I am."

"Hope you've got experience and hope you're good."

Hawkes grinned at the man's challenge. "I'm both." Well, he *was* good, if not experienced. He thrust his hand forward. "Cooper Hawkes."

"You just call me Davis," the other said without lifting his hand. "And I'm not here to make friends. I'll tell you flat out that I don't need any more help—even though the foreman thinks I do. And I don't trust anyone."

Hawkes balled his hand into a fist before lowering it. "We won't have any problems."

"Good," Davis said, then stared at Hawkes oddly for a moment.

"Is something wrong?"

"No," Davis said, but there was something visibly bothering the man. "Hey, why don't you get up to the seventh and relieve Mike. I need him in the trailer to go over some holoprints."

"On my way." Hawkes turned on his heel and strode toward the building. He thought he heard Davis utter something under his breath, but couldn't be sure, for the drone of the powersuits grew louder the farther he moved.

The disc about anti-grav crane signals that Hawkes had studied the night before was, in a word, dated. All day the operator squinted at him and shouted over the link that "We don't use that signal anymore, boy! Ain't you been around sites lately?" It was fortunate for Hawkes that the operator was somewhat familiar with the signals of the disc. By dusk, Hawkes was directing the operator to set the last girder down atop two vertical I-bars. A powersuited laborer stood next to each bar, ready to heat-seal the girder into place. Hawkes felt triumphant for the first time in many months. Finally, he had made it through a first day on the job and had not been fired. Not only that, with this job, he got to work around people. He would never be alone.

"Hey! He's going wide! He's going wide!" one of the laborers shouted.

Hawkes hadn't noticed it, but the operator, who did not have a clear line of sight down onto the bars, had let the girder go wide, and now the anti-grav field between the crane's nozzle and the girder fluctuated violently, turning the air into billowy heat waves of friction. Hawkes struggled to remember the signal for the operator to increase the anti-grav field, but hadn't had to use that signal all day; it was tucked too deeply into his memory.

A sound like a scream erupted from the crane.

"It's coming down!" one of the laborers shouted.

"Otto! Get the hell—"

Under a twilit sky that seemed at peace with the universe, Hawkes watched in horror as the girder broke free from the crane's field and plunged toward a point between the two I-bars, a point presently occupied by one of the laborers. Sparks and blue spiderwebs of random energy encompassed the man's suit as the girder swiped him—but miraculously—did not pin him to the concrete floor. The other laborer went to his friend. Hawkes dropped to his knees, grasped the girder and slid off to let himself be suspended three meters in the air. He dropped to the floor and ran to the two laborers.

The man who had been hit leaned against an I-bar for support. "I'm all right, Shell," he said to his co-worker. "Suit caught most of it." The hydraulic pump casings that ran across his shoulder and down the back of his suit's left arm were smashed and bubbling with fluid.

Shooting him a scowl, Shell stepped up to Hawkes. "What the hell happened? Didn't you see him going wide?"

"It's not his fault," someone said from above. Hawkes looked up to see the burly crane operator staring down from a girder. "I've been telling Davis that beast ain't been holding a charge all week. Wouldn't have been any field problem were she fully charged."

Hawkes couldn't be sure if the operator was covering for him or telling the truth. In any event, he felt his breath begin to even. He considered apologizing to Otto, but that would mean admitting his guilt. Instead, he simply said, "No one was hurt. That's what counts."

Shell reduced the gap between himself and Hawkes. "Keep it up and the next time someone will get hurt."

The operator's voice boomed from above. "It's his first day. He's trying hard. And we got shitty equipment. So cut him some slack. I'm going to talk to Davis about this crane."

As the operator's shadow passed over him, Hawkes turned away and started for the lift. He felt the heat of the laborers' gazes on his back.

An hour later, Hawkes sat alone at a table for two in a restaurant dome about four blocks north of the site. *The Borealis*, once famous for serving chef's salads made with hydroponically grown Martian vegetables, had fallen on hard times. The salads were no longer imported, and Hawkes's drink was watered down. He wished he could share his dinner with someone, anyone. He hated eating alone.

Then Davis emerged from the shadows of the dining area. Hawkes set his drink down and lifted his brow in recognition. "Hey."

"Hey, Cooper." Davis said, pausing before the table. "Barring that little incident, you had a pretty good day. Can you leave?"

Hawkes frowned. "I've already ordered. And it's not like I have the credits to pay for food that I'm not eating."

"A few of the guys and I are going out. They're waiting for us outside." Davis withdrew his wallet and slid out a gold voucher. I got this. We'll take you to a real restaurant."

Mildly stunned, Hawkes rose. "All right."

After Davis paid for Hawkes's uneaten meal, they left the restaurant. Outside, the night air was cold and smelled a lot more like the falls Hawkes had sampled from discs than its true semi-polluted self. Perhaps Mother Earth was, as the scientists had said, bandaging her own wounds. Davis led him into an alley that opened up into a cross street.

But when they reached the end of the alley, the cross street was a dead-end at both sides. And from behind a wide row of trash tubes stepped a quartet of familiar men: Brown, Tatum, Shell, and Otto. Hawkes had met Brown and Tatum while riding the lift. Tatum was a good-natured redhead with a beard that was too sparse to be dignified. Brown was an ex-military man in his fifties with the body of a twenty-year-old.

Hawkes smiled, but there was a slight rumble in the pit of his stomach, a rumble that meant more than hunger. "Hey, guys. You ready to eat?"

No one returned Hawkes's smile. He took a step back, then shot a look to Davis, who was now no longer a construction supervisor, but a predator. "There was nothing wrong with that crane," Davis said.

Though his boots were heavy, certainly not running shoes, Hawkes managed to get moving. He bolted away from the men and into the alley. There was no need to speculate if the others were following. The sound of their boots thundered in Hawkes's ears.

All right, assholes. Now let's see what you've got.

The bravado was necessary. It would, at least, keep him from collapsing in fear, at most, give him the false hope he needed to keep going. Hawkes already knew he wouldn't be able to outrun them forever, but what hurt worse was the fact that he had quite obviously lost the job.

But at least he had lost the job because they blamed the girder incident on him. He hadn't lost it because of who he was. . . .

They trailed him for three and a half blocks, drawing

the attention of nearly every pedestrian. Hawkes was amazed that even old Brown was still locked onto his target. He took another look back at his pursuers—and something got in the way of his boot and he went tumbling to the asphalt. He scraped his cheek, and his nose struck the ground hard enough to break a blood vessel. He pushed himself up and kept on moving, wiping his bloody face on his shirtsleeve and feeling a new fire in his left ankle.

"Guy? You all right?" someone from across the street asked.

"Fine!" Hawkes shot back without looking. "And what kind of night are *you* having?"

Ahead was the construction site, as good a maze as any in which to hide. His breath ragged, he ran past the billboard and let himself wash into the cold sea of silhouettes and the deeper darkness. He heard one of his pursuers, he couldn't identify which, call his name.

Out of the darkness grew a row of girders piled six high. Hawkes took a path between the girders, then found himself on the east side of the building. He weaved into the scaffolding to shadow-hug the wall, and there, grabbed a cold metal support pole. He paused to catch his breath.

"Hawkes!"

The voice belonged to Davis. And the supervisor sounded too close to pause any longer. Hawkes ducked out of the scaffolding and jogged north. As he neared the corner of the building, someone came out of the gloom, and there was the abrupt sensation of a fist connecting with his jaw, followed by the just-as-sudden notion that he was falling backward toward the merciless dirt. And then he was down, dazed and out of breath.

"Don't ya hate when that happens, Hawkes?"

Hawkes pushed himself up on his elbows to see Shell moving toward him. Hawkes guessed the man would attempt to leap onto him, effectively pinning him to the ground.

Rolling onto his side, Hawkes drew back one leg as Shell advanced. He kicked Shell in the shin, and the man yelled and buckled to the ground.

Shell's agony would bring the others, and knowing that, Hawkes rolled onto all fours, then shot to his feet. He began to feel the rage within him, but thankfully, it was still under his control. He just needed to get away. That's all. No more trouble.

He looked to the north, to the chain-link fence around the construction site.

Then he heard the shuffle of feet and was gang-tackled by Brown, Otto, and Tatum. They piled on top of him as if he were inches from the end zone, about to carry the ball in for the winning touchdown. Otto's chest pressed into Hawkes's face, and he felt someone else punch him once, twice, in the ribs.

"Get off of him," Davis said from somewhere above.

The three men complied, but as they did so, they seized Hawkes's arms and legs. Hawkes fought against their grips, but with a man on each arm and Brown holding his legs, he wasn't going anywhere.

Davis's deep voice sounded again. "Check him."

Otto stepped over Hawkes, still holding his wrist. The laborer dragged Hawkes around, onto his stomach. Brown released his legs, but before Hawkes could do anything, the man jammed his knee into the base of his spine.

It had dawned on Hawkes when Otto had first forced him onto his stomach. But Hawkes hadn't wanted to believe it. They couldn't have known. Hawkes was sure no one had told them. And he was sure that his behavior hadn't betrayed anything. It took most people a long time to figure it out, and even when they did, sometimes it changed things, sometimes it didn't. But in the past few months it had only meant trouble. And here he was. And they were about to find out what he was.

Hawkes felt Brown's palm sweep across his nape and lift his hair. What Brown and the others stared at was the navel-like indentation at the base of Hawkes's head, the one that often made people gasp.

"I knew it," Davis said, now hovering over Hawkes. "A tank. I can smell 'em. Like an animal."

Hawkes felt Davis kick him hard in the side, just below his ribs. He stifled a moan.

Davis blew air in disgust. "I told the foreman I had a feeling about this guy. Get him up."

Brown rose from Hawkes, and Otto and Tatum dragged him to his feet.

"Hold him," Tatum told Brown. "Got my cutter on me. I'll get a couple meters of fiber optic and we'll bind him."

Tatum turned over Hawkes's wrist to Brown, then crossed to a coil of cable lying on the ground below the scaffolding. Meanwhile, Hawkes tried to bring his arms together in an attempt to pull away from the men, but even though most of their lifting was assisted by power-suits, simply wearing the heavy suits had turned the laborers into heavily biceped bruisers. What they lacked in intelligence they easily made up for in brawn. Hawkes relaxed his muscles, then shot a look to Davis.

The angular supervisor's gaze was fixed on something. Hawkes followed the man's line of sight until he came upon a girder that had yet to be cut. It extended some two meters beyond the scaffolding and hung about three and a half meters above the ground.

"Cut off another two meters," Davis told Tatum.

At that, Hawkes once again pitted his muscles against those of the laborers . There was no way that he would wind up like old Sam, or Johnson, or Browkel. Each of them had swung from a line because they were tanks. There was no way that would happen to him. No way. Not with his rage.

Tatum was back with the fiber optic cable. He and Otto pulled Hawkes's wrists behind his back while Brown tied them. What little struggling Hawkes managed was answered by Otto's hard wrenches and

Tatum's gouging fingernails. When Brown was finished with his wrists, the man moved to Hawkes's ankles. Otto and Tatum stepped on his boots to immobilize him.

Davis stepped up to Hawkes and seized his chin. "I had two uncles die in the A.I. War 'cause the tanks wouldn't fight."

Hawkes jerked his chin out of Davis's grasp. "The In Vitro platoons were dissolved when I was a kid. I had nothing to do with it."

"Then you're even more worthless."

"I never asked to be born."

"Great, then you can ask to die."

Davis gestured with his head to Tatum, who dropped a fiber optic noose around Hawkes's neck. Brown and Otto each shoved a hand into Hawkes's armpits, lifted and then carried him to a position beneath the girder. It was a reflex action to be sure, but Hawkes looked up. Beyond the girder, the night sky shone with a brilliance that he hadn't seen until now. For a second, he imagined he could float away, float away from all of it, all of the pain. Away from the word and its meaning. *Tank.*

"You listening to me?" Davis asked. "I said you can ask to die. Now, go on . . . ask."

Hawkes leveled his gaze on Davis, a gaze he let burn into the man.

"ASK!"

Defiance could take the form of a look, a word, an action. Thus far, Hawkes had used the first two against Davis. Yes, they had bound him, but they had not gagged him. Hawkes gathered spit in his mouth, then let it fly.

Davis's nose sustained the damage. The big man spun away, wiping his face and swearing under his breath.

Tatum threw the fiber optic cable over the girder, then pulled Hawkes's noose tight. Hawkes felt the noose begin to bury itself in his neck as his feet left the ground.

No! This isn't it! I'm not going like the others. They

don't know my rage. They haven't seen it. But they will. Have to . . . losing . . . can't . . . breathe . . .

He looked down. Davis smiled sardonically. Then Hawkes glanced at Tatum, and the idea struck.

Hawkes grimaced as he summoned from his body every minute particle of remaining strength. He pulled his knees up into his chest, then, with a jerk of his shoulders, he twisted his body toward the slack-jawed Tatum. As he swung within striking distance, he kicked out with his bound feet.

Tatum finally understood what was happening, but it was too late. The laborer's horror registered on his face a moment before Hawkes's boot turned that look into a twisted knot of agony. The man released the fiber optic cable as the blow sent him backward toward the scaffolding.

Hawkes hit the dirt, gasping, noose still around his neck, wrists and ankles still bound together. He rolled onto his back, tucked his knees into his chest, then pulled his bound hands apart, creating about a three-inch gap between them. That would be enough. Hawkes let out a roar as he pulled his bound hands down and around his feet, feeling his shoulders shudder on the brink of dislocation. He sat up, still bound but with his hands in front of him. He fumbled with the knot of the cable binding his legs. Brown was no seaman. It was a simple double knot and Hawkes untied it quickly. He didn't bother unspooling the cable but rather tore his legs apart—just in time to drive a foot into the attacking Otto's gut.

As Otto went down, the laborer cleared a clean line of sight to Shell, whom Hawkes was surprised to see on his feet. The man came at Hawkes, then launched himself into the air.

Utilizing a similar defense as he had when first encountering the man, Hawkes rolled onto his side, and this time kicked up, roaring again as he caught Shell's good shin while simultaneously deflecting the rest of him out of the way. Shell screamed and went down in a heap of spent energy and dust.

Once on his feet, Hawkes turned in time to spot Brown, who'd drawn back a knockout punch that was now on an express delivery toward Hawkes's jaw. Hawkes ducked while balling both hands into fists. He straightened and sent a double-fisted uppercut into Brown's chin with such force that it lifted the man off of his feet, then propelled him backward.

Though Shell, Tatum, Otto, and now Brown each filled the air with sounds that were not unlike those made by the survivors of an A.I. battlefield, and, in effect, Hawkes *had* created a battlefield, Hawkes heard only one sound:

Thump-thump . . . thump-thump . . . thump-thump . . .

That was how it was when the rage took hold. He shot a look at Davis, then snarled at the man. Davis frowned at the sound, then glanced to a graphite pipe lying amid a pile of scaffolding poles. The man darted toward the pipe and came up with it. He beat the pipe into his palm and grinned darkly.

Hawkes waited until Davis got close enough, then he seized the dangling end of the noose around his neck, drew back with the cable, and whipped Davis in the face.

"Ahhhhhh!"

The graphite pipe fell from Davis's hand and rolled toward Hawkes. Scooping up the pipe, Hawkes started for Davis, letting out a cry that came from somewhere deep within.

Davis headed for the street. Hawkes would not let him get away. At this point, it would be more reasonable to simply take off. Hawkes had nearly lost his life. Why push his luck any further?

But the damned rage wouldn't permit that. The damned rage smothered reason.

Hawkes was only about ten meters behind Davis by the time the supervisor was about to hit the street.

Davis picked up the pace, but just as he was leaving dirt for asphalt, he was cut off by an armored, Philadelphia Police cruiser, its lights strobing, its siren screaming with multiple wails controlled by the button-happy cop inside. The car squealed to a stop.

As two helmeted officers dressed in paramilitary black jumpsuits with heavy flak jackets exited the car, Davis ran past one of them, and—to the cops' and Hawkes's surprise—opened up the rear door of the cruiser, threw himself onto the back seat, then slammed the door behind him.

Hawkes raced up to the car, drawing back his pipe. One of the officers seized his arm, but Hawkes managed to reach the cruiser and bring the pipe down onto the wire-protected rear window.

"GET OUT! GET OUT OF THERE!"

Pounding again on the window, Hawkes growled and fought back against the officers' attempted restraint.

"Get back, Willy," Hawkes heard one of the officers say.

Then, abruptly, Hawkes was free. He faced the cops, who now pointed their IM pistols at him.

"Drop the pipe."

"He's crazy, sir," Davis yelled from within the car. "He's a *tank*."

Hawkes bashed the car window at the mention of the word, and the cops took a step back.

"Go on. Get out," one of the officers told Davis. "You're settin' him off."

Davis opened the rear door farthest from Hawkes, then nervously stepped out. He shot a furtive look at Hawkes before sprinting off back toward *The Borealis*.

How could these bastards let Davis go?

Feeling muscles tightening and his nerves fraying, Hawkes slammed the pipe against the patrol car side window, shattering it. "He tried to hang me!"

There was no more reason, no more reality. There was nothing but rage, a fire that burned so hot and so bright that if anyone on the outside were able to look at Hawkes, really look at his soul, they would be blinded and incinerated. He stepped to the driver's side window of the auto and bashed it in. He moved toward the windshield and pounded, pounded, POUNDED!

He barely felt it hit him. He looked down and saw a tiny, dart-like projectile lodged in his chest. A circular wave of energy pulsed through his body and blasted him to the ground.

The cops charged around, and the cuffs they used on him felt strangely like the fiber optic coil, but that hadn't been real, had it? It all felt like a dream now, a numb, laughable memory. But when he swallowed he felt the pain of where the noose had been, then realized that it was still around his neck.

three

Shane Vansen stood near the curb, staring down into a puddle that rippled with light rain and was cast in the harsh glow of a street lamp. Though her reflection kept changing, she continued to try to find herself in the pool of expanding and colliding ringlets of water, to try to find that pretty, twenty-one-year-old woman she should be.

But that woman wasn't there, only a blurry image that suddenly *felt* appropriate. She mused that her reflection might be distinct if none of it had happened. . . .

Running a thumb under her duffel bag's strap, she adjusted its position on her shoulder. She tightened her grip on the mixed bouquet of flowers, then started for the dark, fenced-off house. Only three people remembered a time when the home was idyllic, a place of warmth where spirits soared and dreams were fostered. As she moved toward the gate, she noted, as she always did, the faded sign posted there:

> **NO TRESPASSING. KEEP OUT.**
> **BY ORDER OF THE UNITED STATES NAVY.**
> **SAN DIEGO, CALIFORNIA.**

She shuddered.

Following a crack in the driveway that ran all the way up to the front walkway, Shane turned and stepped to the front door. Then, as lightning flashed, revealing to her just how overgrown with weeds the place really was, she looked to the second floor. The windows had been boarded up, and then those boards had been torn off so that the gangs could take shots at the house and chuckle over the sound of shattering glass. In a way, she was glad the boards were gone; their absence made the house look slightly more lived-in, though it would still need a complete renovation. She averted her gaze and stepped onto the stoop.

The last time she had been here, the door had been broken in; now it was inside the house, clinging to a single hinge. Leaves, twigs, and other debris littered the foyer's concrete floor. The carpeting had been torn out of the house long ago, and the walls had sustained wounds from any number of weapons. At the foot of the stairs, beer cans and plastic six-pack holders lay strewn amid a sea of junk food wrappers. On one of the walls adjacent to the staircase, someone had spray-painted the words: NUKE THIS EYESORE! Shane kicked her way through the garbage and mounted the stairs. Lightning flashed again, and she welcomed the fact that its light illuminated her path. The wooden stairs were warped, and creaked from disuse. She reached the second-floor landing, feeling her chest begin to pound. She froze, listened to the sound of the rain outside, then shushed herself. She drew in long, slow breaths.

You're all right, Shane. You wanted to come here again. Remember?

It was right behind her, but she didn't want to look at it. Not just yet. She needed control. She swallowed, realizing her mouth was dry as a desert, then moved her tongue nervously over her teeth. Another breath. Shush. Another breath.

She turned toward the bedroom door. Then she closed her eyes and strode forward, sensing when she reached the threshold. She opened her eyes and—

—there was Daddy at the window, looking very handsome in his United States Marine Corps uniform. He lowered the lace curtain and turned to

Mommy. "They're coming! The lights!" *Daddy looked very worried—*

Shane blinked hard. No, her father wasn't at the window. There wasn't much left of the window, and the lace curtain lay dirty and torn beneath it. She shot a look to the corner of the room—

—and there was Mommy in her Corps uniform, and she looked even more worried than Daddy. Mommy held Kim's hand and carried Shane's youngest sister, Lauren. "Come on, Shane." *Mommy rushed around the bed to the closet, let go of Kim's hand, then opened the door. She got on her haunches, looked at Kim for a second and then kissed her. She put Lauren down and kissed her, too.*

"Mommy, I don't want to . . ." *Shane bit her lower lip and felt like she was going to cry.*

"I love you," *Mommy said.* "And you have to be strong now. Shane . . . take care of them. Remember how I told you . . . "

Shane felt her hands tremble. "Mommy, no . . . don't . . . "

Daddy burst into the room. "They're here! Hurry!"

She lost her balance and had to lean against the closet door for support. She forced herself to look up into the closet at the small hatch set into the ceiling. She shed her duffel bag and set the bouquet down on top of it. She swung her foot onto the knob of the closet door, and gripped the metal grillwork of the shelf. With a grimace and a groan, Shane drove herself up, quickly shoved open the hatch, got a hold on the frame, then pulled herself into the crawl space.

Sitting with her feet still dangling down into the closet, and hunched over a bit to avoid hitting her head on the rafters rising at a forty-five-degree angle away from her, Shane tried to repress a chill as she surveyed the nearest floor beams visible in the gloom. They, like the backside of the ceiling panels, were covered with a thick coat of dust and spanned by cobwebs. She found a particular floor beam and ran her fingers across it. Feeling what she was looking for, she stopped.

Of course, they were still there. She removed her hand and squinted at the wood—

—and sat between a shivering Kim and Lauren, holding them, they holding her. Each girl clutched the wooden brace with her free hand. Her sisters were breathing loudly, and Shane looked at Lauren, who was on the verge of screaming. She placed her hand over Lauren's mouth, and Lauren bit her. Shane winced as her tears came, then she shot a look through the grill of the air duct to see if they had been heard.

Long shadows rose across the bedroom walls. They looked like the shadows of people, but then one of them spoke, and he sounded like a computer, like the soldiers Daddy had warned her about.

"On the floor!"

Mommy and Daddy were shoved to their knees, and they held their hands behind their back like when they stood at attention. Shane saw the shadow of one of the soldiers raise his arm.

BOOM! BOOM!

Intense white light filled the room and razored through the slits in the air duct's grill and—

—the crawl space was dark and silent again. But then thunder clapped and a strong burst of wind swept over the house. Shane looked down, not realizing until she did so that she had been gripping the floor beam the way she and her sisters had that night.

She sat for a long while, her breath growing calm but her memories still locked into a sick loop that ran from the time she was five until the present.

That night, the road of her life had made an abrupt turn. A pair of shots had changed her from a little girl with loving parents to an orphan. She had fought with the bastards who had wanted to separate her from her sisters. At least Uncle Roger had stepped in—though forced—and had obtained custody of them. But Roger had been barely able to be an uncle, let alone both a mother and father. So Shane, over the years, had assumed the role of both sister and mother to Kim and Lauren. She hadn't wanted the role. She had just wanted to be a kid. Now, she wasn't going to get Kim away from the clubbing lifestyle, or get Lauren back into school. And every time Shane tried to discipline them, they would laugh at her, or blame her for their screwed-up lives. Well, she wasn't going to let them blame her anymore.

"I've been asking you why for sixteen years," she said softly, her voice sounding hollow and unfamiliar to her. "Just tell me there was a reason. Tell me they died *for* something. . . . And tell me why I did . . . nothing."

Sometimes she imagined a reply. This time she did not.

She climbed down from the crawl space, picked up her bouquet, and placed it on the floor where her parents had been murdered. With no one to hold her, she wrapped her arms around herself and stood there, squeezing out tears. It might have been a minute, an hour, a lifetime; she didn't know, but finally, she lifted her head and opened her eyes.

She crunched across broken glass to the window. The rain had stopped. She listened to the residual drops trickle through the leaves and limbs of a great oak in the yard.

A new sound cut into the night, the voice of distant fighter-jet thrusters echoing in the sky.

The jet called to her.

Shane probed the heavens, feeling the wind begin to dry the tears on her cheeks. As the sound faded, she turned from the window and fetched her duffel bag.

Outside the house, she considered delaying, to take one last look at the place, but instead she stared into the sky. The storm clouds were breaking, and the light from the crescent moon bled through them. Near the moon, a bright blue star glimmered.

"You're not that far away," she whispered.

four

Nathan and Kylen left Overmeyer's office and
headed for the cafeteria. The furor of the meeting had
left them famished.

"We'll have a last meal together," Nathan said angrily
as they strode down the drab, purely functional hall.
"God. I still can't believe how they screwed us."

"We can't spiral out of control on this. We have to
think it out." Kylen's even voice was meant to settle
him.

But there was no settling Nathan. "Yeah. We can *easily* reach a decision on this one. Yeah, over burgers and
milk shakes we can figure out what's going to happen to
the rest of our damned lives!"

They turned the corner and reached the door of the
cafeteria. A small, digital sign mounted there spelled out
the word: CLOSED.

Nathan charged the door, hammered the sign repeatedly with his fist until it broke free, emitting a tiny fury
of sparks and smoke, before it hit the tiled floor.

Kylen shook her head. "You done?"

"I . . . I need some time . . . I just . . . I dunno . . . I
gotta get out of here." Nathan jogged past her and broke
into a full sprint down the hall.

"Nathan?"

He reached the door to the stairwell, yanked it open
and began a double-time ascent.

*Screwed me. Screwed me. Screwed me. I give. You
take. Give. Give. Give. Take. Take. Take. Come here,
Nathan. Let me slap you in the face. Come here, Nathan.*

Let me boot you in the ass. Come here, Nathan. Let me show you just how much you're only a seven-digit number with spaces in between, a seven-digit number as replaceable as toilet paper. . . .

Oh, and by the way. Come here, Nathan. I'm done screwing your professional life. Now, let me ruin you personally.

Nathan burst onto the roof, wholly out of breath. His temples throbbed and it seemed he'd lost control of his hands: his fists would not unlock. He ran through a row of tiny, meter-high satellite dishes, then slowed to a stop a short distance from the edge of the complex. A wall about knee high ran along the perimeter of the roof. Still panting, Nathan wandered to the wall and looked down at the lot below.

The ground traffic was heavy. Techs, engineers, colonists, administrators, and security personnel came to and from the complex. The monorail that shuttled people out to the launch pad was just coming into the station.

Nathan imagined what it would feel like to let himself fall from the building, to soar in the air and be at peace for a brief moment, at peace knowing that the decision had been made and there was no turning back. From the moment his feet would leave the rooftop, gravity—not the senators nor board of governors—would be in control of his fate.

He remembered when he was a kid and had jumped off the roof of the family farmhouse, thinking an umbrella would float him safely to the earth. Nathan wondered how many other kids across the globe had tried that same stunt.

What am I doing?

Turning away from the ledge, Nathan withdrew from the breast pocket of his jumpsuit a journal the size of an old paperback book. He opened the journal, took up the pen he used as a bookmark, and wrote the date at the top of the blank page. He moved the pen to the next line.

And all he could hear was that voice in his head. *Give. Give. Give. Take. Take. Take. Work hard. Dream. Get screwed.*

Reaching for anything to replace his angry mood, he turned back to his last entry and read:

04-08-04

2100

Tomorrow is the simulated launch. I tried to call Mom and Dad but first they weren't home, and then there was a problem with the link. At least I got to talk to John and Neil. Neither of them knew what to say when I told them I would miss them. Dad's got them bottling up their emotions, just like he had me doing. But they'll learn, like I did. All it will take is a woman like Kylen.

Ah, Kylen . . . she's . . . God . . . beautiful. She's got me feeling things I've never felt before. She's got me imagining what our family will be like on Tellus. I've painted a whole future in my mind. That's it. That's what she does, she draws out my dreams and she turns them on their sweetest sides.

All right, she gets me choked up and makes me get all melodramatic and mushy, as Dad would say. But when I think about it, when you're going to go on a sixteen-light-year journey with someone, you'd better damned well like them.

Or, in my case, love the hell out of them.

Nathan clapped shut the journal. He sighed, then lifted his eyes to the stars.

I want to be there . . .

Then, at that moment, it was as though he were wiped out of existence by a supernova and reborn with a clear, invigorated mind. Toggles were thrown, connections were made, and sunrise was not far off. He thought of his relationship with Kylen in terms of the solar system. Yes, it sounded bizarre at first, but then he saw the link. Quickly, almost frantically, he opened his journal.

Nathan wrote furiously for perhaps fifteen minutes. At the sound of the rooftop door opening behind him, he shoved his pen into the journal, then closed and pocketed it. He looked over his shoulder to regard Kylen.

"Thanks for . . . the time."

"You all right?"

He faced her. "I, uh, I'm sorry about that back there."

"Forget it."

Kylen ran her thumbs along the chain holding her photo tags. The tags were not unlike old-style military dog tags, but were unofficial and had digital images of Kylen and himself on them. Her picture was perfect. His was of some monster who only slightly resembled him. Usually Kylen kept them tucked into her bra, but now she had them out. Obviously she had been looking at them. She let one hand fall away, then held the tags with the other.

Nathan frowned. "What do we do now?"

"Everyone is down saying good-bye to their families."

He nodded absently.

She took his hand. "I never thought we'd be saying good-bye to each other."

"Then let's run away . . . "

She dropped his hand. "To a life of what? If we break the contract no one will employ us. We'll be indentured servants to the colonial program for twenty years."

Nathan gritted his teeth and cocked a thumb over his shoulder. "Did they keep their word to us? The program was all I ever believed in. And now there's nothing."

He wasn't sure why, but she appeared more hurt than she should have been by his last remark. He repeated the words to himself, and then he realized that it sounded as if he had never believed in her, only the program. And that wasn't true.

"Kylen, I didn't mean for it to—"

"You believed in equal rights for In Vitroes," she said, sidestepping his apology.

"Not at the expense of *our* rights. We've trained. We've sacrificed. We've dreamed . . . together. They're stealing that." He jerked away from her. "Our lives are over."

She stepped closer to him. "Nathan . . . we're not dying. Maybe we just have to find another dream."

Moving to the ledge, Nathan paused to stare at the rocket. He wanted to be aboard so badly that not only could he taste the desire, but every other sense was wired to the notion and blistering from an overload. "Kylen, there are twelve billion people in the world. Less than a thousand have the honor of going into space. In three hours, one of us will leave—forever—on the most powerful and complex machine ever built. One of us will travel faster than light, farther than most people will ever go, to a planet with eight moons, with a waterfall six times the width of Niagara and a tropical rain forest the size of Europe. It's a place with a better life." Slowly, he faced her. "And because of what they've done, one of us will be left behind to always wonder: Would my life have been extraordinary if I had gone?"

Kylen bit her lip, and for a moment looked like a wounded little girl. Then she straightened and showed nothing but her business side. "We can't spend the last hours we have together as victims. We have to . . . somehow . . . take control."

Nathan felt his brow lift, almost involuntarily, but not quite. He had spent so much time being pissed off at the system that it hadn't occurred to him until now that there might be a way to bypass it.

No, there was definitely a way to bypass it. Any lock can be picked, any code broken. The trick would be to get help. And Nathan knew where to start.

"What are you thinking, Nathan?"

"Nothing."

five

"Nathan, you're out of your mind. I won't do it. No."

"We're talking about a seventy-kilogram differential between projected and final. Nobody's going to lose their job over it."

Colonial systems analyst Alex Foster shook his head, his triple chin wagging. The bear of a man leaned forward in his chair, pushing aside the laptop computer on his desk to make room for his arms. "Buddy, I know how you feel. When I heard, I felt like shit, too. But what's done—"

Nathan smote his fist on the desk top. "Is *not* done. All you have to do is pull up the cargo database and change one number. Then give me a couple of crate codes. That's it."

"I don't have the—"

"Bullshit. You've got clearance." Nathan crossed to the door of the small office, then thought better of leaving. He turned back. "Alex, I'm begging. My life, I swear, my life is in your hands, man. Help me."

Foster leaned back in his chair and pillowed his head in his hands.

"Please . . . "

Lowering his gaze, the systems analyst sighed.

On his way to the cargo warehouse, Nathan realized that he wasn't going to be "right back" like he had told Kylen. He hoped she would do the right thing. His failure to return would mean that she would go on with the mission. He was saddened about not saying good-bye, but then again, he shouldn't feel that way. There was no need for a farewell.

Though the senators and governors had taken away his right to board the rocket, they hadn't taken away his I.D. tag, and that got him past the sentries posted at one of the warehouse's north side doors.

Inside, he stopped to make a quick survey of the hangar-like facility. Row after row of white polymer crates were being loaded onto the flatbeds of cargo vehicles by techs in clean suits. The crates would be taken out past the two great open doors on the west side of the warehouse and delivered to the launch tower. Judging from the cargo vehicles' present positions, Nathan figured that the last row of crates to be loaded was the one that paralleled the south wall, and that was a coincidence in his favor. The crate he wanted was in that row.

Keeping his head low, Nathan strode into the warehouse. The internal lights were mounted so high on the walls that they cast a weak glow over everything, and Nathan's passage was concealed mostly in shadow. He reached his destination without incident, for the techs were hustling to load crates and were much too intent on their work to notice a passerby.

Moving up the row, Nathan scanned the cargo. About midway up, he found it. The box was a perfect cube, with a width, length, and depth of about two and a half meters. Its I.D. plate read:

TELLUS COLONY: 85759448##-67854
Docket 347-89-789***
MOBILE WEATHER STATION
AND BALLOON ASSEMBLY

Nathan pulled his journal from his breast pocket and opened it to the back page. There he had written two sets of six numbers that Foster had given him. He knelt before the crate's access panel, then looked up at the small keypad on the crate. As he keyed each number, it was digitally displayed above the pad. The crate's seal blew, and Nathan put away his journal and pulled the panel back toward him, revealing the small weather station and balloon assembly. His original idea had been to squeeze between the sampling rods of the station and rest his head on the silk pile of the balloon. But his memory had painted the space between the two as much larger than it really was. In any event, there was no other option, so he would have to contort himself to get into the crate, shove an arm here, a leg there, perhaps have a knee up near his earlobe.

And, indeed, once he was inside the box, his knee was flirting with his ear. He nearly screamed as he leaned forward, seized the panel and slammed it shut. The lock beeped twice: an arming signal. Now, one thing stood between leaving the crate or dying in it. Nathan set the tiny acid bomb's magnetic base onto the rear casing of the crate's lock. He slid his finger over the destruct button, getting a feel for it. That done, he fell back into the darkness and breathed deeply.

After a moment, already bored and his pulse still on the rapid side, Nathan fingered the light on his watch. He had synchronized it with the launch clock, and now saw that there were two hours and forty-one minutes remaining until liftoff. He guessed he would have to stay in the crate for at least another two hours, and that prospect made the walls seem to move in a little tighter, the weather station and balloon assembly press on him a little harder.

Nathan swam nude at the foot of a great waterfall. He went under the water, and when he came up, Kylen stood before him in the thigh-high water. She was pure, unencumbered by a bathing suit, her golden locks wet and glistening in the alien sun. He went to her, and her skin was soft and warm and her head fit perfectly on his shoulder.

"*Don't leave me,*" *she said.*

"*Never.*"

"This one's a bitch. Get Mike over here and we'll triple-team 'er."

Nathan snapped awake, tried to move, then remembered where he was.

"All right, here we go."

Suddenly, Nathan felt he was in the air, but only for a moment. The techs set the crate gently onto the flatbed. Nathan was jerked forward as he heard the muted sound of the cargo vehicle's engine race, and then the motor fell back into a steady whine.

I'm on my way. I'm on my way. System bypassed.

He forgot all about his confined space and reveled in what he had done and was doing.

The techs brought his crate to the launch tower, placed it on the elevator, then rolled it into the access arm toward the hatch of the launch vehicle's supply deck on level eight. He wasn't sure when they actually moved the crate into the vehicle, but the sound of the techs locking it into position on the floor confirmed that he had arrived.

How long do I wait? Will I be able to hear them seal the supply deck hatch? Listen. . . .

Sure enough, he heard the muted slam of a hatch.

One . . . two . . . three.

He hit the acid bomb's destruct button, then closed his eyes and tucked his head into his chest. There was a hissing sound, a terrible acrid odor, and then a *POP!* Sensing that the lock had been disengaged, the seal broken, Nathan placed his palm on the crate's panel and pushed. The panel dropped outward.

His leg came out. Then an arm. His head, shoulder, another arm, and, finally, his other leg. Though he stood, he still felt like the pretzel he had become. He tried to shake off the stiffness, but it would linger at least as long as the time he had spent in the crate. He looked around the circular room. A sole work light illuminated a wall marked: THIS AREA NOT PRESSURIZED. He shifted back to the crates locked onto the floor, then began checking I.D. plates. One, two, three ... eight ... ten ... fourteen ...

Come on! Come on! Where are you?

He glanced at his watch. 01:53:36.

The crate he wanted was, of course, last in the first row. But at least it wasn't the last one in the *last* row. Were that the case, he would have had to examine nearly sixty crates in the subdivision of gear. Nathan opened his journal, found the correct code, plugged it in, then unlocked the rectangular crate, a box approximately three meters wide, three high, and five long. The interior was divided by shelving, the top shelf containing twenty or thirty flight helmets. Nathan went through them, pulling out and trying on several before finding one that fit. Below the helmets were the oversized silver suitcases that contained the flight suits. Above the handle of each case was an I.D. plate that supplied the model number and dimensions. Again, in this department, Nathan could not fudge. The suit had to fit him snugly. He wouldn't even entertain the idea of a pressure leak. Foster had asked why he didn't want to simply bring along his own suit; but wearing it or carrying the suit and helmet, concealed or not, would have brought questions from the warehouse sentries. The idea had been to make it as easy as possible to get on board. He had planned to worry about the problem of the flight suit later.

Later sucks, Nathan thought.

Then an idea struck him. Instead of going through row after row of the suitcases, checking I.D. plates, he went directly to the bottom right case, the last one.

"Son of a bitch."

The dimensions of the suit within were not just close to Nathan's requirements, they were exact.

A noise came from the other end of the supply deck: someone was opening a hatch.

Nathan snatched up the suitcase, tucked his helmet into the crook of his arm, slammed the crate shut, then scrambled toward a ladder. He mounted it, skipping every other rung as he climbed. Emerging into level nine, another supply deck, Nathan shot toward the nearest row of crates and took cover behind it. The crates on this level were much larger than those below, forming rows that rose nearly three meters.

"This is the third check, sir."

"If we forgot anything, we're fired."

"Yeah, it's not like they can come back for it."

"All right. I've got one thirty-seven."

"Check's good. We're set."

The hatch slammed shut.

Nathan threw the latches on the suitcase, pulled out the flight suit and stepped into it. He removed his watch, dug his fingers into the attached gloves, then buckled the watch over his protected wrist. He zipped up the suit's two inner linings, then the outer. To start the pressurization system's warm-up sequence required him to press a trio of buttons located at his left breast. A soft whirring told him the sequence had been initiated. He grabbed his helmet and headed up the supply deck to the next ladder. Once he reached the top of the ladder, he found the expected pressure hatch. The code to these hatches was known by every colonist, and in a moment he was on the next deck, sealing the hatch behind him. He straightened and stepped into the garden, glancing briefly at the wall marker:

LEVEL TEN: PRESSURIZED: HYDROPONICS

Plants, vegetables, and fruit trees, all weaving vine-like through growth racks, encircled the room. Tubes of water led in and out of the holding area. Thin bands of florescent grow lights formed concentric circles on the ceiling and ringed the walls. The juxtaposition between every other level and the garden had always struck Nathan. There was something telling about slapping the natural against the synthetic. It made the natural look that much better and the synthetic look that much worse. It was the natural that would buy him a flight to Tellus now. His suit's pressurization unit would run only eight hours before requiring a recharge. The garden was pressurized. However, he would, as always, follow safety precautions and pressurize his suit for liftoff.

He searched the garden for something he could use to restrain himself for the launch. Coming up empty, he went to the perimeter and dug his gloved hand into the crack where one of the flexible water tubes met the wall. He found another tube to his right and did the same. After rocking himself forward and back several times, he decided that, with a little luck, he would make it through the liftoff. He withdrew his hands, fetched his helmet, put it on and sealed it to his flight suit; then he engaged his pressurization unit, the helmet's comlink, and the O_2 knob. Air flowed. He resumed his position on the wall.

By now he hoped Kylen was boarding the rocket. Her presence would be all Governor Overmeyer needed to know the decision had been made. A horrible thought occurred to him, but he dismissed it. No, she was on board. He was not stowing away only to discover that she had opted to stay on Earth. She wouldn't do that. She wouldn't.

He rolled his wrist, checked his watch. Fifty-five minutes to go.

In the time that followed, the various communications from Mission Command were a symphony building toward a final crescendo. And, when there were forty-five minutes left in the countdown, the words Nathan wanted desperately to hear, the words he had sweated over, now buzzed in his ears.

"Tellus, you are a GO. Initiate primary launch sequence. . . ."

"Sequence engaged."

Then something odd happened. Mission Command went dead. No signals. Nothing. Twice the vehicle's pilot tried in vain to contact the center.

Nathan waited. And waited. His jumpsuit was soaked, his mouth dry, and his trembling grew.

A sound. A hatch blowing. He looked at the ladder, then let his gaze sweep up to the ceiling. Xenon beams poured down through the circular hole and into the garden.

No! They can't know! Foster didn't double-cross me, did he? He fixed the weight. I saw him. And he gave me the codes. No, it wasn't him. Then . . .

He was breathing hard enough to take notice of it, and a dark awareness crawled over him. His hand went to a pack mounted at his hip. The pack, labeled OUT-FLOW, the one containing three slits for the release of CO_2, had betrayed him. Or, rather, he had failed to consider the extra CO_2 he would release into the garden. That was it. That was how they got him.

Tearing his wrists free from the water tubes, he looked left, then right, for a place to hide. Boots hammered on ladder rungs. Lights flashed. He unfastened his helmet, removed it, then unzipped his suit down to his navel. He dug out his journal, flipped through the pages and tore free the entry he had been writing on the complex's roof. He put the free page and the journal back in his pocket.

A xenon beam hit him square in the eyes.

Blinded, he tried to move back, but the muzzle of a sentry's stunner jabbed his shoulder blade. His heart felt as if it were dropping to his ankles as he raised his hands.

They said nothing as they escorted him up the ladder, one in front, one behind, and led him onto the next deck, the colonist compartment.

He spotted Kylen up ahead among the rows of people to his left. She unsnapped her flight restraints and began to get up.

"No! Kylen! It has to be you!"

Nathan sprang past the sentry in front of him, pulling out the page he had torn from his journal.

Kylen's visor was up, and her eyes brimmed with tears. He embraced her, then pulled back and handed her the paper. "I wrote this for you. Read it when you land."

Hands came down hard on Nathan's arms, and the sentries began to drag him away.

"I . . . I . . . can't leave . . . "

"I'll find you." He wrenched an arm free, an arm that was immediately reseized. "I *will* find you."

The sentries jammed him into the tunnel of the hatch that led out to the white room. On the other side, Nathan shot a look back into the hatch and saw Kylen; she was holding her photo I.D. tags. She thumbed the corner on her picture, activating the voice recorder, and said, "I believe in you." Then she threw the tags to him. They landed at his feet. Once again, Nathan broke free from the sentries, scooped up the tags and held them in his fist.

"No more from you," a sentry said tersely.

The man shoved him to his knees and slapped magnetic cuffs around Nathan's wrists. Nathan looked to the hatch. Kylen's tears ran freely, and then a tech blocked his view of her and proceeded to seal the vehicle's hatch. The sentries pulled him to his feet.

"Give me what you got in your hand," one said.

"Better kill me first. Only way."

The access arm began to pull away from the launch vehicle. Nathan closed his eyes and tightened every muscle in his body.

They shoved him in a PRT 2000 escort van, made him remove the flight suit, which was colonial property, then drove him toward the seashore road that paralleled the launch center. The hard-faced security chief, who sat on the passenger's side, spoke with Governor Overmeyer on the hands-free link. Nathan could hear the governor's voice:

"Let him go. All charges dropped. And Nathan, if you're listening. What you did was stupid. But, yes, I know why. And I might've done the same myself. I'm sorry."

"Sir. You're going to have to put this on the director's voice mail before launch," the chief said.

"I'll do that now."

"Thank you. And good luck."

The complex blurred by. Nathan felt nothing. They let him out at the gate, and he barely heard the vehicle leave. He dragged himself away, pebbles rolling under his feet. There was no sky, no earth, no love, life, or dreams. Just a road leading nowhere. He passed in front of a sign.

TELLUS-VESTA
FRANCIS R. SCOBBE COLONIAL LAUNCH CENTER
CORPUS CHRISTI, TEXAS

Suddenly, to his right, far, far in the distance, out over the dark horizon, a brilliant white light rose swiftly, illuminating a trailing plume of smoke. He froze, and after a moment, the sound of the launch reached him, a deep thunder that rumbled across the desert.

His gaze burned as he tracked the rocket's path, higher, higher, higher . . . then it disappeared.

six

"Why'd you enlist?" she asked, sounding like a convict asking him what he was in for.

Nathan touched the photo tags hanging from his neck, then shrugged. "Just did."

The bus lurched. All the young recruits were thrown forward.

A lean, dark-haired young man seated two up from Nathan shouted, "Jesus, driver, this damned humidity is gonna kill us. We don't need any help from you."

Nathan gazed out the window, then once more regarded the young woman seated next to him. She had a kind of sandy look to her, hair that had many shades of brown, and brown eyes to match. She appeared about to say something, then pursed her lips.

Not exactly in the mood to be friendly, but not wanting to put her off, Nathan extended his hand. "My name's Nathan."

"Hi. Shane Vansen."

They exchanged a polite grin, shook hands, then she wiped perspiration from her forehead.

"Hot."

"Yeah."

The guy who had shouted to the bus driver took Nathan's and Shane's cue and reached across the aisle to a young African-American woman. "Mike Pagodin."

Taking his hand, she replied, "Vanessa Damphousse. See, there's a P-H in there you say like an F."

"Damp-fooz. Damp-fooz. 'Sthat French or somethin'?"

She lifted her shoulders. "Doesn't matter. My friends call me 'damn fool'."

Pagodin chuckled over that. "It's gotta tough ring to it. My friends call me 'Pags'—like I'm a dog or somethin'."

She grinned. "Nice to meet you, Pags."

"Hey, I know it's only the first day," Pags began, raising his voice for all to hear, "but any guess as to when we get our planes?"

A few of the recruits murmured their guesses, but no one spoke up with certainty.

Nathan resumed staring through the window. They were approaching the base, and set into the lawn to the right of the main gates was a steel sign that boldly proclaimed in large, white letters:

UNITED STATES MARINE CORPS AVIATOR CAVALRY LOXLEY, ALABAMA

The gates opened automatically, and the bus driver saluted the two MPs posted before the sentry gate inside the fenced perimeter.

From his present angle, Nathan could see what appeared to be a main complex surrounded by several support structures. Off to the far left was a group of long, rectangular buildings that were presumably barracks. To the immediate right was a string of more than twenty small aircraft hangars. Behind them were many more rows of hangars, some so large that Nathan thought they could house a Tellus launch vehicle.

The driver turned down a road that gave them a clear view of the tarmac before the smaller hangers.

Abruptly, Shane leaned over Nathan and pointed to something outside. "That's why I joined."

A group of soldiers marched in formation. Nathan had seen formations around the colonial complex while he was in training, but this group was not like any of those. Even with a quick glance, it was clear to him that they were elite. They sported tight, high-tech flight suits of a design Nathan had never seen before. Black boots and matching berets completed the indomitable look. On their backs were two lines that suggested angel wings.

"Very cool," Nathan found himself saying.

"That's the 127th Attack Wing," Shane said. "The Angry Angels. The best there is . . . or ever will be."

"They lack one thing," Nathan said.

Shane looked at him and frowned. "What?"

He grinned. "Us."

She returned a grin and nodded, then focused her attention back on the Angels. "Someday that'll be me."

Nathan wondered if he or Shane ever would become part of the Angels, then considered whether they'd ever achieve the more immediate and realistic goal of just becoming flyers. Looking at the 127th made it all seem parsecs away. However, some of the men and women did not look that old or that experienced. They only marginally intimidated him.

But there was one who stood out among the Angels, a man built as sleek and rugged as a Marine Corps Condor or Hammerhead fighter. Nathan guessed him to be in his late thirties. There was a mix to the man, a blend of wisdom, toughness, and mystery. Nathan read somewhere that for centuries, soldiers with battle experience wore a gaze known as the "thousand yard stare." It was a look that this guy seemed to have, but Nathan would never know for sure until he himself had battle experience. It was safe to say that the pilot had been there. Probably had seen a lot of action in the A.I. War.

"You looking at him, too?" Shane asked.

"Yeah," he replied softly. "Looks like he's been around."

"My parents were Marines."

"Career officers?"

She nodded.

"They retired?"

"Dead."

Nathan swallowed. "Sorry."

The bus's brakes squeaked as it came to a stop. The young Asian man seated across from Nathan and Shane stood up and squinted at the windshield. "They're gonna yell a lot, aren't they? I hope they don't yell as much as I've heard they do."

He saw Shane take note of the recruit. "He's screwed," she whispered to Nathan.

The bus door opened. A drill instructor's hat, better known for roughly the past two centuries as a "Smokey the Bear campaign cover," appeared at the front of the bus and rose to reveal the man under it. Stocky and mustached, the black man with dark eyes like the muzzle of a shotgun looked more than capable of dealing out enough death to satisfy his superiors. He frowned and shook his head as he eyeballed the recruits. If he had spoken, he would have said, "You are one sorry bunch of cherries."

But he had probably said that to more than enough recruits in his day, Nathan speculated, so perhaps he was keeping his derision to himself.

There would, of course, be plenty of time for that later.

"All right, *herd*. Listen up," he began without introducing himself and apparently having decided that browbeating could not wait. "You ah now at the United States Marine Corps Space Aviator recruit dee-po', Loxley, Alabam-er. When you left home, you were under Momma and Dadda's care. You are now under mine. From here out, you will NOT speak, eat, sleep, or take a dump until you are told to do so, and the first and last word out of your slimy holes will be *sir*. Do you maggots understand me?"

Nathan, Shane, and the rest of the recruits answered, "Sir, yes, sir."

"LOUDER!"

Nathan stole a look at the Asian guy, who flinched.

"SIR, YES, SIR!"

"That's good. And here is something else you had better get used to. You are not going to be happy here. You are not going to have fun. Some of you came here to fly. Most of you will never do that. Most of you will flunk out or freak out or slit your throats. It is my job and the job of my fellow D.I.s to reach down into your guts and see what the hell we got there. Do we got Marine Corps Space Aviator or do we got a shivering sack of shit? So far, I see shit." The drill instructor held his nose and marched down the aisle, using his fist to pound any recruit who strayed too far out of his or her seat. After returning to the front, he released his nose and said, "Upon the command you will have approximately thirty seconds to fall out of this bus. Any questions?"

The guy named Pags raised his hand. "Sir, when do we get our planes, sir?"

"EVERYONE OFF THE BUS!" The drill instructor pointed at Pags. "EVERYONE BUT YOU! MOVE! MOVE! MOVE!"

Nathan fell in behind Shane as they hustled toward the front of the bus. The Asian recruit was in front of Shane, and as he crossed from the steps of the bus to the tarmac, he slipped and fell onto Damphousse.

She cocked her head. "Hey, watch it!"

"Uh, sorry."

Outside, two more malicious-looking D.I.s stood and barked, "GO! GO! GO!" at everyone. Nathan observed the painted shoe prints on the tarmac. He found a set and stood at attention next to Shane. Then he remembered his photo tags and tucked them quickly into his shirt. No need having them out to be scrutinized by the D.I.s.

In a minute, Pags assumed a position on the other side of Nathan, having survived his one-on-one ordeal with the drill instructor on the bus. "I don't believe this crap," he said under his breath.

"You're lucky you don't have any bruises," Nathan

said, hoping his voice had been muted enough by the shuffle of other recruits so that the D.I.s hadn't heard him.

"Just my ego so far."

Another drill instructor, the fourth, paraded in front of the line of recruits. On the planet for some forty-odd years, the guy had probably spent at least twenty-two of them with the Marine Corps. The scowl he wore looked permanently hatcheted into shape on his face. Nathan tried to find the man's eyes, but all he had were two thin slits of leathery skin. Of course, his uniform looked painted on and perfect, creases so sharp they could cut glass. "I am Gunnery Sergeant Bode-juss. Spell it B-O-U-G-U-S. Spell it wrong on any of your paperwork and lose a day's leave. I will unfortunately be your senior drill instructor. I am here to turn you disgusting feces into United States Marine Corps Space Aviators, capable of invoking bowel-wrenching terror in the hearts of your enemy."

Thus far, the D.I.s had spoken a whole lot about shit, twice labeling the recruits as the smelly, sticky stuff. Training for a colonial expedition had been much more reserved, conducted by soft-spoken geniuses instead of loudmouthed bulldogs.

Bougus moved nose-to-nose with Damphousse, intentionally invading her personal space. She drew back a little. "WHY ARE YOU HERE?" he barked.

"Sir, to find a direction, sir!"

"A direction? Are you lost?"

"Sir. I, uh, I suffer from a sense of disconnection and—"

"ANSWER THE QUESTION!"

"SIR, YES I AM, SIR. LOST, SIR."

Bougus took a step back, then raised a thumb and stuck it to his chest. "Do I look like a road map to you?"

"SIR, NO, SIR!"

"WELL, I AM A ROAD MAP!"

Turning away from Damphousse, Bougus continued

to move down the line. "I will guide you and you will learn. If you pukes manage by some miracle to leave my academy, you will be weapons, focused and full of purpose. You will pray for war. You will be proud, hot-rod rocket jocks of precision and strength, tear-assing across the cosmos, huntin' for heaven."

Nathan saw the young Asian recruit stiffen as Bougus passed in front of him. The D.I. moved on, and the recruit emitted a sigh of relief.

Bougus stopped, spun and rushed into the Asian recruit's face. "WHAT'S YER NAME?"

For a moment it seemed the young man had forgotten. Then, in a squeaky voice, he managed, "Wang, Paul Wang, Officer."

Bougus drew back as if Wang had a disease. "OFFICER? I AM NOT AN OFFICER! I WORK FOR A LIVING." Suddenly, Bougus swiped his "campaign cover" from his head and slapped it down hard onto Wang's. "Son. Do you have a cranial-rectal inversion?"

"Uh, a what, sir?"

"A CRANIAL-RECTAL INVERSION. I THINK YOU DO. I THINK YOU'RE SHITTING IN MY HAT RIGHT NOW. IS THAT RIGHT, SON?"

"SIR, NO, SIR!"

Bougus ripped his hat from Wang and replaced it on his own head, pulling the brim down to eyebrow level. Wang made a tiny sound, a remote, high-pitched and extremely short squeal that betrayed his fear.

"Did I hear a sound outta you, Wang?"

Hyperventilating, Wang vehemently shook his head no.

"I did. I heard a sound outta you." Bougus put his lips only inches away from the young man's ear. "I bet it was your war cry. Lemme hear your war cry, Private."

"Ahhhhhh . . . "

Half of the recruits, including Nathan and Shane, broke into laughter.

"SHUT YOUR HOLES!" Bougus directed his attention

to the black D.I. from the bus. "Sergeant Maxwell. Let this pantywaist hear a Marine Corps war cry."

Maxwell, who stood at parade rest some half-dozen meters away from the recruits, suddenly charged wild-eyed at Wang. "AHHHHHHHHHHHH!"

Wang closed his eyes. The sergeant stopped short before running him over. Maxwell took a step back. "OPEN YOUR EYES!"

Bougus crossed to face Wang. "NOW LEMME HEAR YOUR WAR CRY!"

Wang was in hell. "Ahhhhhh . . . "

Then Bougus and Maxwell added their voices to Wang's. Wang reacted to this, intensifying his scream to the volume and pitch of the D.I.s. Finally, the trio broke off.

Nathan looked at Shane, who rolled her eyes.

Bougus gave Wang his deadpan. "In space, no one can hear you scream, unless it's the war cry of a United States Marine."

Shane shook her head slightly.

Bougus moved to her. "Why'd you join my Corps?"

"Sir, to defend my country, sir."

Bougus actually smiled, and his teeth were actually white. "'To defend my country?' Are you crazy? We have no enemies. YOU'VE MADE A TERRIBLE MISTAKE!"

To Nathan's surprise, Shane held her ground, undaunted. "Sir, no, sir."

"ARE YOU CALLING ME A LIAR?"

"Sir, the best way to maintain peace is to maintain a strong defense, sir."

"Are you running for office?"

Nathan blurted out a snicker, then quickly composed himself.

Too late.

Bougus regarded him. "You think that's funny?"

"SIR, NO, SIR."

"Why not?"

"SIR, I DON'T KNOW, SIR."

"DO YOU BELIEVE IF YOU SAY IT IS FUNNY YOU WILL OFFEND ME?"

"SIR, YES, SIR."

"YOUR PRESENCE HAS ALREADY OFFENDED ME. AND NOW YOU HAVE TOLD ME THAT MY WIT IS NO GOOD. I THOUGHT I AMUSED YOU." He softened. "Come on, tell Uncle Frank the truth. I'm funny, ain't I?"

Nathan knew Bougus was baiting him. But any answer at this point would be wrong. "SIR, YES, SIR."

"Well I don't want YOU to be the only one laughing. Amuse ME with twenty-five!"

Beside him, Nathan heard Shane stifle a giggle, then, from the corner of his eye, he saw her cringe.

Sergeant Bougus, still wielding a near-full stockpile of verbal missiles, aimed his gaze at Shane. "I'm glad we're having such a fun time! You too, on your face. ONE ... TWO ... THREE ... FOUR ... I LOVE THE MARINE CORPS."

As Nathan did his push-ups with Shane, the two of them counting in unison, he listened to Bougus and Maxwell.

"Are all these worms accounted for?" Bougus asked.

"Short one guy. The tank."

Nathan hesitated, then resumed his punishment. Just what he needed, a *tank*. He had joined the Corps on the possibility that somehow, sometime, he would get to Tellus and see Kylen again. Now he would have to serve with a living reminder of why he wasn't with Kylen in the first place.

He hadn't even met the tank. Already he hated him.

"Twenty-two ... twenty-three ... twenty-four ... twenty-five." Nathan rested his stomach on the warm tarmac a moment before hauling himself to his feet. His arms and shoulders were sore, his palms full of grit. Wiping sweat from his temple, he turned to Shane. They both were breathing too heavily to speak, not that they would've wanted to with the D.I.s hovering nearby.

A military jeep came from around the corner of the

main complex and pulled up to the line of recruits. The MP driving got out and shuffled to the passenger's side to let out a lanky man with chestnut-colored hair. The prisoner's hands were locked behind his back. After withdrawing a remote from his belt, the MP aimed it at the young man's hands. Freed, the prisoner slipped the magnetic ringlets from his wrists and tossed them back to the MP.

"All yours," the MP told Bougus, then laughed over some private joke as he headed back to the jeep.

Bougus glared at the MP, then craned his head slowly, dramatically, to regard the prisoner, who remained standing where the MP had left him.

Nathan was not a great judge of character, but based on the new arrival's escort, his appearance, the smirk on his face, he looked like an edge-walker who projected a serious air of rebellion.

Bougus approached the prisoner, then stood shoulder-to-shoulder with him, staring at the horizon. "I know all about you, Mr. Cooper Hawkes. The judge thought it would be—*cute*—to sentence a tank to the military."

Hawkes bowed his head.

"I want you to know," Bougus continued, "that I fought alongside your people. So I know."

Nathan couldn't believe what he was hearing. It sounded as if Bougus had suddenly found a kindred spirit in the tank. Hawkes's people were veterans, so now the recruit would share that special relationship, one reserved only for veterans, with the D.I. It was bad enough serving with a tank. But to serve with a tank who was teacher's pet?

"Yeah, I know all about tanks," Bougus restated. "They're lazy and they don't care about anyone or anything."

Nathan could not repress his grin. Bougus sounded wonderfully malevolent. And then the D.I. crossed in front of Hawkes, challenging the tank to respond.

"I won't let you down," Hawkes said.

Were he not in uniform, not a D.I., not standing on the tarmac of a Marine Corps base, the proximity of Bougus's face to Hawkes's could have been taken for the prelude to a kiss. "The only thing you're gonna let down is your face on the deck. Gimme fifty, right now!"

Bougus swung away, and the other D.I.s swarmed around the tank to back up Bougus's order. Hawkes dropped to his hands and knees and began.

Without warning, Bougus steered straight for Nathan. "What are you doing standing up?"

"SIR, I HAVE COMPLETED THE TWENTY-FIVE PUSH-UPS, SIR."

"I DIDN'T SEE NO TWENTY-FIVE FROM YOU OR HER. GET YOUR SNOT HOLE BACK DOWN ON THIS DECK."

"SIR, PERHAPS ONE OF THE OTHER DRILL INSTRUCTORS SAW, SIR." Nathan looked to them; they shook their heads negatively.

"DOWN!"

Nathan and Shane complied, and as they counted off, Nathan saw Hawkes look up at Shane and wink. She reacted with disgust. Nathan stared at the tank, kindling the fire in his gaze.

seven

Kylen lay on her bunk, staring across the tiny cabin at Yolanda. Her friend took a seat on the floor near the wall, pulled her knees up into her chest, then hugged her legs.

Yolanda lowered her head slightly and formed an exaggerated pout. "This is my impression of you for the past six weeks."

"When they create a law against sulking then maybe I'll stop."

"I've been trying—and it's gonna happen now."

"What?"

"We're going to talk about—"

"No, we're—"

"Yes, we are. We're going to talk about *him*."

Kylen asked herself why it had to be Yolanda's business. Yes, she knew her friend was trying to help her get over the grief of saying good-bye—perhaps forever—to Nathan, but to force her to speak about him would only make things worse.

She voiced that sentiment. "Don't make me. I think that if I just don't talk, just don't think, then this thing I have in me will wash away."

Yolanda's brow rose. "Girlfriend, you're fooling yourself. In a little while we're going to make wormhole insertion. Now's the time to let go . . . leave it all back here—in this part of space. You'll come out on the other side renewed."

Kylen threw an arm over her eyes. "I'll never let him go."

Yolanda *tsk*ed. "You don't have to forget him. Just get him out of your heart."

"What if I don't want to?"

"Then you're going to *waste* what will be the most exciting time of your life. You're starting a new existence on a new planet. And you're going to mope around, looking back instead of forward?"

"It would've been more exciting *with* him."

Yolanda sighed deeply. "Girlfriend, let me put this into perspective for you. We all said good-bye to a lot of people, people we may never see again for the rest of our lives. Do you know what it was like for me to leave behind my parents and sister?"

Kylen stiffened. She jerked her arm off her eyes and sat up. "I know all about that," she began, feeling her chest warm. "It's not the same. I said good-bye to my parents, too. But we both knew that signing a colonial contract meant I would be traveling light-years away. We had time to think about that. We had time to prepare for it. Nathan and I got a few lousy hours."

Her friend unclasped her arms and pushed herself to her feet. "All the time in the world is not enough to prepare for a good-bye. One hour . . . a millennium . . . there's no difference."

"But they threw it at us—just before launch! There *is* a difference."

Yolanda shook her head negatively. "How the pain comes doesn't matter; it is . . . always the same."

Kylen reached back and seized her pillow, then threw it against the cabin wall.

Yolanda crossed to the bunk and sat at its foot. "Easy."

Kylen beat her fists on her thighs. "Oh, I could choke those senators and every governor—Overmeyer included."

"I guess they were smart to seat you away from the In Vitroes. You probably want to choke them, too. And they're as innocent as you."

Kylen massaged her eyelids, realizing that Yolanda had tricked her into a conversation about Nathan. She felt the growing soreness of tears. "I told you that I didn't want to talk about this."

"It's gotta come out. We gotta get it out." Yolanda sounded serious, and a trace desperate.

"Why do you care? Why do you have to keep doing this to me?"

"Your parents aren't here. And you'd do this for me. I can't tell you how many times my heart was broken and my mom and sister comforted me. Heartbreak and solitude don't mix. I'm in your face—and I'm here to stay."

Kylen flashed a wan smile. "Should I thank you or kill you?"

Yolanda lifted an index finger and placed it on her chin, thinking it over with mock seriousness. Then she brightened. "You can buy me lunch on Tellus. Now. Tell me everything you hated about Nathan."

Frowning, Kylen looked away. "Hated? Why?"

Yolanda tucked a stray lock of hair behind her ear. "The idea here is that I ask you to do something and you do it—for your own good. You keep questioning the process instead of riding the wave. All that does is get me frustrated and you pissed off because I'm not supplying answers to questions about the process." Yolanda huffed. "All right?"

"He's got a temper. He's got some nervous habits, I guess—don't we all—like when he hasn't shaved for a day or two he'll constantly rub at his beard."

"Good. What else?"

"He drifts off a lot . . . you'll be talking to him and he's gone, not even listening. I used to tell him that he was already on Tellus."

"Do his feet smell?"

Kylen felt her lips curl into a full grin. "Yolanda!"

"Really. I dated a guy once—whew! Got him right the hell outta my bed."

Kylen cringed.

"Well?"

"No. His feet do not smell. I can't believe we're talking about this. We're on a colonial cutter bound for an alien planet and the topic of conversation is foot odor."

"You think you guys would've married?"

That one hit Kylen in the back. "I thought we were talking about—"

"Process again."

She let her mind drift into a place that she had, for the past six weeks, forbidden it to go. It was the vision she had of her life on Tellus with Nathan, of their home, their garden, of when she carried their first child and they stayed up on cool, dry nights smelling the cinnamon in the air and watching her belly twitch with life. They would be a family and teach their children about Earth and create a world that was even better. And all of it would come to pass because they believed in each other.

"This one you can leave alone if you want to," Yolanda said. "The answer's obvious."

"Then why did you ask?"

"It's what you say around the answer that's helpful."

"So I couldn't have said yes or no."

"Not that you couldn't have . . . you wouldn't have."

The link speaker crackled a moment, then the ship's captain spoke. "ETA to wormhole: five minutes. All personnel to assigned stations." He repeated the message as Yolanda rose.

Kylen scooted out of the bunk, moved to her friend and embraced her. "Thanks," she whispered.

"I don't know if we got him all out of there. But just think about what I said. New life ahead. Old life here."

"I will."

"Coming with me?"

"Go on ahead. I'll catch up."

Yolanda left, shutting the hatch behind her.

Kylen went to her bunk and slid out the paper Nathan had given her. She still had not read it. She would wait, as he had asked her. Yolanda would want her to read the paper now, then toss it. Instead, she folded the paper once more, making it smaller, and decided she would take it—take him—with her.

I'm sorry, Yolanda.

She left the cabin, and within two minutes was suited and sitting next to her friend, strapped to her seat in the colonist compartment. She kept Nathan's note tucked under her hip, hidden from Yolanda's view.

A panel in the ceiling flipped down, and a three-by-five-meter video screen descended and locked into place. After a buzz, multicolored snow filled the screen, then an image rolled and stabilized: a forward view into space.

In the center of the viewer lay the wormhole. It made space look as if a plug had been pulled and the universe was being sucked down a cosmic drain. Unlike a black hole, which drew the light and life out of everything around it, wormholes occasionally spat back glowing particles from the other side. Kylen was not into the physics of the whole thing, just the beauty of it. The swirling. The blue and white and yellowish light.

"It sure is pretty," Yolanda said. "But I can't help thinking of it as an orifice."

"You mean like a mouth?" Kylen asked.

"I was thinking of—"

"Oh . . . "

Yolanda nodded. "Yeah. And we're headed right up it."

"ETA to wormhole: forty-five seconds . . . "

A forked tongue of blue light rose up out of the wormhole and then dissipated.

Yolanda gasped. "My God, the thing's hungry."

"Twenty seconds . . . "

Kylen put her hand on Yolanda's wrist. "I know what we're going to talk about over lunch."

"What?"

"Some of *your* heartbreaks."

"Oh, no. That's level-seven info. Priority."

"Ten seconds . . . "

"Oh, shit," Yolanda said. "Here we go."

Together, they counted off the remaining seconds. Before they got to one, if felt as if a hand vised itself around the cutter, a hand that was, in fact, the gravitational pull of the wormhole. Kylen thought she heard the hull groan in protest.

Strange, elongated shapes made of light or darkness, depending upon which caught your eye, shot at them and rolled past the screen. Then the cutter shook violently. The time-matter effect that her instructors had warned her about took hold. Kylen looked down at her hand, and when she moved her fingers, it seemed the action was delayed. She thought about moving her thumb. What felt like a second passed, and then the thumb moved as though underwater. She glanced at Yolanda, who lifted her arm up and down in the odd slow motion produced by the wormhole.

"Seeing it on discs is one thing. Experiencing it is another," Yolanda said. Her words were as altered as her movements. Indeed, Kylen could discern them, but they were much lower in pitch than normal and bore the slur of a drunkard.

A small circle of normal-looking space expanded from a point of nothingness in the center of the viewer, surrounded by the rushing walls of the wormhole. The diameter of the circle increased steadily until it swallowed all four corners of the screen. For a brief moment, a fuzzy, multi-colored ringlet, a ghost image of the wormhole, appeared against the starfield, then it came at the screen and vanished.

"Wormhole exited. Switching to aft view," the captain said.

As the colonists broke into a round of applause, the wormhole was displayed on the viewer. The abyss looked exactly as it had when they had entered it, only now, to Kylen's relief, it shrank as they moved away from it.

"I believe forward view contains something you might

want to take a look at," Overmeyer said coolly, trying to suppress what Kylen knew was a wellspring of joy.

There it was. The magnificent green and blue planet of Tellus. Two of its eight moons, one full, one a waning gibbous, glistened in the distance. The planet's atmosphere created a hazy halo that was more than a little fitting. Had she arms, they would have been outstretched, welcoming the colonial cutter.

"Proximity beacons located. Signals are good. Retro rockets engaged."

For a moment, being in the cutter was not unlike being in the full inertia of an abruptly slowing ground vehicle. Kylen's harness tightened automatically, then slackened.

Studying the planet, reveling in its beauty and feeling her heart thumping faster and faster, Kylen didn't realize what she was doing until it was too late.

I'm excited? Yes! I want to be here. This is it. It's what . . . we . . . dreamed of.

Suddenly, it was a rainy day at the beach, and feeling good about anything was an act of betrayal. He wasn't with her to share in it.

"Trans-Tellus injection complete . . . prepare for entry."

The colonists around Kylen slapped shoulders, blew kisses, and waved fists in the air. Yolanda was no exception. She threw off her strap and tried to give Kylen a hug, though her flight suit and helmet were in the way.

"We're here!"

"Yes we are," Kylen said, hearing the lack of emotion in her voice.

As Yolanda buckled herself to her seat, Kylen furtively withdrew Nathan's note from beneath her thigh.

I'm not on the planet yet, but this is close enough, Nathan, and I can't wait anymore . . .

She began reading the note, hearing Nathan's voice in her head:

Five billion years from now, maybe to the day, the sun burns ninety percent of its hydrogen. A balance is destroyed. More energy is created than released. Quickly, in a few million years, the sun radiates all of its potential power.

The star swells. Mercury. Venus. Earth. Disappear. Swallowed. The sun truly, finally, touches the sky. Life vanishes.

Eventually, the sun shrinks, decreasing to the size of the Earth, which reappears from the Red Dwarf's grasp. With no gravity to hold it, the Earth slowly floats away.

She looked up from the page to the viewer. They were streaking toward the dark side of the planet. A large land mass, mottled green and brown, was half-draped in darkness at the bottom of the screen. She tossed a quick look to Yolanda, saw that her friend was deeply involved in a conversation with the doctor, Drake, then turned back to the note.

Elsewhere . . . stars are born. Other star systems, older, larger . . . continue to breathe. The Solar System dies of crib death. If that's what it takes . . .

An explosion rocked the craft. Kylen slammed back into her seat, the note falling from her grasp. The ceiling above the viewer caved in, dropping the screen in a shower of wires, deck, fire, smoke, and sparks. Cabin lights went out. Amber-colored backup lights winked on in their place.

"Yolanda! What the hell was that?"

And even before she could get the question out of her mouth, Kylen had turned to look at her friend and saw that the young woman's visor had been shattered by a knife-like fragment of flying deck plate. A mist of blood dotted the inside of the visor, obscuring Yolanda's face.

"Yolanda!" Kylen shook her friend who wasn't moving. Yolanda didn't react. "You can't . . . no . . . ohmygod."

Another explosion threw everyone to the right, as if tossed by an eight-foot breaker.

"We've got damage . . . level ten . . . level five . . . what the hell are —"

Internal power died. Darkness. Screams of terror echoed off the shattering, spark-spewing hull of the compartment.

Kylen thumbed off her restraints. She climbed out of her seat, adjusted the O_2 flow knob on her helmet, then rushed to the nearest porthole.

Her jaw dropped as she watched three trios of spacecraft strafe the cutter with weapons' fire. The many eruptions, some distant, some inside the compartment, nearly sent her to the floor. She kept a strained grip on the sill of the porthole and studied the flat, black, triangular fighters. Sleek dorsal fins jutted from their backs, fins that, like the fighters' wings, narrowed to sharp tips at the rear of the craft. The metallic sharks wheeled sharply around for another run. She backed away from the porthole as they targeted the cutter.

A direct hit sent her crashing to the floor. Her visor smashed against the deck but didn't crack. Her right thigh shuddered as a small shock ran through it, and suddenly, her airflow was gone. She unfastened the latches on her helmet, then twisted it off. Smelling the frayed wires and smoke, she resisted the temptation to pull in a long breath. She chanced a little air, then coughed and began to choke. Through tearing eyes she saw that nearly every control panel in the compartment billowed gray smoke illumined by the random flashes of overloads. She crawled forward, reached and found Nathan's note, even as the ship vibrated with a force that threatened to tear it apart. She felt the cutter dip into the planet's atmosphere like a sinking ocean liner. With the air growing thin, and salvos of alien fire still blasting off pieces of the craft, she pressed Nathan's note to her lips and closed her eyes.

eight

"Where are they?"

"Don't see 'em yet."

"You ain't gonna see 'em until it's too late."

"See if you can pull them up on LIDAR."

"Nothing. No contacts."

"Give them a minute. They'll show."

"Yeah, rushing the bad guys is rude."

"PEOPLE. CUT THE SKIPCHATTER UNLESS YOU GOT SOMETHING IMPORTANT TO SAY!"

A glassy black sea speckled with light lay serenely before Nathan. He adjusted his grip on the stick of the Marine Corps SA-43 Endo/Exo Hammerhead fighter, then checked the heads-up display superimposed on the canopy. Data bars within the HUD told him all systems were in the green. He looked above to the LIght Detection And Ranging image. The LIDAR was devoid of enemy craft, yet he knew they were there. He grew tense within his helmet and pressure suit, then reminded himself that he was at the tip of a spearhead of warplanes, and each cool, mean craft, with its forward-swept wings that supported proximity guns and multiple laser cannons, could bite a lethal chunk out of anything it encountered.

But then he re-reminded himself that an ace can fly a piece of garbage made from tape and coat hangers and still inflict heavy casualties on the enemy. Pilot equals everything. Was Nathan up to the task? He knew one thing. His inexperience kept creeping into his voice. "All right. Let's check them again, people."

"Come on, Nathan," Pags moaned in Nathan's link.

"Do it," he replied flatly. "My twelve, low and high, is clear."

"Red Leader, R-Three. My two to four is looking good," Shane said.

"This is R-Two," Wang began unsteadily. "And, uh, we're okay over here."

"R-Four?" Nathan asked.

"What do you think?"

"R-Four. Report properly."

"Our six and three are full of nothin' but space."

"R-Five. You're up."

A loud yawn crackled through Nathan's link. "Yup."

"Yup, what?"

Hawkes dropped his voice in an overwrought attempt to sound serious. "Seven, six, and five, low, high, and any other ways you wanna look at them, are clear."

"R-Six. I'm clean all around," Damphousse reported.

Something flashed on Nathan's periphery. He turned his head. It seemed the stars blurred as though suspended above a barbecue pit. Then his heads-up display went wild:

Blip-blip-blip-blip-blip-blip.

Six targets knifed into his two o'clock. His NAV system was already plotting an intercept course and targeting locks were already hovering across the display.

"This is Red Leader. Six contacts at two o'clock. Confirm."

"Red Leader, this is R-Three. Confirm. A-0-A: fifteen degrees." Shane sounded intense.

And then Pags, all business, added his voice to hers. "R-Four. Confirm. Check six."

Nathan's suit kept him too cool to sweat, and there was definitely something unnatural about that. His pulse, rocketing at least as fast as the Hammerhead, should be accompanied by clammy palms and soaked brow. He eased back on his stick while he checked the

LIDAR. The bandits were moving behind the wing. "R-Five, check six! R-Five, check six!"

He waited for a few seconds. Nothing.

"Hawkes! Answer me!"

Dead air.

Nathan looked back to take physical account of the wing. Wang was on the right, Shane the left, both in the first division. Pags, the tank, and Damphousse made up the second division. He focused on the tank's fighter, directly behind him. Though he couldn't see Hawkes, he imagined that the pilot had his feet kicked up on the console and was snoring. Or, perhaps, was flying nonchalantly with his link turned off. Either way, the tank was screwing up royally.

"Enemy craft have us locked on!" Shane announced.

Nathan's HUD showed that the bandits had banked left and rolled around to the wing's six o'clock. "Juke right! Buzz east!" he ordered.

Nathan cut the stick, rolling his Hammerhead tightly in an evasion tactic that he hoped the others would follow. Indeed, the HUD confirmed that one, two, three, four Hammerheads were behind him as he came out of the roll, pulled the stick back, and engaged full thrusters to begin a seventy-five-degree climb.

Four? There should be five of our wing behind me. And I know who's not following. . .

"Hawkes!"

The tank's fighter continued on a straight path, oblivious to bandits, orders, and the universe.

"Hawkes!"

Nathan looped around, sticking to his original plan to fall low and then come up at the enemy's six.

"All fighters! Break off from leader!" Shane cried. "Nathan! YAW TO EVADE!"

"R-Three! What are you doing?" he asked, dumbfounded.

Then Nathan's jaw nearly fell in his lap as looked

dead ahead. The LIDAR sounded an alarm to underscore the nightmare image:

He was headed straight for Hawkes's fighter.

A yawn from Hawkes sounded through the link as Nathan tried—at the last possible second—to drive his stick forward and dive beneath the oncoming fighter.

The nose of Hawkes's Hammerhead, with its small, slightly upturned forward wings, filled Nathan's view. Then the thermoplastic canopy shield abruptly shattered amid a torrential river of fiery hell.

"Pags, look—"

"Oh, shit!"

"Pulling up! Can't hold . . . "

"Adiós."

Nathan saw the other ships go down like dominoes behind him, one exploding after another, complex machinery and fragile flesh and bones turned to wreckage and ash in the vacuum of space.

Punching straight up, Nathan's gloved hand connected with the plastic. "Damn!" His cockpit powered down and the canopy rose slowly. He looked over his shoulder and spotted Sergeant Bougus leaning into Hawkes's cockpit. The D.I. appeared to be floating in space.

"YOU'RE DEAD! YOU'RE DEAD!" Bougus waved a hand, gesturing to the other ships. "THE ENTIRE WING IS DEAD BECAUSE OF YOU!"

The starfield around the ships faded into the antiseptic white walls of the simulator room. The only section remaining of the Hammerheads was their cockpits, each interlinked with the others to simulate attack formation fighting.

Unfortunately, they simulated it a little too well.

Nathan hung his head out of his cockpit and shot back a menacing look. "You stupid tank!"

Shane had her gaze locked on Hawkes. "What were you doing?" Her tone sounded as if she were giving him the benefit of the doubt.

"Screwing up is what he was—"

"YOU TWO SHUT THE HELL UP, YOU'RE DEAD!"

Shane looked at Nathan, pursed her lips and shook her head. Nathan nodded then glared at Hawkes.

The tank smiled. "What're you so upset about? This ain't real."

Bougus went to seize the tank's collar, then made a quick fist and held himself back. Nathan dug his own fingernails into his palm. Bougus shouted, "SOMEDAY, NUMBNUTS, IT WILL BE REAL!" Then the sergeant grew quiet, a volume that seemed much more dangerous to Nathan. "You'll be in the middle of a hairy-assed furball and you will"—he resumed his shout—"DIE! With you around, the wing doesn't have to fear the enemy!"

Nathan gritted his teeth. "I should have blown your ass away."

The tank fired off a look that had challenge written all over it, and Nathan imagined himself taking the look, chomping down on it, swallowing it, then vomiting it back into the tank's face.

And then Bougus was in Nathan's face. "Is that right? GET OUT! GET OUT OF THAT COCKPIT! EVERYONE . . . OUT! OUT!"

Nathan unplugged the computer cable that attached his flight suit to the cockpit, then hustled out to join the rest of the recruits.

"OVER HERE! TOGETHER!"

The group formed a semicircle around Bougus, with Nathan and Hawkes on opposite ends.

Bougus turned to Nathan and pointed to the tank. "You! Grab his ass!"

Nathan grimaced. "Sir?"

"THAT'S AN ORDER! GRAB IT! EVERYONE LINE UP AND GRAB THE ASS OF THE MARINE NEXT TO YOU!"

As Nathan grasped the tank's butt, he saw Pags maneuver himself to a place behind Damphousse. She smirked at Pags. Nathan withdrew his hand from the tank as Shane stepped in front of him. He reached out to grab her.

Hawkes then cut between Shane and Nathan, blocking Nathan's hand. The tank locked a paw into position on one of Shane's cheeks.

Nathan's breath quickened. He considered yanking the tank around and beating the lousy pilot's face into a purple sheen, but then Bougus would take him into the latrine and do the same to him. Resignedly, he resumed clawing the tank's butt, feeling the bile build at the back of his throat.

"YOU FEEL THAT MARINE'S ASS? THAT'S YOUR ASS!"

"Ouch!" Shane looked back at the tank and scowled. *The bastard!*

"You may fly in individual rockets, but you're a TEAM. If you risk your ass, you risk the team's. You people have been here six weeks and still ARE NOT *gung ho.* Have you already forgotten what that means?"

Damphousse raised her hand and spoke. "I remember, sir. It's Chinese—and it means working together."

"DO YOU KNOW WHAT A RHETORICAL QUESTION IS?" Bougus asked her.

"YES, SIR!"

"NO, YOU DON'T! SHUT UP!"

Nathan thought that when it included tanks like Cooper Hawkes, working together was not just an impossibility, it was a violation of natural laws. Hawkes was a reckless loner, a maverick, and dead weight. Bougus would do well to flunk him out of the academy, thus getting that weight off the wing's back.

"Now. If you Marines do not learn to work together, then that fatty clump of flesh in your hand will be blown to every speck of the galaxy—and yours will follow it."

Nathan sensed that everyone was letting the D.I.'s words sink in, but he thought the whole demonstration was a joke. What was sinking deeper into him was his hatred for the tank.

"Sir," Pags said, dropping a word into the silence, "maybe Coop would do better in a real plane, sir. I know I would."

The tank craned his neck to regard Pags with a quarter-smile.

Bougus crossed to Pags. "I'm afraid of you in a SIMU-LATOR! Now get back in your pits. We'll do it again 'til it's right! MOVE!"

Shane slapped away Hawkes's hand then shot Nathan an unreadable look. She headed for her cockpit.

Nathan paused a moment to stare down the tank, who, in turn, stared him down. His fists and arms trembled. Then, deciding that the weaker man would be the guy who turned away first, Nathan held his ground and his gaze, even after Bougus walked up from behind him and asked, "Problem with your feet?"

"Sir, no, sir."

The tank grinned sardonically, then marched away.

Nathan lowered his head and ambled back toward his simulator.

"I got both your numbers, West and Hawkes," the sergeant warned. "And anything but *by the numbers* from you two now and I'll be dining on both your livers."

"A nice White Zinfandel would go good with that, Sarge," Pags suggested.

"GET IN THAT PIT!"

nine

Neon stars twinkled behind a flashing rock.

"'Sthat an asteroid or a hemorrhoid?" Pags asked. "It does look more like a—"

"He asks that every time we come here," Shane moaned.

Though he'd seen it before, for the hell of it, Nathan casually inspected the sign above the bar.

Pags could be right.

He followed Shane, Wang, Mr. Hemorrhoid, and Damphousse into Asteroids, and was quickly enveloped in the sights, sounds, and smells of the place. Dimly lit, the club was a throng of humanity freshly squeezed from concentrate. Leathernecks from the base nursed drinks at nearly every table, and others gathered in cliques about the bar. Bottles flashed, liquor flowed, and music videos wailed from speakers and flickered from wide screen projectors. Wafting in the air was a trace mixture of potpourri, perfume, and cologne. The talk, Nathan guessed, was either about sex or flying, or, more interestingly, sex while flying.

Damphousse squinted and went up on her toes to see over the crowd. "There's a place over there. Let's grab it."

They crossed, seized, and immediately occupied the table. Pags signaled to the waitress, a cute blonde who winked at him and, in short order, returned with beers for everyone.

Nathan glanced perfunctorily at the empty stage behind their table, then sipped his beer.

Damphousse picked at the front of her pants. "You think I could ever talk the Marine Corps into pleats?"

Pags poured himself a mug of the frosty stuff, then used the rest of his bottle to fill Wang's mug. "See, if I were runnin' the Marine Corps, I'd give recruits planes on the first day."

Nathan chortled. "War's good business—but that idea ain't."

"He's right," Damphousse said, tipping her head toward Nathan. "The loss of fighters and lives would be tremendous—if today's a good indicator of—"

"Not in defense of Pags," Nathan said, cutting her off. "But today didn't mean jack. Actually, without Hawkes, we probably would've done all right."

Shane nodded. "At least he got his act together on the second run."

"And you've gotta admit," Pags began, then took a sip of his beer, "the son of a bitch is a crack shot."

Nathan rolled his eyes. "They probably rigged that into his genes."

"It was six on six and he got three, one off my tail, one off Wang's—and one off yours, Nathan," Damphousse reminded him. "Not in defense of him."

Nathan drew a line in the sweat on his glass. "I'll concede that he's good. But a team player? I don't think so." He connected the line with two others, forming the letter F: the tank's grade in the academy.

"I invited him to come with us," Damphousse confessed.

Wang set down his drink. "I told her not to."

"We can get him to play on our team," Damphousse said, leaning forward as if it was somehow important to her, "if we just try to understand him."

"Why do you care?" Nathan asked. "If he doesn't hack it, he doesn't hack it."

"I just think it's a shame that—"

"Speak of the devil," Shane said, then elbowed Nathan. The tank entered the bar, his gaze sweeping over it.

He spotted Nathan but acted as if he hadn't. After one more inspection of the place, Hawkes went to the bar and slid onto a stool. He signaled to the bartender, then shot a look back at Nathan, reacting to the fact that Nathan was still looking at him. He gave a slight nod of his head, then looked away.

Yeah, you'd better stay over there, tank.

Damphousse pushed her seat back. "I'm going to see—"

Nathan pointed an index finger at her. "He wants to be alone."

"How do you know?"

"Trust me."

"Didn't Hitler say that?"

"Don't bother him, Vanessa," Shane said. "Maybe later he'll soften up and come over."

Nathan raised his brow. "In which case I'll be gone."

Damphousse pushed her seat under the table. "All right. I won't get in the middle of this. But Nathan, you're going to have to stop this animosity. There's always one or two rogues in every group. Get used to it. You don't have to hate this guy."

She didn't know. He wanted to, at the moment, lapse into the fact that he had rallied for equal rights for In Vitroes, and those "equal rights" had resulted in a colonial quota system that had backfired in his face. The woman he loved was light-years away because of equal rights for In Vitroes. It had been easy to hate Hawkes, and then the tank had, by way of his attitude and actions, made it even easier.

But Damphousse saw only the surface.

A tall figure walked into the bar, backlit by the red neon glow from the sign outside. As he came closer, a face materialized from the shadows: it was the Angry Angel from the 127th, the one Nathan and Shane had seen from the bus window, the pilot with *the stare.*

Hawkes noticed the pilot's entrance and watched as the Angel found a lone seat away from everyone at the corner of the bar. The Marine fingercombed his hair, took a pretzel from a plate near him, then munched. Hawkes nodded to the Angel, who managed a slight nod in return. Then both men ignored each other.

"Does he know that guy?" Shane asked.

"Probably not," Nathan said, then looked at his empty beer mug. "I'm ready for another. Pags? Another round?"

"Oh, yeah."

He regarded Shane, who froze as she stared at something out of Nathan's view. "You chipping in for round two?"

"The Angry Angels . . ." was all that came out of her mouth.

The elite pilots of the 127th Airborne paraded into the bar as though it were enemy territory they had just conquered. Arrogant and humorless, the three men and one woman moved to a table of their liking, and, without a word, the recruits drinking there fell over themselves to give up their seats. One young man even lingered behind to wipe off the table with a napkin.

"That's odd," Shane said.

"What, the fact that vets bully cherries? Been going on since we were grunting and fighting with clubs and stones."

"No." She looked at the Angel at the bar. "How come *he* isn't with them?"

Nathan studied the Angel at the bar. The pilot didn't even acknowledge his squadron. He seemed fascinated by the veneer of the counter top. Then Nathan looked at Hawkes. The tank studied his beer.

Without warning, Shane rose and steered herself toward the Angels' table.

"Hey, maybe you'd better—" Nathan cut himself off since she was already out of earshot. He adjusted his seat so that he could watch her.

Arriving before the table, and probably a little short of breath, Shane said, "Uh, 'scuse me."

They ignored her, the three men listening intently as the woman spoke.

"Sorry to interrupt . . . "

The female Angel broke off and joined her fellow Marines in fixing their nervous fan with a cold, steely look.

"I just wanted to tell you all how much I admire and respect the 127th."

The men looked at one another, smirking.

The woman smiled condescendingly. "Thanks. Thanks a lot. We'll have four pitchers of draft and a couple of shooters."

The group immediately wounded Shane with their sniggers and laughs. She seemed to grow pale and glassy-eyed with the realization that her heroes were creeps.

Nathan slid out of his chair, regarding Pags as he did so. "Be there. If I need you."

Feeling a nerve thump in his neck, he went to the Angels' table, crossing in front of Shane. "She's not a waitress."

"I think we hurt her feelings," the tallest Angel said. "Come and sit in old papa Slayton's lap and tell him all—"

"She's a Marine. Now . . . apologize."

The tall Angel rose, knocking over his chair. He was six-feet plus, and from Nathan's angle, looked nearly seven. "Until she graduates . . . she's slime. Now . . ." he began, spacing his words for effect, "you . . . apologize. To me." He glanced in the woman's direction. "And to Collins."

Nathan considered the situation, which boiled down to mathematics. He was rather deft at the problems they had thrown at him in flight school, physics problems that dealt with aerodynamics, lift, vacuum maneuvering, what have you. Often, he'd click off his calculator and work out the problem long hand, the way a good pilot might switch off his NAV system or LIDAR and fly by the seat of his pants. One learned the true nature of the beast that way.

To get the present equation to balance required the addition of two more variables, variables who sat back at his table. He gave a subtle look to Pags, Wang, and Damphousse. They looked worried. They were not moving.

I'm about to get a beating.

Shane shifted in front of Nathan as the rest of the Angels stood. She was up to something; perhaps she had a few words that would dilute the tension. "Hey, what's the farthest you guys have flown?"

"Four-point-eight light-years," Collins said, without having to think about it.

Shane grinned, then her expression soured. "That's how far you can shove your apology."

The tall guy, Slayton, plowed through the table. He kicked a chair out of his way, threw Shane aside, then slapped away Nathan's fists in order to bring his beefy hands down on Nathan's shoulders. Slayton drew back his bereted head, then, gripping Nathan with what had to be all of his force, brought his forehead down onto Nathan's.

In a flash, Nathan was gazing at the ceiling, which became a starfield for a moment, then blurred back into wood and rafters. He rolled away, shot to his feet, and took a defensive stance as a surge of dizziness passed through him. Shane arrived at his side, her small but formidable fists raised and ready.

Collins came at Shane, releasing a high kick that Shane dodged. Shane's reply was a solid right into Collins's stomach, a punch that, astoundingly, had no effect. Collins smiled, then backhanded Shane across the face so hard that it sent her flat onto her back.

The other three Angels surrounded Nathan, Slayton assuming a position directly in front of him. "There's an interesting sound that a nose makes when it breaks," Slayton said. "Kind of a pop, as if you poked a hot sausage and let out some of the steam."

"YAAAAAAHHHHHH!"

Nathan looked back and saw that Pags had launched himself from a tabletop and now sailed through the air. Pags wore the look and sounded the cry of a pissed-off psychopath. Sergeant Bougus would have been proud.

Pags collided with Slayton and the Marine standing next to him. The two Angels crumpled under the human missile.

Exploiting Pags's move as an avenue for escape, Nathan delivered a roundhouse right to the standing Angel. The Marine fell back over his chair and hit his head on the leg of a table.

"Nathan!"

He spotted Shane being choked from behind by Collins. Running toward the two, readying his fists to do some pounding, he was caught off guard when Collins shoved Shane aside and sent a knee into his groin. Doubling over, he spun and collapsed onto his side.

"Come on, bitch! You gonna get some!"

"We're gonna get in a lot of trouble for this."

Nathan didn't have to look up to know that Damphousse and Wang had joined in what was now an all-out brawl. As the fire in his crotch subsided, he stretched out, got on all fours, then finally managed to rise. He noticed that Hawkes was eyeing him from the bar. The tank repositioned himself on his bar stool, as if he was considering whether or not to help. Then Nathan looked to the other end of the bar, at the Angel. He, too, appeared to be mulling over a decision to join, but just then, the Angel glanced at Hawkes, and there was a look that passed between them, a look Nathan read as: "You help your side, then I'm helping mine." Once that look was exchanged, neither man made a move.

At least the math problem has been solved.

Then again, as Nathan took in the sights of Shane getting thrown into a table of recruits, Wang taking an uppercut and then a kidney punch, and Damphousse getting her arm twisted so far behind her back that it looked about to snap off, he reasoned that even with good numbers they were still going to get the crap beaten out of them.

As least they'd go down as a team. A unit.

Seeing that Slayton was open and not looking in his direction, Nathan rushed to the gawk, pulled the guy's jacket up over his head, effectively blinding the Marine, then unleashed a triplet of punches.

Wang staggered away from the Angel who was clobbering him, then summoned what little strength he appeared to have to kidney-punch the Angel holding Damphousse.

"Ahhh!"

Free, Damphousse rubbed her sore arm a moment, but that moment was interrupted as Collins grabbed the back of the Damphousse's hair and drove her head into a table.

Slayton, jacket down and already recovered from Nathan's beating, seized Wang by his belt, lifted the pleading young man over his shoulder, then tossed him like a rag doll onto the empty stage.

Nathan drew back a fist, about to catch an unsuspecting Slayton in the cheek.

An emergency broadcast tone cut off the music videos, and then every wide screen in the bar displayed the bold letters:

SPECIAL REPORT

Lowering his fist, Nathan regarded the nearest screen. Everyone around began to do the same.

The seal of the United Nations flashed on the screen, then the logo dissolved into the image of a heavyset man behind a desk. He blotted sweat from his balding pate with a handkerchief, replaced the garment in the breast pocket of his suit, then leveled his bow tie. He looked to someone off-stage, nodded, and then faced the camera. Superimposed on the screen was the name:

**SPENCER CHARTWELL
PRESIDENT OF THE UNITED NATIONS**

An eerie, bone-chilling silence, save for the tone, slowly pervaded the bar. No one moved. The tone ceased. The bartender lifted a remote and thumbed up the sound on the main tuner above the bar.

Shane threaded between Wang and Damphousse to stand next to Nathan. "What do you think—"

Nathan put an index finger to his lips.

"Not since the moment of creation has our universe changed so infinitely, so desperately, so quickly. Tonight—for the first time in the brief history of mankind—we are truly of one planet. Last evening, we confirmed that the landing party of the Tellus colony was massacred, unprovoked, by an alien civilization of tremendous force."

Nathan felt the word come crawling out of his throat, but barely heard himself utter it. "No." He gasped. "No." An invisible hand clenched his heart and shook it. Chills spidered up his spine. His ears rang. Then his senses shut down. The world became windswept ice, and it was hard to remain standing.

"Two hundred and twenty-five are dead," Chartwell added. "Twenty-five are unaccounted for."

Twenty-five. Kylen could be among them. He was back in the bar, the glacier behind him. He took a step toward the screen, and only a laser cannon could have severed his gaze from Chartwell.

"Because of destroyed communications, we have only now learned that the Vesta colony suffered the same fate. The alien civilization has not responded to any of our attempts at communication. Of this race we know nothing. The only clue to their people is the bloodshed they left behind.

"My fellow citizens of Earth, no matter where you stand on this planet, either beneath the sun's warmth or in the cold of night, storm clouds of war gather over our home. Soon, they may fall in unceasing thunderbolts. We must stand together against the deluge, for we cannot possibly retreat."

In the pause, the 127th gathered up their fallen berets and headed for the door. The lone Angel at the bar fell in behind them. Nathan saw Hawkes yawn, then turn apathetically away from the screen and pick up his beer.

Kylen might be dead!

Nathan now rode the loops and rolls of his emotions as if they were a simulator. One second he was on the enemy's twelve, coming dead-on, target locked, the next he was staring at Kylen, who lay in a pool of blood. Should he continue to hope? Or would that only make the truth more painful?

WAS SHE DEAD?

He had to know.

When things got tough, as always, Nathan got running. He charged toward a hallway that ended at the rear exit of the bar.

"Hey, Nathan—"

Shane's cry faded behind him. He shot out of the club and into a narrow, moonlit passage between the bar and rear wall of another structure. Stumbling to the wall, he visualized himself beating his face against it, but he already knew he didn't have the guts for that. He draped an arm across the stone and rested his forehead on his wrist. He thought of Kylen, how she might have suffered. He placed her in scenario after scenario, in life-and-death struggles with the aliens or floating helmetless in the silent void of space until she was caught by Tellus's gravitational pull and burned up in its atmosphere. To someone on the planet, she would be a tiny, shooting star.

Nathan pushed away from the wall and drew the photo tags from beneath his shirt. He looked up and spotted the twinkling blue light, center of the system that would have been their future. Then he stared hard at the tags, not realizing his knuckles were whitening as he held them. He touched the corner of Kylen's tag, and her voice came from a tiny speaker:

"I believe in you."

ten

When Nathan and the others returned to the base, they witnessed a light show worthy of the Las Vegas strip. Every room in every building and barracks was illuminated. Moths fluttered in the beams of the powerful pole-mounted spots, which lifted the tarmacs out of the shadows. The runway lights repeatedly chased to the horizon, and the lights of fighters pulsed and rose as each craft thundered toward the stars, toward battle. Crisscrossing the service roads were the headlights of ground vehicles which seemed to be driven by mad speeders but were, in fact, controlled by carriers on urgent missions. Lording over it all was the tower's main beacon, its powerful narrow beam rotating and casting the hangars and complex in a rhythmic, alternating pattern of light and gloom.

Nathan ached with the desire to get into the fight. He was more than ready for a little payback.

Unfortunately, they were assigned to temporary gopher detail and attached to the anything-but-glamorous cargo crews. They slaved until 0500, fetching crates, double-checking invoices, and sometimes, as Pags put it, "just getting in the damned way. We oughta be flyin'." At 0500, they were ordered back to their barracks to clean up and change. Chow was at 0600. At 0630, they were to report to hangar nineteen to receive new orders.

Cranking the knob all the way to the left for full heat, Nathan planned to stay as long as he could under the shower. He kept his eyes closed and tilted his head back to let the water stream onto his face. Somewhere along the line there was a moment where his mind emptied. Either his lack of sleep or the shower had made it so. He no longer worried about Kylen's fate, about his future, about the war. There were only the million tiny rivers cascading over him, the tranquil, hypnotizing music of the water seeping down the drain, and the arms of warmth that cradled and rocked him.

"Come on, West, you're usin' up all the hot water," Wang shouted, his voice echoing too loudly off the tiled walls.

"Wang. I know fifteen silent ways to kill a man. Come here. Let me demonstrate one of them."

"Just hurry up. Please."

He sighed, the spell broken. Kylen . . . piloting . . . the war . . . all coiled around him.

During breakfast, Nathan's spirits lifted a little. Someone once told him that bagels and cream cheese were the food of the gods. At least they made him feel better. He remembered sitting in a doctor's office, waiting for his preliminary colonial physical. He'd read an article about how foods affect one's moods, but there had been nothing about bagels and cream cheese in the report. Chocolate made people happy, peanut butter made people alert, and steak made people aggressive. Judging from the article, what the Marine Corps ought to be feeding its people now were T-bones so big that they hung over their plates and slices of German triple-chocolate peanut butter cake for dessert. They would have many divisions of happy killers all singing:

> *From the halls of Montezuma,*
> *To the shores of Eridani,*
> *We will fight our planet's battles,*
> *In space, land, air, and sea.*

After chow, Sergeant Maxwell escorted the recruits to hangar nineteen and left them at the threshold of an open door that was, Nathan estimated, five stories high. This was arguably the largest hangar on the base. Indeed, as he had suspected earlier, a Tellusian launch vehicle could be housed within the structure. It seemed nearly a kilometer to the rear of the hangar, and cargo trucks and support vehicles raced into and out of the place. A division of landing troops marched inside and filed into an APC that was a hybrid of jet car and tank. The armored personnel carrier rolled out of the hangar and up the ramp of one of at least a dozen gigantic Inter-Stellar Troop Transports. The ISTTs, Nathan had learned, needed only half the fuel of a colonial launch vehicle to make orbit; they utilized some kind of new technology that combined fusion with anti-grav principles.

"What do we do now?" Wang asked.

"Oh, don't worry. Mr. Congeniality will be around," Pags said.

And, as if on cue, they heard a voice from the rear:

"We ... are at war. HOO-YAH! This is what Marines pray for."

Nathan, along with everyone else, snapped to triangular attention. He was at the tip of the triangle, with Hawkes and Shane standing at the rear points. Wang, Damphousse, and Pags formed their triangle to his right, with Damphousse leading off. Nathan glanced at her. She looked at once horrified and exhilarated.

In sharp contrast to her, the tank scowled. He probably didn't want war. All he wanted was to do his time and get out. Do what he had to do. Just enough. Get by.

Asshole.

Nathan was about to flip Shane a look when Bougus proceeded to the front of the squadron and continued:

"From here out every move is crucial. All personnel, vital. While combat-ready pilots are dispatched into battle, you have been assigned a training mission, nonetheless imperative to the global war effort."

"Sir, permission to speak, sir," Pags said.

Bougus found a spot a few inches from Pags's face and paused. "Granted, but if you're gonna gnaw at me about your plane, then—"

"Sir, I want my plane, sir."

The sergeant eyed the rest of the squadron. "You people hear that? This hamster thinks he can fly. Anyone ever seen a flying hamster?"

"There *are* squirrels that can—" Wang started.

"HOLES SHUT! Now, I know how anxious you people are to die, so listen up." He moved to face the group. "You will proceed via military heavy launch vehicle to Space Station Goddard. There, you will board an Internal Solar System Cargo Vehicle and proceed for eighty-four hours to the planet Mars.

"You will be issued rationed supplies: food, air, and water. You will also be issued one Urine and Fecal Collection Device. A yellow flashing light on the flight suit indicates full capacity. I know some of you will forget that. Do your buddies a favor—don't.

"Your mission is to repair a malfunctioning Mars Tracking Drone vital to interplanetary communication. If successful, you will proceed to Accelerated Flight Training. At which time"—Bougus stared wide-eyed at Pags—"you will be assigned a plane and *then* be considered combat ready. From this moment, until we win this war, the only easy day was yesterday."

Since they were on a training mission, the Marine Corps wasn't going to waste valuable space aboard an ISTT for the squadron. Instead, the recruits were, as Bougus had mentioned, going to hitch a ride on an MHLV, the commuter bus of the military. The short-winged rocket was at least twenty years old and sat nestled on a launch platform even older.

As they rode in a small transport toward the vehicle, Damphousse remarked, "We're going in that? I think not."

"It'll get us there," Hawkes assured her.

"What makes you so sure?" she shot back.

"My luck."

Nathan hissed. *Yeah, and mine, to be stuck with you.*

They reached the platform, caught the elevator, then were led by a pair of MPs to the main hatch.

The passenger compartment of the MHLV was no colonial launch vehicle. The seats were worn and torn, the walls scuffed where equipment and personnel had dragged along them, and more than half of the overhead lights had burned out. A cursory look at the consoles told Nathan the redundancies went back three instead of the usual six. A main failure, say in the compartment's pressurization system, followed by two more failures of backup systems, and that would be it. There wasn't much technology standing between the Marines and a vacuum that had a nasty habit of turning people into red and gray mush.

"Thank you for flying Marine Corps. Now bend over and kiss your ass good-bye," Pags instructed, not even trying to make a joke. He found a seat and collapsed into it.

"All right. Everyone relax. She don't look like much, but she'll get us where we're going," Nathan said.

Shane looked him straight in the eye. "You sure?"

He shook his head no. "But I feel better saying she will. Confessing it, I guess."

Hawkes fell asleep during the countdown. Nathan wondered if the tank were trying to prove something, or if he simply was so tired that even a rocket launch wouldn't wake him.

At six seconds, the engines ignited. At three seconds, tons of thrust and flames created billowy clouds that were visible through a porthole. At one second to go, Nathan did, in fact, feel the urge to follow Pags's earlier instructions.

She was a temperamental rocket and, though a veteran,

still anxious and unsure of herself. She trembled through the troposphere, the temperature around her decreasing at a rate of about one and a half degrees Celsius for every 305 meters she climbed. Once the sixteen or so kilometers of troposphere were cleared, she punctured the stratosphere, then the mesosphere, and, at about the 644-kilometer mark, she smoothed out into the ionosphere.

Her pilots were good. No doubt about that.

"I'm thinkin' a martini would work right about now," Pags said.

Hawkes stirred, then his eyelids flickered open. "We there yet?"

"I wish," Damphousse answered.

"Hey, hasn't it dawned on any of you?" Wang asked.

Shane gave him a quizzical look.

The young Marine answered himself. "We're going to *Mars*."

Hawkes yawned, one of the few things he was good at. "So what."

Wang looked at Nathan. "Hey. You ever been on another planet?"

"Accused of being on another planet, yes, but literally, no. Tellus was going—" He cut himself off.

Shane frowned at him. "Tellus?"

He had trouble meeting her gaze. "Nothing. Forget it."

"How about you, Shane?"

"Uh, well . . . "

"Well what?" the tank asked, furrowing his brow.

Shane looked at her knees. "I was very little. During the war my parents were stationed on Mars for a short time. I don't remember much."

"All right," Wang said, brushing off the strain in Shane's voice. "At least we have someone with experience among us."

"Don't look to me," Shane corrected. "Like I said, it's all a blur."

The overhead link buzzed, then the pilot spoke. "Now in Earth orbit. ETA to Space Station Goddard: seven minutes."

Through the porthole, Nathan saw the convex Earth arcing across the top of his view, giving him a brief flash of vertigo. Europe was a brown smudge with clouds pasted on it as if by a preschooler. The white spiral of a hurricane tore a hole in the center of the Atlantic. Beneath the planet, hanging by an imaginary thread, was a gleaming, expanding, ivory-and-silver dot. Soon, the station was in sharp relief, a lone, angular lifeboat floating in a night where straight lines were imposed by man.

Goddard was the result of twenty-five years of multi-national funding. The largest orbital platform yet built, the station had fourteen individual and diverse habitats, and sixteen research facilities within a university that rivaled M.I.T. Layover accommodations were not very glamorous, but anyone who wasn't assigned to Goddard never spent more than a day or two there. As it was, Nathan figured they'd be lucky to have an hour touring the place.

Once the MHLV docked with the station, they were joined by four other recruits. Lynn Bartley was a tall blonde whose feet, Nathan guessed, would have been more comfortable on a California beach than in a pair of standard issue Marine Corps boots. Ken Carter was a dark-haired young man absolutely awed by his surroundings but trying desperately—and unsuccessfully—to hide that fact. Charlie Stone, a tall African-American who, in street clothes probably still looked like a Marine, made it a point to shake hands with everyone, a handshake that augured the power contained within his muscular arm. What Michele Low lacked in height, she made up for in charm. The graceful young Asian woman spoke in a captivating lilt, and, for a moment, Nathan felt guilty about staring at her.

They were ordered to report immediately to the

Internal Solar System Cargo Vehicle's boarding platform, gate seven, flight number 08790. No time for touring.

As the ten Marines walked in line through the tunnel that led to the ship, Pags complained, "Not even five minutes for that martini."

"I hear the in-flight film is one of those old science fiction classics, *Aliens*," Damphousse said.

"That was back when they used real actors, wasn't it?" Bartley asked.

"Yeah," Stone replied. "I think so."

One by one the squadron members stepped through the hatch into the cylindrical troop transport. Nathan was last in line, and before he entered the craft, he stole a look through a large, rectangular, slightly convex viewport. On his left, the ISSCV's troop cylinder jogged straight out into space. The gray hull of the craft had been repaired too many times and was impaled by rotating dishes and antennas of various sizes. Nathan thought that the engineers who had designed the troop carrier must have been fond of Italian food: the craft was like a tube of manicotti, but it was being stuffed with Marines instead of chopped ham and ricotta cheese.

Nathan went inside and a tech sealed the hatch behind him. There were no seats in the cylinder. He and the others strapped themselves to the wall and stood, waiting for launch. When it came, it was soundless and pleasant, the anti-grav units dampening nearly all of the force.

"We moving?" Low asked.

Nathan pointed to the porthole. "Take a look."

Goddard shrank with surprising speed. While the others joined Low as she took in the view, Nathan unfastened his straps. "Listen up. They've done it for us already, but let's meet up in the supply room and double-check our gear."

"Yeah, right. Never trust cargo techs," someone muttered.

The ten Marines barely fit in the small, square cabin

at the end of the troop cylinder. Shelves weighted down with allotted supplies covered three of its walls.

Nathan suggested that each Marine gather and report on his or her water and air tank status, suit and helmet integrity, and personal supply of Meals Ready to Eat.

While Nathan was hunched over, amid the shifting and clattering of personnel, something hit him on the side of his neck and stuck. He slid off the rubber, diaper-like part of the Urine and Fecal Collection Device, held it up, then looked to the end of the cabin.

Hawkes stood in the threshold, a cocksure grin plastered on his face. "Think that one's yours. How 'bout a demo?"

Low, Bartley, and Stone broke into laughter. Shane, Wang, Pags, and Damphousse knew better and stifled their chuckling. Carter hadn't been paying attention.

"I'm not as full of it as you are," Nathan retorted, then resumed going over his gear.

Once all supplies were accounted for, they changed into their olive-drab skivvies then unfolded their bunks from the walls. Less than a meter separated the top from the bottom bunk, and the aisle down the center of the tube was narrowed so considerably that passing meant getting intimate.

From his bunk on the top, Nathan couldn't help but wonder why Shane stood next to hers, apparently reluctant to climb onto the mattress. Sweat beaded her forehead as she gazed with dread back and forth from the bunk to her palm.

"Shane. You okay?" he asked.

"Yeah. Just give me a minute."

"You getting a little space-sick?"

"More like claustrophobic."

"I think we got something for that in the medi-kit," Damphousse said, sitting up in her top bunk, two down from Nathan's. "I'll check." She climbed down and headed toward the supply room, but Shane snagged her arm.

"I'm all right, Vanessa. Don't worry about it."

"Sure?"

"Yeah."

With a doubtful expression, Damphousse returned to her bunk. After one false start, Shane disappeared beneath Nathan's bunk.

Stretched out on his mattress and leaning on an elbow, Carter addressed the group. "Hey. I heard they had an army of six million."

Bartley, pounding some softness into her pillow, stopped to look at Carter. "They can't know that, can they?"

Carter shrugged.

Nathan rolled over and now he had a view of Pags, who couldn't get comfortable in his bunk. The Marine tossed and turned as if lying on a bed of ants. Finally, he settled down and turned to Stone, who bunked across from him. "You think they got better planes than we do?"

Stone nodded. "They gotta be more advanced."

Nathan repressed a chill, and he guessed he wasn't the only one moved by Stone's assessment.

"I knew we couldn't have been alone," Damphousse chipped in. "But now that we're not, I don't know what's scarier, being alone, or"—she cut herself off, shuddering visibly, then eyed Pags. "Do you think you'd be scared if you saw one?"

"If it looked like Sergeant Bougus."

Wang, bunking below and two across from Damphousse, half-grinned, then his gaze went distant. "I'll never forget when I was a kid. The first time I saw an A.I."

"What did you think?" Shane asked, sounding more than just casually interested.

He pursed his lips in thought. "I don't know . . . they looked perfectly human, but something inside me could tell."

"I felt that way when I saw my first In Vitro,"

Damphousse said, then put a hand to her mouth and looked down at Hawkes, who lay a few bunks away, cupping his head in his hands. "I didn't mean nothing by that, Coop."

The tank did not react. His eyes were open, and certainly his ears were functional. Obviously he was used to the remarks, numb to them.

Taking a long breath through his nose, then rubbing his eyes, Nathan told no one in particular, "Hit the sack. When the time comes to face them, we'll all hack it fine." He folded his pillow the way he liked it, and was about to close his eyes when he heard Shane's bunk creak, and then saw her stand. She kneaded her palm with the thumb of her other hand.

"Why don't you let Vanessa get you something?"

She looked like a little girl, thinking it over, her lower lip protruding a bit. Then she wiped the sweat from her brow and nodded resignedly.

eleven

The psychiatrists had told Shane to record her dreams on paper. She had questioned their use of the word *dreams*.

Not dreams. It's the dream. It just keeps happening and happening.

She played out variations of it, switching around acts, beginning with the climax and working her way back, beginning at the middle and spiraling outward so that the start and end ran simultaneously.

But the result was always the same.

While she listened to the hum of the troop carrier's instruments, she felt that the cabin was too small, her bunk too cramped.

The way the crawl space had been.

Shane knew she was going to dream; it was simply a question of how intense the nightmare would be. With Nathan's bunk seemingly pressing down on her, she couldn't help palming the plastic, wishing she could drive it away.

I have to sleep. We went from the bar to cargo detail to the MHLV to the station to this ISSCV. My eyes hurt. I feel like I weigh a ton. Come on, Shane. Close your eyes.

She obeyed herself, and as always, the point when she actually fell asleep went unnoticed. Sometime during the night, the flecked darkness was burned away by a wrathful white light.

Shane lifted the door of the crawl space.

"Kim. Lauren. Stay here!"

She dropped into the hole and hit the floor. Looking forward, she saw her dead parents lying on their stomachs, cast in the twin shadows of the A.I. soldiers. The cyborgs' eyes were obscured by infrared visors, and their chins, though pink, looked as hard as the black armor plates strapped to their bodies.

One of them brandished his pistol and—

Shane sprang away, even as the closet exploded behind her. The pretty school clothes Mommy had bought her burned furiously, their hangers melting off of the rod.

"Take her out," one of them said tersely to the other, his voice sounding tinny, unnatural.

Darting toward one of the soldiers, Shane dropped to pass through the killer's legs; then, from behind, she tore away his pistol. Fumbling with the weapon, she finally wrapped her trembling fingers around it, took aim as the soldier faced her, then, at point-blank range, blew a hole the size of a basketball in the cyborg's chest. Fragments of blood-covered metal and wire splattered on the wall behind the soldier. He crumpled to the floor and lay there, writhing spasmodically.

Shane turned to the other soldier, who, in one fluid motion, ripped the pistol away. He took a step forward, training two weapons on her, his gaze unreadable, his mouth unflinching.

She backed away to the window, thinking she might be able to crash through it and fall to the bushes below. Pressing her arms against the cold glass, she stiffened and braced herself.

Then the A.I. soldier spoke, his voice strangely familiar. "They had to die, Shane. Even here you can't save them. Even here."

Shane balled her hands into fists, but then relaxed the hand that Lauren had bitten. "Liar."

"Do you know how many of us your mommy and daddy slaughtered?"

"You're not . . . human."

"What does that mean, little girl?"

She glanced at her parents. *"You killed them! And THAT means YOU deserve to die!"*

"Isn't your life better now without them?"

"How can you say that?"

"They never loved you. They loved the Marine Corps."

"What do you know?"

"I know everything about you." He raised his infra-visor.

And Shane saw that the soldier was herself, her bloodshot eyes rising from the shadowy plains of her face.

"It's me," the soldier said, *now sounding feminine, sounding exactly like she should, exactly like herself.*

"You killed Mommy and Daddy!"

"Yes, Shane. I did. . . . "

She felt someone shake her. The nightmare rushed out of her head, making her feel as if she were sinking through her pillow. She realized she was out of breath and soaked in her own sweat. After gingerly opening her eyes, she saw Cooper Hawkes staring at her from his bunk. He looked fascinated.

Shane wanted to duck under her blanket, but she felt the need to say something, to sort of cover up what he had seen. She cleared her throat. "Sorry I woke you."

"Wasn't asleep."

They lay there, looking at each other, saying nothing, just there, alive, breathing, at a loss.

Finally, a curious thought worked its way into Shane's mind. "Don't take this wrong," she started softly. "I'm just wondering, I've always heard that In Vitroes can't dream."

Hawkes, revealing no pity for himself, answered matter-of-factly, "I dream."

Shane nodded, and her curiosity blossomed. What did the tank dream about? She leaned back and gazed at the blank plastic base of Nathan's bunk.

Then, as if reading her mind, Hawkes supplied, "I know they never lived, but when I dream I see my parents."

She shivered, then rolled onto her side to face him. "Me too—only I have nightmares about mine. The same one. Since I was five."

"What happens?"

Shane discussed her dream with few people. And she had found that talking about it was nearly as hard as experiencing it. Hawkes was moving pretty fast, not that she sensed he had any romantic or sexual intentions, but rather, he was diving headfirst into one of the most painful and private experiences of her life. She could either clear the water for him, or drain the pool and let him hit fiberglass.

"My mother and father were Marine Corps officers in the Artificial Intelligence War," she told him, half-regretting it as she spoke. "One day, an A.I. patrol attacked our house."

They're coming! The lights!

"My mom hid me and my sisters in a tiny crawl space in the attic. I saw them—"

The shadow of one of the soldiers raised his arm.

"—kill . . . my parents."

Hawkes appeared sympathetic, but there was something missing in his expression, something she couldn't discern. "Your sisters still alive?"

She nodded. "That night, during the attack, my sister Lauren tried to scream, but I kept my hand over her mouth. She bit me." Shane held up her palm. "I still have the scars."

Before she realized what was happening, Hawkes reached across the aisle to take her hand in his own. She felt a little awkward but still trusted him.

"That must've hurt."

"Yeah," she said softly. "And you know what's weird? My sisters and I aren't close. I guess I'm the parent they need to grow away from. And maybe they've always reminded me of . . . "

Hawkes looked up, puzzled.

"You know, they've always looked to me my whole life. I want to get away from people looking to me. I enlisted for me. *My* life. I don't want to take care of anyone for a while. Does that sound selfish?"

Hawkes shrugged, then ran his thumb across her scars.

"So what happened with you?"

"What do you mean?"

"With the cops . . . "

He sneered, looking away into some hidden memory. "One of those things."

"You didn't kill anybody, did you?"

"Not yet."

"You thinking of—"

"I'm just pissed off."

"Why?"

"I wake up every day shortchanged."

"I don't —"

"'Cause I'm a tank, all right?"

She hadn't intended to exasperate him. She slid her hand under his, now holding him. "I'm sorry if—"

"You didn't." He sighed. "Some guys I worked with tried to hang me."

Shane flinched. "Ohmygod . . . "

"Yeah, my timing was pretty bad on that one."

"Things are going to change. It's already happening."

"Sometimes I think the only peace for me is six feet under."

"Now *that's* selfish."

"How?"

"What about the people who care for you?"

His grin was sarcastic.

"Really. Think about it. Did you ever lose anyone?"

He looked deeply into her eyes, as if probing for something. Leaning over, he gently placed his finger around the back of her neck. He pulled her close. She thought he needed someone more than ever now, someone to hold.

But then his grip tightened on her neck and he drove her face into his. He kissed her hard and tried to pry open her lips with his tongue.

Shane craned her head, pulled away, then drew back a fist and punched him in the mouth. His head lolled back to collide with the hull. Caging her desire to scream, she gruffly whispered, "What the hell was that?"

Grimacing, Hawkes ran an index finger over his teeth, checking to see if they were all there. He wasn't exactly in a position to answer.

"How does 'did you ever lose anyone' translate into 'please stick your tongue down your throat'?"

His eyebrows drew together. "I don't know much about stuff like loss and nightmares. So don't get all in an uproar."

"You don't know much about women, either."

He turned on his side, his back to her. "What man does? Oh, I'm sorry. That doesn't work. What man or *tank* does?"

"Let's get something straight right now, otherwise—"

"Give it a rest. I won't be around much longer anyway."

Shane faced the hull, pulling her blanket over her shoulder. She hadn't thought about it until now, but she wondered if anyone had been listening.

Twice Nathan had held himself back from jumping down and pummeling the tank. He had known that would embarrass Shane to no end. He had let her handle the situation herself, and, to his mild surprise, she had been the one to whack Hawkes.

When Shane had told him that her parents were dead, he guessed that they had died of illness or natural causes. For some reason, he had not made the connection between their service in the Marine Corps and the Artificial Intelligence War.

She had seen her parents murdered. Her inability to

sleep in the cramped bunk and the favoring of her palm all made sense now. Nathan tried to put himself in her position. He imagined himself in the crawl space with his two brothers. And then he imagined the pleading eyes of his mother and father a second before they got their heads blown off.

No wonder she couldn't rest.

And now he couldn't. He looked across the cabin to the opposite porthole. The sun was two-thirds its normal diameter and half as bright. For a moment, he couldn't find Earth; then he spotted the azure planet with its tiny speck of a moon floating nearby.

It was funny to admit it, and it made him feel childish, but he was homesick. He remembered going away to summer camp when he had been seven or eight, and after about a week, something had come over him, a sense that he might never go home again, never see his brothers or parents again. He had started crying and couldn't stop. One of the counselors had had to take him into her office and assure him that in another week he was definitely going home. At first, he hadn't believed her, but then she had called his parents and they had told him not to worry, that they loved him and would see him soon. It had taken him a couple more days to fully shake off the feeling.

It would take much longer now. Nathan was nearly twenty-one million kilometers away from home, and he felt that the farther away the ISSCV took him, the stronger the longing would become.

He closed his eyes, dug his head into his pillow, and tried to fall asleep.

twelve

Bored out of his skull, and unwilling to hazard a conversation with anyone, Hawkes tried to kill the hour before they made the Mars orbit by reading the briefing.

The Marine Corps had provided them with a detailed background on where they were going and what they were supposed to do there. The Marine Corps thought of everything.

Mars, fourth planet from the sun (no kidding), diameter: 6,788 kilometers. Mass, a large number in grams, mean density . . . what? Rotation period: 1.02 days. Revolution period: 1.881 Earth years. Two moons: Phobos, Deimos. And nothing about the data on those two kidney stones really caught his attention. He scanned down to the subheading: DESTINATION.

The report said they would touch down in the Hellas Plains as close to the tracking drone as best estimates permitted. Apparently, about 3.8 billion years ago, a giant chunk of something had struck the Martian surface. What was left now was an impact basin over 1,600 kilometers in diameter and centered at 293 degrees west, 42 degrees south. Within the basin were some 2,600 smaller craters and three channels: Dao Vallis, Harmakhis Vallis, and Reull Vallis, the largest channel in the southern hemisphere. Some of the oldest recognizable volcanoes on the planet were supposed to be near Hellas.

As for weather, the temperature would be a balmy minus-30 degrees Celsius by day, and one should take a sweater along if going out at night, when it dropped to minus-80 degrees Celsius. The report provided an atmospheric breakdown, all of which was to say that if your suit was breached, you'd be gasping to pull .1 percent oxygen out of a 96 percent CO_2 environment. Good luck.

"Hey, Coop. Put that down and take a look at this," Damphousse beckoned.

He rose and crossed to the porthole near Damphousse's bunk.

Mars's red and orange surface features rolled slowly by. Hawkes spotted a canyon that he remembered was about the size of the United States. Vast craters and channels pockmarked and grooved the surface around the canyon. He wondered how close the ship was to Hellas.

"I didn't realize it would look this bright," Damphousse said.

Her excitement was infectious. Hawkes felt a smile come over his face. "Huh. It's . . . "

"Nearly time to fold 'em up and prepare for final approach," West finished.

Hawkes sent a glare the hotshot's way, then crossed back to his bunk. He rolled up the briefing and, as did the others, proceeded to make his bunk, sheet-in hospital corners, blanket pulled quarter-bouncing tight. He lifted the bunk up into the wall, then squirmed into his restraints.

Shane stood directly across from him. She pretended not to notice him, but every once in a while he caught her looking.

Mr. Hotshot West started a conversation with her. While watching Shane giggle over West's pathetic wit, and barely hearing the pilot's twangy notification that they were entering Mars's atmosphere and were in for a little chop, Hawkes made a decision about the way things were going to be down on the planet.

Sergeant Bougus had told them that the mission was to be a joint effort, commanded by the entire squadron. Hawkes had wondered what had happened to the military chain of command. Then he had reasoned that not assigning a team leader was probably part of the test. Bougus had told them they had still not learned to work together. Indeed, without a leader, they would all be responsible for what happened.

But West was carving out a position of leadership for himself. His authoritative tone was enough to make Hawkes realize that Mr. Hotshot thought of himself as team leader, despite the fact that the position was supposedly nonexistent.

If, for any reason, Hawkes felt that West was overstepping himself on the planet, then a small war would come to Mars.

The chop wasn't as bad as the pilot had made it sound. Hawkes had experienced rougher rides aboard commercial airliners. The bad news came a few moments before touchdown:

"Wind's blowing a little too hard over by the tracking drone. I'll get y'all in as close as I can, but you're still gonna have a little hike."

A chorus of moans followed.

"I'm trying to think of something important to say when I set foot on Martian soil, something I'll always remember," Wang said. "Anybody got an idea?"

"Oh, come on," Carter groaned, splashing water on Wang's fire. "It's not like you're going to be the first man to step on the planet. You're making too big a thing out of this."

Hawkes usually kept to himself during most of the bantering, and the present conversation was no exception—especially since there wasn't any famous "First In Vitro On Mars" speech for him to emulate. And, in truth, the whole affair seemed anticlimactic. Yes, there was an element of suspense and adventure associated with coming to a new world, but the fact of the matter was that they were here to fix a broken tracking drone. They weren't well-muscled or buxom heroes embarking on a great quest to save the world. They were repair persons with sagging guts and underwear that failed to cover their big cracks.

"I got it!" Wang announced. "I'll dedicate each step to the important people in my life."

"Hey, yeah," Damphousse said. "This step is for my father. This step is for my mother . . . "

"All right, we don't need the whole list," Carter said.

"Hey, Nathan. You got anyone you're going to dedicate a step to?" Pags asked.

"Sure. Family . . . friends . . . "

"Someone who was part of the Tellus colony mission?" Shane asked West.

Mr. Hotshot didn't answer her. Interesting. West might know someone who was part of the Tellus mission. He had reacted strongly to Chartwell's announcement back at the bar. And maybe now he had a score to settle with the aliens. Hawkes would definitely have to watch this one. Perhaps West's private agenda would be his undoing. Perhaps Hawkes could make sure of that.

Touchdown was simply touchdown, occurring without incident. Damphousse, Wang, and a few of the others rushed to get out of their straps.

Hawkes took his time. Once free, he looked around, then thought he'd try something. "All right everyone, suit up, then get a buddy and check equipment. Don't forget about your links."

Surprisingly, the group complied, even West, without so much as a double take.

Fully suited, West crossed to the air lock. "We'll go five at a time, take a look around, then haul out the gear," he said. "And yes, Wang, you can be in the first group. Pags. Stone. You two grab a couple of persuaders for insurance. Low. You handle the GPS."

"Already have it," she said, tapping the small, rectangular, positioning device clipped to her waist.

Hold back. Don't go off on him yet. Let him push it a little farther . . .

Pags and Stone returned from the supply room, each

toting an M-590 photon rifle. They joined Damphousse, Wang, and Bartley in the air lock, then disappeared behind the door.

Through his helmet's link, Hawkes heard them gasp, nearly in unison.

"This is incredible," Damphousse said.

Wang began dedicating each of his steps, then Pags and Damphousse joined him.

Carter was annoyed and wasn't shy about it. "People! Turn off your links while you're doing that!"

The door opened and Hawkes filed into the air lock with the rest of the Marines. The inner hatch sealed and the outer hatch slammed onto the ground, abruptly revealing the Hellas Plains.

"Join the service and see *other* worlds," Low muttered.

They crossed onto the sandy Martian soil. According to the briefing, high levels of iron oxide gave the landscape its rust color. Beyond the other five camouflaged Marines who had fanned out for a better look, Hawkes could see faint columns of dust that swayed like charmed cobras above the dunes. There wasn't much to view past the sand, save for a pink-gray sky that dimmed into the horizon.

Hawkes turned and headed back toward the troop cylinder, his legs feeling odd in the weaker gravity.

"Hawkes, where are you going?"

He stormed past West without answering. Then, a few steps from the air lock, he paused and looked back at the group, most of whom had their backs to him. "Hey! What're you doing, looking to buy real estate? There's a war on. Everyone back inside and break out the gear."

Then, as he had suspected they would, all of the Marines looked to West, and all of them probably couldn't believe that a tank was giving orders.

The visor of Nathan's helmet caught the sun and fired a dazzling reflection at Hawkes. He couldn't see West, but he guessed that by now the Marine's face was flushed. "First we secure our position. Low . . . "

After unclipping the Global Positioning System from her waist, the short Asian woman aimed it at the horizon.

"Our position is out in the middle of nowhere," Hawkes said. "There. Secured. Now. Everyone back inside."

Nathan took a step toward Hawkes, his helmet no longer reflecting the glint of the sun. West's face was red, all right. "The H.I.S.T. manual states—"

"The manual? When they drop us in the middle of a hairy-ass furball, you gonna take time to check the manual?"

West appeared flustered, at a loss. Perfect. He threw up his hands. "Do what you want. I'd be happy to see you take one the second we're in battle. *We're* doin' it the way we've been told." Hotshot strode away, thinking he was going to get the last word.

"That's right. Follow their rules. They'll just keep takin' from ya . . . and you'll let 'em. You ain't ever gonna get to Tellus that way."

West froze. He bowed his head—

Struck a nerve, eh?

West whirled and then charged at him.

"Nathan!"

"What's he doing?"

"Oh, man. Don't ruin this."

"Somebody's gonna get hurt."

"Don't do it, West!"

"Pags! Stone! Get over here!"

Hawkes lifted his gloved fists. West came within a yard, but was bear-hugged from behind by Pags.

Suddenly, someone grabbed one of his wrists and twisted his arm behind his back.

A lock was opened in Hawkes's mind.

And his rage stepped out, a free beast in the cell block.

Twisting to face the Marine holding him, Hawkes

tried to wrench his arm out of—it turned out to be—
Stone's grip. "You ain't getting away from me, Hawkes,"
the big Marine said, his voice edged with exertion.

Oh, yeah?

One tug, backed by his rage, and Hawkes was free.
He aimed for West, who had broken out of Pags's hold.
Hawkes threw himself on Nathan, and the two of them
went down, digging a shallow crater.

Clinging to Hawkes's suit, West managed to roll him
over and pin him, then jab him in the chest with a right,
a left, another right, before Hawkes could grab West's
suit near the shoulder and yank him off.

Hawkes scooped a handful of sand and threw it at
West's helmet, blocking his view for a second—a second which he exploited by driving his elbow into West's
groin.

"Yaow!"

What's the matter, tough guy?

As West began to curl into a fetal position, nursing
his groin, Hawkes climbed on top of the Marine, ready
to pin him and speak the words Mr. Nathan West desperately needed to hear: he was not, nor had he ever
been, team leader.

But West snapped out of his curl, sent a knee into
Hawkes's groin and kept it there, utilizing it and his
hands to toss Hawkes up and away. One moment
Hawkes had been preparing his victory speech, the next
he was lying supine across the Martian surface.

"Now we're gonna finish this!" West screamed.

Hawkes bolted upright, growling, panting, his temples
throbbing. "Come on. Come on!" As he leaned forward
in an effort to stand, he saw Pags slip behind West and
seize his suit near the neckline.

Then Hawkes felt someone grab his own suit in the
same fashion. Pags drove West down into Hawkes, their
helmets striking each other with such a force that
Hawkes was knocked flat and swore he heard his oxygen supply hissing away.

But the hissing was coming through his link; the volume control must have been maxed during the fight. He gazed to his left and saw West lying beside him, Mr. Hotshot's chest rising and falling.

Slowly, Hawkes went up on an elbow. He tried to blink off the dizziness, but it didn't want to fade. Next to him, he heard West moan as he sat up.

Shane circled around to stand in front of them. Her gaze was directed at Nathan. "What the hell's wrong with you?"

Then she scowled at Hawkes. "And you knock it off. You think we're going to blow it because you two *boys* need to prove something?"

Hawkes stared through her. Neither he nor West acknowledged Shane.

"We're drivin' on," she added, her temper mounting. "So you two had better mature real fast, or—and I swear this—you'll both stay in the vehicle while the rest of us get the job done. Oh, yeah. And your conduct will show up in all of our reports."

"Right on," Stone said. "Act like kids, be treated like kids."

Shane stomped away, and Hawkes noticed that everyone was looking toward her, impressed. She stopped, lowered her head a moment, then faced Michele Low. "Now, Low, tell West our position."

Like everyone else, the young woman wasn't looking at West but at Shane. Hawkes felt the trace of a grin pass over his lips. They wanted Shane to be the team leader.

Visibly shaken by the fact that everyone was staring at her, Shane looked off, plainly disgusted.

Hawkes wouldn't mind if Shane were the boss. She was smarter than West, and tougher. Trouble was, she didn't want the job. Hawkes's luck.

Finally, Low made it known who she wanted to follow. She took a step toward Shane, holding out her GPS. "We're on the southeast rim, 45 by 271."

"I heard they were getting ready to terraform this sector. That true?" Wang asked, in a weak attempt to lift everyone out of the awkwardness of the moment.

Pags withdrew a copy of the briefing from a hip pocket on his suit. He unfolded it, studied it a second, then crossed to Shane. "The tracking drone is about four klicks east from here."

Shane nodded, then shut her eyes—as if preparing for the bad medicine of being leader—and said, "Okay. We'll gear up and move out." She kept her head bowed and started for the ship with Wang, Low, Damphousse, and Stone following.

Then the others fell in line, including West, who had miraculously managed to get up. Hawkes rolled onto all fours, then tried once, twice, to stand.

A shadow passed over the soil. It was Pags, proffering his hand.

"I can get up myself."

"Probably. But it looks like you could use a hand— and I'm offerin' one."

Hawkes tried to read an ulterior motive in Pags's expression, but there seemed nothing but honesty there. He glanced at the hand, then took it.

On his feet, Hawkes brushed dirt from his arms and knees. "Ain't easy for me to recognize a helping hand."

"If that's a thank you, don't worry about it," Pags answered. "Someday you'll pay me back."

Hawkes didn't like owing anything to anyone, but it was too late. At least Pags didn't seem the type who would call in the favor any time soon.

It was odd, but for the first time since becoming a Marine, Hawkes felt that he belonged. Someone had reached out to him, someone half-blind to who he was. Maybe he wouldn't get himself thrown out of the Corps after all. Maybe he'd stick it out. Who knows what could happen then?

thirteen

By the time they were two kilometers closer to the tracking drone, the Martian wind waged a private war against the Marines. Twice Nathan felt himself about to topple, and twice he struggled to stay on his feet. The wind foretold something Nathan didn't want to consider, but it reared its ugly head nonetheless.

His first thought: send the tank out there alone to confirm or deny the horrible fact. But Shane wouldn't like that, and he was tired of fighting with Hawkes anyway. Better to just ignore him. Let him screw up and wash out on his own. That wouldn't be too hard for him.

They trudged single file, ascending an enormous red sand dune, Shane at point, Nathan close behind. Their footprints were swept away in seconds, giving Nathan the eerie, disoriented feeling that the group had simply appeared in the middle of the dunes.

"I'm no expert," Stone said. "But I remember reading something from a disc once about a Martian dust storm back in 1971. Within seven days it encompassed a sector 6,000 kilometers across. I think it took like another two weeks to envelop the rest of the planet."

"Now here's a man who knows how to build morale," Pags quipped.

"Low, why don't you grab a satellite image—just to settle my stomach," Carter said.

"Good idea," Nathan added.

"On it."

"This sucks," Wang said.

"The hike, the planet, the Corps, what?" Damphousse asked.

"I think I got a rock in my shoe."

"Impossible. You're sealed, pressurized."

"I'm telling you I got a rock in my shoe."

"Uh, excuse me," Low said. "But Shane, I think you'd better take a look at this."

Nathan put his hand up, signaling the group to halt. He and Shane went to Low, who held up the pocket-sized Satellite Image Receiver so that they could see a digitized view of the plains taken from orbit.

Low pointed to a dark blob that Nathan wanted to believe was dirt on the screen. "Don't even say it," he told her.

Shane sighed deeply and slumped. "Say it."

Low touched a button on the SIR. The image zoomed in on the blob. A data table appeared on the right side of the screen. "Storm is moving at three klicks per hour, with wind speeds varying from a hundred to two hundred kilometers per hour at its eye."

"Damn," Nathan said, then looked away.

"All right. So we ride it out. Three klicks an hour. What's the storm's diameter?"

"Well, it's not exactly circular, but I know what you're looking for. It'll take about fifty-five minutes for it to pass over our position."

"This sucks," Wang said. And it was obvious he wasn't talking about a rock in his shoe.

"I say we turn around and beat the thing back to the ship," Bartley offered. "We don't have shelter. And those winds . . . we don't know what's flying around in them."

"*We* might be flying around in them soon," Pags said.

Stone hesitated, then said, "At the risk of sounding like a cliché, we're Marines, first in, last out. I'd rather face that storm than a couple of wings of those aliens."

"I'm in," Damphousse said.

"Me too," Wang added, resignedly.

"Aw, hell, let's do it," Carter grunted.

Damphousse pointed to Hawkes. "What about you, Coop?"

The tank scanned the horizon, holding a hand up to his helmet to block the glare. "We came this far . . . "

Pags folded his arms across his chest. "What I wanna know is if we're gonna ride this storm, then how the hell are we gonna do it? Just stand here and see what happens?"

Nathan looked to Shane. "We don't have—" He cursed at himself for opening his mouth.

"We'll hold hands," Shane said.

Carter snickered. "Yeah, right."

Shane went to the man and seized his hand. Then she turned and snatched Wang's hand. "We're a team," she began slowly. "*Gung ho.* Working together. We sit in a circle, no one out of sight, no one out of reach. We keep our heads low, our gear packed tight, and we wait."

"And pray," Wang added somberly.

Nathan found himself smiling at Shane. An incredible woman had emerged from a tortured child. He still had a lot to learn, but she, she understood the moment better than anyone. He envied her, but that feeling did not go so far as to make him refuse to obey her. In fact, looking at Shane as she inspired the group, he felt utterly proud to know her.

"Hey, if we sit near the crest of the dune, on the back side of it, maybe the side facing the storm will act as a slight buffer," Hawkes said.

Shane bought the proposal with a nod. "Let's do it." She started for the head of the line.

Surprise, the tank has a good idea. He's actually interested in what's going on around him.

It took fifteen minutes to reach the crest of the dune. They settled into a tight circle, made sure their packs were strapped snugly onto their backs, their rifles slung across their chests. Nathan sat between Shane and Pags. He took their hands, then scanned the faces around him: Hawkes looked vacant, Wang licked his lips and swallowed, Low creased her brow in worry, Carter actually looked bored. Pags, Damphousse, Stone, and Bartley wore identical expressions: lost in thought, each assumedly in a personal vision of what the storm would be like.

A circle. Hands held. It was necessary. Practical. Gave them hope. Indeed, they were a group of people sharing an interest: survival. But Nathan couldn't help but see the spirituality of the union. Nathan remembered how, whenever his grandparents would come over for a holiday dinner, everyone would hold hands at the table and say a prayer before eating. Billions upon billions of families had done the same thing over the centuries. Now, ten Marines sat a very long way from home, holding hands and perhaps thanking God in advance for his mercy.

Low broke her grip with Wang and looked at her SIR. "Dust storm ETA: Nineteen seconds!" Frantically, she clipped the device back onto her suit, just as Wang retook her hand.

Nathan felt the ground quiver. He had switched his link so that he could monitor both the troop channel and the external noise of the planet.

He almost wished he hadn't.

The dust storm hit, an invisible, caterwauling hammer striking a continuous blow. Within a millisecond, wind-whipped sand turned day into night and buffeted his suit as if fired from a high-powered weapon.

His nerves made their way to his throat and gave him a keen sense for the obvious. "Hang on!"

Nathan looked back to the once-sharp crest of the dune; layer upon layer of it was being stripped away, the storm filing their shield down to a blunt edge.

Ahead, Cooper, Wang, Low, and Carter, were indistinct amid the torrents of sand. Pags and Damphousse were partly visible, and it shocked Nathan to see that they were being buried. Then he looked down. His lap was gone, covered.

"We might have to stand!" Shane said.

"Let's wait!" Damphousse said. "We'll only give the storm a bigger target that way."

In one sense she was right. But if they were buried over their heads, yes, they could still breathe, but getting out. . . .

Things remained constant for the next twenty minutes, after which two things occurred.

The wind died to about half its former speed, and Shane ordered everyone to stand, which took about five minutes, as they were buried up to their waists.

With his legs sunk in to calf-height, Nathan felt confident about his footing. The surrounding sand aided in his balance. Even if the wind picked up, he still felt rooted enough to resist it.

Then Bartley's earlier question of what was flying around in the wind was answered.

Most of the rocks had collected at the tail end of the storm for a reason that was beyond Nathan. The sand had been bad enough. Now missiles varying in size from plums to grapefruit pelted the Marines.

Wang screamed and dropped to his knees, dragging Hawkes and Low with him. Stone and Carter no longer liked the odds of standing and opted to sit, tucking their helmeted heads into their chests.

A rock hit the back of Nathan's helmet just as Shane yanked him down, and he swore aloud. He leaned forward as far as he could, trying to keep his head low. He was breathing so heavily that he fogged his visor, but he wasn't about to reach back and drop his suit's temperature to adjust for the imbalance.

To someone not in it, the storm presented a curious dilemma: suit-breaching rocks above, swiftly rising sand below. Presently, Nathan concluded that the sand was the lesser of two Martian evils.

Shane called roll for the third time since the storm had begun. Eight names shot back at her over the link, then Nathan added his own.

As the sand continued to rise and the rocks streaked overhead, a few grazing his helmet, Nathan felt the increasing desire to fight back instead of quivering like a coward against a malevolent but flawed opponent. If Low's math was correct, less than one quarter of the storm was left. He could stand and make a mad rush for the clear air beyond, and, perhaps, the others would follow.

Idiot. Is that working together? Yes, you still have a lot to learn. You're not a coward for lying here. Your presence helps the group.

In a few more moments the storm slowly dropped off into a whimper. Grains of sand peeled away from deeper layers, slowly, artistically, silently. Nathan lifted his head and saw his shadow in the sand. He didn't have to look back to know the sky was clear, the sun shining. Were this the moment after a total eclipse on Earth, the insects would begin to hum, and the birds would resume their chirping. Roosters would announce morning at 5:00 in the afternoon.

Looks were exchanged, looks that asked, "Are you all right?"

"There was a time when I used to like being buried in the sand," Carter said.

A cursory inspection revealed that the dune had been through not a meteor shower but something akin to one. The fine sand was freckled with rocks.

"Storm picking up speed and changing direction slightly," Low said, reading her SIR. "Good news. Don't think it'll hit the ship."

"We've burned some valuable O_2 here, people," Shane said, releasing Nathan's hand. "Check your gear and let's hustle."

They stood atop a hillock, looking down at the tracking drone which sat a half dozen meters away. It was like an old piece of furniture sitting in an alien living room, eroded, half-buried in the sand, its solar array foil flapping in the freezing breeze.

"Didn't they count on storms when they built that piece of junk?" Pags asked.

Bartley aimed her directional Geiger Counter at the drone. "Point-oh-one-seven rads."

Damphousse arrived next to Bartley, sloughed off her pack and withdrew the circuit storage box. She opened it and produced three small plug-in modules.

Seeing that Damphousse was on the ball, Shane said, "Good. Replace the transceiver units and let's get back. We have about ten hours of daylight."

"Hey, Coop. Pags. I'll need your help diggin' it out," Damphousse said as she descended the slope.

Pags and Hawkes dropped to their knees before the tracker and used the butts of their rifles to shovel away the sand and small rocks that had collected there. Seeing that they weren't making much headway, Nathan signaled for Stone and Wang. The three Marines joined Pags and Hawkes, and in less than five minutes they were using their gloves to wipe the tracker's legs free of sand.

"All right, gentlemen. Let me in there." Cautiously, Damphousse reached down toward a small, square compartment, its surface etched with line drawings of Earth that the briefing said were the same ones carried by two ancient spacecraft: Pioneer Ten and Eleven.

"There's an eject switch in there somewhere," Low said.

Damphousse found and pressed a button. A small drawer containing a micro-CD slid toward her. She lifted the golden disc from the drawer. "This it?"

"That's the Earth message," Wang informed the group. "They made it a requirement in the twenty-first century that all off-Earth installations had to have one. It has pictures and sounds of Earth in case an extraterrestrial found it."

Hawkes stepped around the tracker, then got on his haunches before another door. "Let me have it."

"What're you doing?" Shane asked.

"Read about this," Hawkes said. "Don't worry. It won't explode."

Damphousse looked to Shane, who shrugged, then gave Hawkes the micro-CD.

The tank tapped open a door, then inserted the disc into a tiny, metallic disc drive. "Everyone. Set your links for proximity scan and lock. You're gonna like this." He tapped a switch.

Nathan, along with the others, adjusted two knobs on the com-panel at his hip.

And his ears filled with slow, sad, passionate music. "Mozart."

"Yeah, I know this one, too," Bartley said. "My sister used to play it all the time at home. It's his Piano Concerto in D-minor."

"K: Second Movement, to be precise," Carter said.

"Why, Carter. I didn't know you were a connoisseur of the arts," Damphousse said.

"I'm not. There was a list of the disc's contents in the briefing. Guess I was the only one who read that part."

"If only this had been our first contact with them." Shane groaned and looked askance to Nathan. "They never would have killed the colonists."

Nathan was about to say something, but thought better of it. He listened to the music, tones like waves that bobbed him and carried him closer to Kylen. There was no way of knowing how the aliens would have responded to this. Ironically, it might have incited them to even greater violence. If Shane wanted to believe that a first contact of this nature would have prevented what had happened, then that was all right. But Nathan had already tried, convicted, and sentenced the aliens to death. Their first contact with him would be a salvo of laser fire from his fighter.

Mozart was cut off, replaced by a Scottish Highland fling with heavy bagpipes blaring.

"Aw, I was liking that," Stone said. "Put it back, Hawkes."

"If they had heard this," Wang began, in a poor attempt at a Scottish accent, "they would've wiped us out a long time ago. And I wouldn't have blamed them."

"Hmmm. I'll see if I can skip a sector—" Hawkes stopped himself, or rather was drowned out by what had to be the strangest thing Nathan had ever heard.

The Marines broke into laughter as a singer seemingly shouted over noise that was supposed to be music but sounded more like a racing combustion engine.

"What the hell is that?" Damphousse asked.

Nathan glanced at Pags, who moved subtly to the racket. "I know this," Pags confessed. "I heard this in my twentieth century history class. This was called rock 'n' roll. I think this group was called . . . The Pink Floyd. They went like this." He spread his legs and fanned an air guitar, bouncing from side to side, then dropped to his knees and leaned back as far as he could, his face contorted in agony or pleasure.

Nathan chuckled.

"But Pags, this ain't The Pink Floyd," Carter said. "It's The Ramones. Listen. You'll hear the title of this one. They called it the 'Blitzkrieg Bop.'"

But Pags wasn't listening; he was too caught up in singing along. "Hey. Ho. Let's go! Hey. Ho. Let's go!"

BOOM! BOOM!

The thunderous sounds had come from behind him—
BOOM! BOOM!

—and then overhead.

"Look!" Carter shouted, pointing to the near horizon.

A fiery streak arced eighty degrees across the sky and vanished behind the summit of a volcano. The sky above the volcano strobed with flashes of light so intense that, for a second, Nathan could see the lava lines of the elevation before he had to shield his eyes.

Pags gasped. "Whoa!"

"One one thousand. Two one thousand. Three one thousand . . . "

An explosion echoed Shane's words, followed by a quake that knocked Hawkes onto his butt and made Nathan and the rest of the Marines fight for balance.

"On Mars," Shane said, even before the tremor ceased. "About fifteen or twenty klicks out."

"A bolide, maybe?" Bartley guessed.

"A ship?" Wang asked.

"If it's one of ours, then that crew might need help," Low said.

Shane considered the horizon. "Twenty kilometers there, twenty back. That cuts into our O_2 ration in a big way."

"I'll lower my O_2 flow during sleep," Pags said, his tone just shy of begging.

"Me too," Damphousse added.

Nathan studied the others. Hawkes looked doubtful, but he didn't voice an objection. Everyone else appeared as charged as Pags.

Shane looked to him for a decision. He nodded, and she addressed the group. "We all go. Check supplies at regular intervals and report."

Nathan removed his rifle from his shoulder and pointed its business end at the volcano. "I got point. Stone, you're pulling rear guard."

The big Marine brandished his weapon. "Ready, willin', and loaded."

fourteen

Nathan led the Marines toward the fallen object, leaving the repaired tracker and the dunes far behind. Their orange halogen helmet lamps did little to rob the night sky of its beauty. The stars shone nearly as brightly as they did from a vantage point in space. Mars's two moons, Deimos and Phobos, were up from their daytime slumber. Deimos appeared as Venus, perhaps a tad brighter. Phobos was a little smaller than Earth's moon but someone had taken a hammer and chisel to it, banged the once-perfect sphere into an irregular lump of coal, then dug out long, parallel grooves as if in preparation for canals.

As the team hiked around the volcano, the plains gave way to the lazy rises and falls of the hardened lava flows. Jagged boulders occasionally obstructed their path, then became more frequent the farther they trekked.

Nathan grew tired of kicking stones out of his way and decided to simply step on them, despite the fact that he could lose his balance. He forged on, growing weaker.

Then he slipped, caught his balance, lost it, then caught it again. If it wasn't the wind knocking him over . . .

"I'll take point for a while," Shane suggested.

He agreed and she crossed in front. He shot a look back to Stone. "How are we doing back there?"

"Fine, if you like rocks," Stone moaned.

They came upon a small but steep hill that Nathan

guessed hid a valley beyond, a valley in which the object had presumably made impact. Above the crest of the hill, he spotted a mysterious orange glow that, from this angle, appeared to be emanating from the rock itself.

He grabbed Shane's shoulder. "You see that?"

"Yeah, come on," she said excitedly, slinging her rifle over her shoulder.

"You'd better—"

"You cover me," she said.

Throwing her hands forward to help her keep balance, Shane climbed the steep hill. Nathan followed and found it increasingly difficult to keep up with her while holding his rifle.

She dropped to her chest just before the peak, then slid forward to peer furtively over the other side. "Holy shit . . . "

"What? What?" Nathan picked up his pace, and, after an eternity plus thirty seconds, lowered to all fours and crawled beside her.

The hill dead-ended in a nightmare cliff that would kill anyone who went over it, even in Martian gravity.

But that wasn't what Shane had commented on, nor was it the reason Nathan's mouth went dry.

Littered with boulders, the valley was a natural maze of rock that had a trench newly dug through it. At the far end of the trench lay a black metallic craft, partially masked by two boulders and veiled in its own smoldering. He heard Shane click her night vision face shield into place and he did likewise. Night became a green day, but the craft remained a mystery.

"Is it a Mars orbiter?" Shane asked.

By now, the rest of the Marines were spreading out along the crest of the hill, crawling on their bellies as if under concertina wire.

Stone dropped his NV shield over his eyes. "Maybe it's a classified recon ship."

"Yeah," Carter agreed. "Something to do with the war."

"Damphousse, West, Pags, and me. The rest of you provide cover."

Hawkes, who had assumed a position next to Shane, nudged her. "You want me to go?"

"Stay here. In case something happens."

"You trust me that much?"

"Yeah. I guess I do."

"Thanks," he said, surprising Nathan with the level of sincerity in his voice. He edged backward on his hands and knees.

Shane, Pags, and Damphousse followed Nathan around the north side of the hill and into the valley. The beams of their lamps sliced into a fog that prowled at their knees and mixed with the fumes of the wreckage. Nathan's breath was so labored that he feared he'd short out his suit's exhaust system. The resultant breaths of the others created an unsettling, odd metronome that marked the seconds as they drew closer to the craft.

"Radiation levels?"

Pags, who had taken Bartley's directional Geiger Counter, consulted a gauge on the instrument. "Let's say we don't stay long."

Nathan tossed a glance back at the hill, spotting the heads of Hawkes and the others. They readied their M-590s, throwing their weight from elbow to elbow.

He moved around a boulder that stood some three meters taller than himself and froze as the craft came into full view, just a dozen or so meters away.

Like a pair of shark's teeth glued together and fitted with metallic skin polished to a breathtaking luster, the ship hinted at the potential for great speed and incredible atmospheric maneuverability. It had no identification markings, and its dorsal fin and right wing had been torn to ribbons by either laser fire or boulders, the latter seeming more likely since there weren't any scorch marks on the ship's hull. The nose of the craft was buried in the soil, but there was a bump in a likely place for a cockpit.

Nathan edged forward, his light and the lights of the others crisscrossing over the craft. *Chic-chic.* He locked his rifle. Pags crossed in front of him. "Hey," Nathan said. "What're you—"

"I'm taking point, West. Relax. We're a team. Remember?"

"Yeah," Nathan murmured. "Just stay close. And wired."

"Michael Close-and-Wired Pagodin. That's me."

Pags moved to the left side of the craft where a half-open hatch invited entrance.

Damphousse, her gait stiff, her head sweeping from side to side, let her rifle lead the way to Pags. "What the hell is it?"

"Looks like it's open," Pags said. "There's electronics, a console of some sort." Pags used the barrel of his rifle to shove the door aside—

—something fell toward him.

"Ahhhhhh!"

Pags drew back as it dropped to the rocky surface. A yellow light flashed on the Marine's suit: his Urine and Fecal Collection Device was full. He sighed, his cheeks reddening.

Nathan grimaced as his light illuminated an alien body lying on its side. It was a shade of gray that Nathan speculated was not its natural color, as if it were pale from death. The muscularity of the thing was either natural or heightened by armor; it was hard to tell flesh from synthetic material. Some sort of grillwork took the place of or was a face. The thing was short a few fingers and probably wore boots, which would account for the smoothness of its feet. Some sort of fin jutted from the middle of its chest, not unlike the dorsal fin on the spacecraft; however, the appendage hung half-off and, along with the being's heavily ribbed chest, was slick with a liquid that resembled crude oil.

Nathan voiced his thoughts. "It looks like . . . I don't know . . . Like it's . . . like it *was* . . . alive."

ZZZZ-POP-POP!

"What the—"

Something came from the left and sprayed across Nathan's face plate. He cocked his head and saw Pags falling onto his back, intestines and pink viscera spilling from a gaping hole in the Marine's abdomen. A smoke ring pulsed as the young man's arms and legs repeatedly pounded the dirt.

"Pags!" Damphousse screamed.

"West! Report!" Hawkes demanded.

Nathan hit the deck as Damphousse seized the now inert Pags, lifted the Marine over her shoulder and took off. Nathan crawled to the ship, put his back to it, then, with Shane at his side, unleashed a volley of unforgiving M-590 photon fire.

"Got a sniper, Hawkes! Somewhere northeast."

At that, a fireworks show fueled by six Marines lit up the sky, bolts of energy razoring down and blanketing the probable position of the sniper.

The hull above Nathan's head took a hit that ricocheted to strike the ground a meter away, blasting up a cloud of debris. Under a shower of residual sparks he faced Shane. "We gotta move!"

They darted toward the path they had originally followed into the valley, a path marked by the tallest boulder and a few remaining boot prints. They ran stooped, to avoid the freeway of laser fire a scant quarter-meter above them. But then she stumbled and fell sideways. Her rebreather tube got caught on the base of a knee-high rock and was torn from her suit. Pressure escaped in a sickening hiss that Nathan heard despite the cacophony of weapons' fire. Then a more terrifying sound rose above it all: her scream.

A ball of energy pulverized a rock face behind her. Then another came. Still another. Blue energy flickered, and lightning-like threads splayed across the stones like varicose veins. In the eerie light, Shane began to choke.

Nathan tried to reattach Shane's tube, but the coupling had been ripped so badly that a tight seal was impossible. He shut down her O_2 flow, then held his breath, threw two sealing latches, and removed his own rebreather tube. He flipped up Shane's visor and stuffed the tube into her mouth. "Breathe," he managed to order.

After drawing in a long breath, trailed by several short, quick ones, Shane cried, "Can't stay here!"

Nathan threw up his own visor and nodded. He helped her to her feet. Arm in arm, sharing a single lifeline, they moved out, threading from boulder to boulder, pausing behind each to switch the tube.

They spotted Damphousse as they neared the edge of the valley. The woman, still with Pags over her shoulder, regarded them with a face creased with exertion. "Move out!"

Not about to protest, they arced around the side of the hill and began their ascent.

Once on the summit, Damphousse lowered Pags to the ground. Wang and Low quickly attended to Shane. They patched her rebreather tube with sealant tape from Low's pack, then repressurized her suit. Meanwhile, Nathan reattached his own tube and thumbed the auto-pressurize button.

He looked at Damphousse, who was now on her knees, weeping softly. "Pags . . . is dead."

Nathan felt the world begin to spin, and he fell onto his back. Hands not his own began to fumble with his suit's control panel. He saw Carter's face flash, then Stone's, then a bright light. He closed his eyes.

"He ain't pressurized," Stone said.

A familiar and wonderful sound commenced: *Hissssssss.* The air actually smelled sweet. He sat up, concentrating on his breathing. He found the rest of the Marines huddled around him, their gazes sweeping the landscape, their weapons at the ready. Shane, still an unhealthy shade of violet, smiled wanly. Over her shoulder, Nathan saw Pags's body. He shivered and gritted his teeth.

"We got a casualty. We're low on air. Whatta we do now?" Wang asked.

"I say we go down there and hunt that mother. We're Marines," Stone said, then eyed Pags. "Time to kick ass."

"No. We spread out and wait for it," Shane said.

"For how long? We don't got time to wait for it," Hawkes argued. "Stone's right. *Pags is dead.* Based on the fire I saw, there's only one of them."

"Yeah. That makes it nine on one," Carter said.

"But if it corners one of us . . ." Damphousse started. "Nathan, you think one of us could—"

He cut her off with a wave of his hand. "I say we strap on our NVSs and assume positions. We'll give this bastard about ten minutes. Then we gotta go."

Shane appeared to agree with his plan. She didn't nod, but she didn't leer at him either.

"No matter what we do. I say we call for an immediate EVAC," Bartley suggested.

"And do what, screw up the whole mission?" Hawkes asked incredulously. "Pags would've wanted us to stick together and complete the mission like Marines. He wanted to fly more than any of us. He'll never get that chance. And neither will we if we don't finish this on our own. No EVAC. Let's go hunting." Hawkes stood.

Damphousse, Carter, Stone, Wang, and Low joined him.

Bartley bit her lower lip and shook her head.

Nathan thrust a hand toward Wang, who helped him up. "Carter, Stone, take west side. Stone, assume a position behind that"—Nathan pointed—"see it? See it over there? That long, fat boulder."

"I'm already there," Stone replied curtly, then he and Carter jogged off.

"Damphousse and Wang, east side. Back on the path.

Now swing really east and we might be able to drive the sucker back toward its ship."

"Where we'll show it a little good, old-fashioned Marine Corps payback," Wang said before leaving.

Nathan looked to Hawkes. "We're gonna be the eagles, and this summit's our nest."

Hawkes struck up a thumb. "What side you want?"

"East," Nathan said.

With a terse nod, Hawkes pivoted and started for his position.

Nathan shifted his attention to Low, whose brow rose in anticipation of orders.

"I need Low," Shane said, trying to get up on her own but failing miserably. "I have a job for her." She faced the Marine. "I want you to see if you can convert the SIR into a thermal imager."

Low nodded, already understanding. "I think we can. There's an uplink code to break, but I don't think it'll be too difficult."

Nathan smiled. "We get an image on that thing—"

"Don't get too excited. *It* might have an imager of its own and is—at this moment—tracking *us*," Shane said. "Now, where do you want me?"

"Here. Stick with Low. At least until you feel better."

"I'm fine. A little groggy, maybe."

"You were violet, now you're somewhere on the light green side," he said.

Before heading for his position, Nathan took one last look at Pags's corpse. The wind rippled across Pags's flight suit. The red mass where his chest had been was covered with a fine layer of dust.

At his self-appointed post, Nathan dug out his Night Vision Sight and clipped it onto his rifle. He squinted at the small screen, trying to pull a glimpse of the alien from the red-tinted terrain. He was already anxious, and in his mind's eye Pags's murder was looped into an endless rerun of carnage. His visor and suit were still smudged with Pags's blood.

You're not dealing with feeble humans. You're dealing with Marines. We're weapons, focused and full of purpose.

The wind got stronger, the dust turning points of clarity into opaque blurs. He cursed under his breath as he scanned the valley through his NVS.

Then, in the shadows near covering boulders . . . movement.

He should alert the others so that they could drive the alien—as planned—into a position where it would be somewhat cornered, either near its ship or against the cliff side. But his desire for revenge had coalesced into a rabid beast that had to be fed.

They might've killed Kylen! They killed Pags!

He jogged around the hill, booting up sand and sliding over rocks as he descended into the valley.

Low's voice came through his link. "West is solo."

"Dammit! What the hell's he doing?" Shane asked. "Nathan? What's up? Nathan? Report!"

Ignoring her, visualizing himself as a nuclear-tipped rocket on a heat-seeking course for the alien, Nathan raised his rifle and sprinted to a boulder. He ducked behind the stone, polished it with his shoulders as he paused a moment to catch his breath. He rolled a dial on his suit's main control panel, dimming the readouts.

"Stone? Carter?"

"Yeah, we've been listening. Moving east to intercept."

"And I'm with you," Shane said.

"Wang and I are closing in, too," Damphousse added.

Nathan didn't exactly resent their help, but he didn't think he needed it either. As far as Shane was concerned, he should've figured that there would be no holding her down.

He crept to the edge of the boulder, stole a glance into the clearing that led to the next jagged rock, saw no sign of movement, then tore off.

At precisely the moment he reached the center of the

clearing, the silhouette of the alien burst from the deeper gloom roughly a dozen meters ahead. The thing, like him, was dodging for rock cover.

Synapses fired, but Nathan's shock had slowed his reaction. He squeezed the trigger of his M-590. The gun spat a trio of bolts at the alien.

But the creature's speed was astounding. It sheered, rolled, and vanished behind a rock in a single, insect-like maneuver, the bolts blasting apart rock faces in the background of its ghost.

The mistake Nathan made was to linger in the clearing to see if he'd shot the thing. Problem was, his assailant exploited the delay to release a round, a round accompanied by the now-familiar and gut-wrenching noise that had come a nanosecond before Pags had been blown away.

ZZZZ-POP-POP!

Despite the skin of his camouflage suit, despite the pressurization, despite the fact that Nathan was already in the air, having launched himself toward the hemispherical shadow of the boulder, he still caught the light of the alien's round on his periphery—a light brighter than burning magnesium—and he felt its heat—something akin to a supernova—as it grazed his shoulder.

He hit the dirt, knees and elbows first, his rifle jarred from his grip. He scrambled forward, came back up with the weapon, then kept on his haunches, trying to decide how long he'd wait before risking a look.

"You spot that fire?"

"Oh, yeah."

"Now hold until you got a clean shot."

"Stone? Circle—"

Nathan switched off his link. No need to be distracted by their skipchatter. If memory served, the thing was about three rocks up, on the left.

If you swing wide and come from behind it . . .

Abandoning the idea of looking before leaping, Nathan rabbit-ran from boulder to boulder. He didn't stop to check each clearing or catch his breath. Though riding the edge of recklessness, he'd stitch a pattern to his position without, he prayed, the alien knowing until a heartbeat before he shot it into salsa.

One rock, two, three, and arrowing toward the fourth—

ZZZZ-POP-POP!

A large chunk of the boulder in front of him erupted with blue webs of energy, then was shaved off to fall into rubble. He swung around to sprint back—

And the alien broke free from a swirling smoke cloud and charged him.

Before he could level his weapon, the abomination dug its claws into his chest, lifted him a half-meter off the surface, then threw him. Nathan floated like a free-thrown basketball on his way toward an unforgiving stone backboard. When he hit the boulder, the air blasted from his lungs and his neck snapped back so hard that he thought it broke.

As he slid down the rock to land unsteadily on his feet, the creature came at him again, vapors and a low trilling escaping through its grillwork. It was then that he noticed it was unarmed. Had it run out of ammo? No time to speculate, for the alien, leaning forward, arms outstretched, fin on its chest looking like a stinger that would finish Nathan, shambled within two meters, arguably point-blank range for someone armed with an M-590.

Nathan fired.

And there was the creature on the ground, slithering away from him, unhurt. It had evaded his shot! The only thing damaged were the peaks of a pair of rocks, both now flat and haloed with dust.

He stood rapt as the thing sprang to its feet and scurried like a roach from the light to gyrate into a crevice between boulders.

Mustering his remaining strength, Nathan staggered forward, then climbed onto the boulders above the crevice, hoping to catch the thing as it emerged from the other side. He found good purchase on a ledge and dragged himself up, the clearing coming into view.

His mouth fell open.

With its back to him, the alien knelt in the clearing. Its trembling arms were raised above its head. Nathan tracked the creature's gaze to Shane, Stone, Wang, Damphousse, and Carter as the group slowly surrounded the thing. He switched on his link, and immediately had to adjust the sensitivity to cut off the panting of the Marines, who were obviously as scared as their prisoner.

Shane looked up at him. "I think it's trying to surrender," she said, her voice cracking.

One shot would finish it. All he had to do was lift his rifle, barely aim and squeeze the trigger. The military biotechs could dissect the corpse at their leisure; they didn't need a live one running around.

He pushed himself a little higher onto the boulder, then lifted his rifle, bringing it to bear on Pags's murderer.

Shane turned her gun on him. "Don't you dare."

fifteen

Shane had tried to talk to Nathan during the hike back to the ISSCV, but he had remained sullen. She guessed she would eventually get him to open up, and so she had let him have his reticence.

They hadn't had to tie the alien; it had come at gunpoint peacefully, as humans also are wont to do. Low had recorded the position of the downed alien ship and had sent the data to the Marine Corps Command Post just south of Olympus Mons. Shane wished she could have seen the looks on the comtech's faces. News of their discovery would become a global event. . . .

Now, with the sun rising over Gledhill crater in the distance, burning off a thin morning fog, Shane stood near a porthole in the troop cylinder, rubbing eyes that yearned for sleep.

"It probably thinks we're gonna kill it," she heard Wang say from somewhere behind her.

She crossed from the window to the doorway of the supply room. Inside, the alien sat in the middle of the room, tied with cargo cord to a storage crate. The others, save for Nathan, were gathered at the threshold, grimacing and covering their mouths and noses as they studied the hideous but fascinating pilot.

The alien's head was bowed submissively, as it had been all the night. Though she had tried, Shane could not detect a single facial feature that she could compare to a human face. Just those lines that were either part of a mask or some type of gills. While some parts of its skin were smooth, perhaps synthetic, other parts, particularly its hands, were covered with gray scales edged with black or green.

"We're gonna kill it?" Stone asked, clamping his nostrils. "I think not. It's gonna kill us with that smell."

"Or at least it's gonna make me puke," Damphousse said, her eyes tearing as she waved the air in front of her face.

"Smells sulfuric," Low observed.

Damphousse took another look at the prisoner. "Must be a scout. Going toward Earth it had to crank the chicken switch over Mars."

"Probably sent a distress call," Wang added.

Shane gazed soberly at Damphousse, then at Wang. "That means there'll be more coming."

Carter edged a bit toward the enemy creature, crouching for a closer look at the thing's head. "There's got to be some way to figure it out."

"Maybe it's in the mission briefing," Stone said sarcastically, then sniffled and strode away from the doorway to return to his bunk.

Hawkes stepped gingerly past Carter and got so close to the alien that Shane felt the sympathetic racing of her heart. The being seemed to tense, scales standing out, head lifting a little. Hawkes held up his palms, trying to indicate that he wasn't going to hurt it.

"Don't get any closer," Shane told him. "It could carry some disease."

He tossed her a cocky grin. "I never had a mother, but you sound like one." Then he focused back on the alien. "It's wearin' an armored flight suit, I think."

"I would hope we're not at intergalactic war with a naked enemy," Wang said.

"What if it *is* naked," Carter proposed. "With that kind of skin, I bet the thing would be impossible to kill in an unarmed hand-to-hand."

Stone sat up in his bunk. "Why don't we let it loose and you two can go outside."

Carter brought himself to full height. "I'm up for it."

"Cut the crap," Damphousse said. "Hey, Coop. Watch it there."

Hawkes's nose was a mere thumb's length above the back of the alien's head. Indeed, he was breathing down the thing's neck. "All right, that's enough," Shane complained. "You're taunting it."

"No . . . I think I . . . see something," he said, distracted.

The alien awkwardly shook its head no.

Damphousse gasped. "It knows some of our nonverbal gestures."

"They've been studying us," Shane concluded. "And we know nothing of them."

Hawkes was reaching down toward a straight metallic line on the alien's right bicep. Shane couldn't bear any more of the tank's interrogation. "Get away from it, Hawkes."

But her words meant nothing to him. He lifted a small metal card from what now revealed itself as a slot in the alien's body. The card had raised points and gleamed in the cabin's artificial light.

A noise on the order of a shriek burst through the alien's grillwork:

EEEEEEYAAAAAA!

Hawkes had obviously pissed it off. Carter began to withdraw a pistol from his holster as everyone else took at least a step back.

Shane glowered at Carter. "Put that away."

The Marine smirked and complied.

Hawkes studied both sides of the card, then held it up.

Immediately, a thought hit Shane. "Maybe it operates the vehicle, like a key."

Damphousse took the card from Hawkes and ran her finger over its surface. "There's some sort of encoded information here."

Hawkes snatched the card back from Damphousse, then stepped around the prisoner and dropped to one knee before it. He shoved the card into the enemy's face, and, in a commanding tone, asked, "What is this?"

The creature did not move, its head hanging. Though it surely couldn't say it, Shane imagined the thing rattling off its name, rank, and serial number in answer to Hawkes's query.

Shaking the card, Hawkes raised his voice. "Explain."

EEEEEEYAAAAAA!

And this time even Hawkes was startled. He fell onto his rump and retreated crab-like from the thing. Then he pulled his sidearm and pushed himself back up onto a knee. He took aim at the alien's head.

Shane swallowed. "Wait, wait, wait, wait, wait . . . "

Strangely, the alien seemed to look to the weapon, then, with a tip of its head, indicated toward Nathan, who had just joined the group in the doorway.

All eyes turned to Nathan, whose gaze was narrowed on the alien. He looked to be gathering spit in his mouth.

"Him?" Hawkes asked the creature while pointing at Nathan.

Shane's heart nearly hit the floor as the alien nodded.

Hawkes waved the card. "What does this have to do with him?"

Once again, the alien gestured toward Nathan with its head. Hawkes moved to Nathan, and an expression of understanding came over Hawkes's face. Nathan's flight suit was zippered down to his navel, and his photo tags had become untucked.

Hawkes grabbed the tags and turned back to the alien. He shook the card. "This"—he lifted the photo tags—"is this?"

It took a second, but finally the creature nodded, a sad nod, Shane thought. Then, curious about the card, she took it from Hawkes.

Wang leaned over her shoulder. "It's like a picture of its family or somethin'."

The mood in the cabin grew dour. The home world of

the aliens was probably light-years away, yet they, like humans, took along reminders of home, of family, of a life they probably fought for. Shane felt an ironic sense of pity as she pictured the prisoner as a father or mother with little ones praying for its safe return.

Yet when her gaze met Nathan, who had collapsed back onto his bunk, he stared back at her with a countenance of ice.

"Maybe we ought to give it something to eat or drink," Low suggested.

Moving its head right, the alien focused its attention on a section of shelving that contained a lone canteen. It nodded over and over, pleading in its own odd way and pulling at its bonds.

"It wants water," Wang said, awestruck.

"Right," Damphousse tossed in. "Hydrogen is the most abundant element in the universe. Makes sense that water's one thing we have in common."

Shane glanced down at the card, then, not trying to hide the melancholy in her voice, amended, "But not the only thing. Give it some water."

Out of the corner of her eye, she caught Nathan springing to his feet. Her head wasn't turned fully in his direction when he stuck his face in hers like a D.I. bent on making a point. "What the hell is wrong with you? We're low on rations already. We're all cut to thirty percent O_2 flow and you're gonna waste water on this *thing*?" He shook his head, a crazed lilt in his voice. *"No! No way!"*

Then he abruptly shifted away from her, elbowed his way into the supply room and spat on the alien. He glimpsed back at everyone, his mouth curled downward, his eyes pained. "This thing killed Pags!" Then he shot a malevolent look at the alien. "God knows who else it's killed."

The card fell from Shane's grasp. She eyed the floor, ashamed. But part of her still knew that showing mercy to the alien was right. It was a first step. The aliens might have murdered, but perhaps they were ordered to do so. Perhaps they were the slaves of an unreasonable dictator. She could speculate for a millennium, but humanity would never learn the truth if it failed to communicate.

Teeth gritted, face flush, Nathan slapped on his helmet before stomping into the air lock.

After listening to her own breath trip over itself several times, Shane picked up the alien card and went to her bunk. She fetched her helmet and hustled off after Nathan.

Outside, the sun was five degrees off the horizon, the distant crater summits crowned in a scarlet haze. Were it not for her mood, Shane would have taken time out to enjoy the Martian sunrise, perhaps a once-in-a-lifetime opportunity.

Nathan stood twenty or thirty meters from the vehicle, a lone violet silhouette staring into the sun. At his feet lay Pags. They had zipped the Marine's body into one of the black body bags Wang had found in the supply room when they had first checked the gear. Wang had chided the Corps, saying that they didn't have much faith in the recruits—and the presence of the body bags was proof of that. Nathan had argued that every Marine should pack a body bag in consideration of the others, but no one had taken him up on his idea. Actually, if they had had the bags during the dust storm, they could've used them as makeshift shelters.

Shane stepped carefully to Nathan. Once at his side, she kept quiet, respecting his thoughts. She could only see his profile, but it was enough to reveal that he shed no tears. He might be numb, beyond crying.

Stealing a glimpse at the body, she had to immediately shut her eyes and fight off a chill. The darkness took her to another time, a time when Kim and Lauren had been crying. Uncle Joe and Aunt Rita, Marine friends of her parents who were not true relatives, had been bawling even more fiercely than her sisters. There had been the blinding flash of rotating lights, the shrill wail of sirens, and the popping of gunfire in the distance. The pungent scent of faraway fires had been carried on the night wind.

Mommy and Daddy had been zipped into black bags.

After blinking several times, she put her hand on Nathan's shoulder. "Nathan, you're out of control. It's more than just Pags. . . . "

Slowly, maybe embarrassed, he faced her and slipped the alien card from her hand. He studied it.

Shane took in a long breath before speaking. "We're at war. It killed Pags because it had to. I hate what happened, you hate what happened. But maybe if we show it what it means to be human . . . who knows . . . one day the killing might stop. It can communicate. We've already proven that."

"Its kind communicates with weapons. With death," Nathan retorted. He handed her the card. "You think it cared about those colonists on Vesta, or those on the Tellus ship?"

"I . . . "

Nathan cocked a thumb over his shoulder in the direction of the ship. "It represents them. And their actions tell me all I need to know."

They both looked back at the sound of the air lock door lowering to the ground. Hawkes, Low, Damphousse, and Wang struggled forward out of the lock, and, at first, it was hard to see what they were dragging.

Then Shane realized it was the alien. She jogged to them, calling out, "What happened?"

Hawkes dropped the arm he was holding. "It killed itself."

"How?" Nathan asked, slowing to a stop before the corpse.

"I gave it a drink. That green foam there spewed from its grill thing. Then it keeled over." She huffed. "I don't know, I just . . . I can't believe it would be that afraid of us." Damphousse stared grimly at the creature.

Nathan went to the recruit and stuck his face in hers. "We're the enemy."

Damphousse shoved Nathan away. "Don't be so glad it's dead. We could've learned something."

Shane wasn't the only one who stared accusingly at Nathan; the others had him under their spotlights.

"Look, I'm just trying to make you people understand what we're dealing with. Now, c'mon."

Shane folded her arms over her chest and watched the five drag the pilot next to Pags's body. Alien and human lay side by side, a haunting prophecy framed in rust-colored sand.

"This is the first time I've ever seen a dead body," Low admitted.

"Stick around," Hawkes told her. "It won't be the last."

Once again, the wondrously surreal landscape was marred by the terrifying reality of death. Shane would be hard-pressed to remember the beauty of Mars. She watched as Nathan returned the alien's card to its bicep pocket, then he straightened and focused on Pags. Shane did likewise.

Wasn't it just yesterday that she was listening to the funny, obsessive Marine?

Hey, I know it's only the first day, but any guess as to when we get our planes?

Sir, maybe Coop would do better in a real plane, sir. I know I would.

See . . . if I were runnin' the Marine Corps, I'd give recruits planes on the first day.

Sir, I want my plane, sir.

sixteen

Nathan stared at the United States flag as two members of the Marine Corps Honor Guard used white-gloved hands to fold it into a triangle before Pags's casket. One of the guardsmen presented Pags's teary-eyed mother with the flag. For a moment it appeared she didn't want the flag, but then she took and held it tightly against her chest. Pags's father wore a callous face, but his anguish was visible in the hand he repeatedly balled into a fist. As Pags's mother collapsed to the folding chair behind her, Pags's father sat, slid an arm around his wife, and let her bury her face in his chest.

Shane, Low, Stone, Bartley, and Carter stood at parade rest to Nathan's right. Yes, their dress blues itched, but Nathan knew that wasn't the only reason they shifted uncomfortably.

A zephyr fluttered through Nathan's hair, and he looked up into it, into a sky he had forgotten was that blue. He was on Earth at last, no longer homesick but surely not at peace. The snare drummer started a roll. That was Nathan's cue to hold a salute. The bugler began to play taps. Nathan's legs stiffened, then his back, arms, and chest. His hand shook and he tried to calm it. Tried.

Pags's casket was lowered into the grave. Hawkes, Damphousse, and Wang stood opposite Nathan. He eyed the grave, then studied Hawkes. The tank appeared especially affected, blinking hard, lower lip quivering as he held a crisp salute. Nathan wondered if the tank knew how to cry, and guessed that the whole ceremony was probably hard for Hawkes to comprehend. Tanks didn't lose loved ones. Then again, they did lose friends.

When Nathan had been ten his grandmother had died. He'd been too scared to go to the wake or funeral. He and his brothers had stayed home. Pags's funeral was the first one Nathan had ever been to. He would have to get used them.

The bugler held his last note, then let it fade into the rustling of nearby trees. The drummer lifted his sticks from his drum.

A wing of five SA-29 Condors boomed overhead, then one plane dropped back and rolled away: the missing-man formation. The jets disappeared, leaving ivory vapor trails in their wake.

It was over. Nathan dropped his salute. People collected their belongings. Family members thanked those gathered for coming.

Nathan felt the need to go to Pags's parents, to talk to them, to tell them their son had not died in vain. He'd read the official report, an objective collected account of what had happened on Mars, a report devoid of Pags's humor and bravery. It made Pags seem like he'd been a piece of machinery that had just happened to be in the way. "... and Pagodin, Michael E. was KIA by enemy sniper fire as he stood near the craft ..." The Marine Corps certainly had a way of processing words.

Nathan took a step toward Pags's folks, then, seeing how distraught Pags's mother was, he hesitated.

A hand slid onto his shoulder. It was Shane. She looked at Pags's parents. "When no one knows what to say, they just say 'it happens' or 'it was fate' or 'it was his time to go'."

"Or 'I'm sorry,'" Nathan added, "which doesn't mean jack. Everyone covers it up with pretty words. The guy's dead, wiped off the planet forever. Nothing pretty about that."

Damphousse approached. "Some of us are going for lunch, then over to Asteroids. You guys want to—"

"Not me." He glanced sidelong to Shane. "You go."

She took his arm. "No one should be alone now."

"I have something I have to do," he told her.

She frowned. "Like what?"

He rolled his eyes.

"Leave him be," Damphousse said, taking Shane's arm and pulling her away from him. "Let's go."

Nathan watched them walk away, then, with his head bowed, dragged himself away from the graveyard.

With nothing in particular to do, but wanting to do it alone, he crossed the street, opting to hike the kilometer back to the base instead of riding in the jeep.

He sensed the approach of someone from behind, then a shadow rose next to his. With mild shock he glimpsed a sweaty Sergeant Bougus. "West, I wanna talk to you."

"Sir, yes, sir."

"I read your version of the mission report. Why does it lack your single-handed and single-minded charge after the alien?"

"Sir, this on the record, sir?"

"Yes it is."

"Sir, I was instructed to write a summary, sir. Which I did. That detail—"

"—was included in every other recruit's report. Lying won't get you far in the Corps."

Nathan picked up his pace, challenging Bougus to do the same. The older man's collar was already dark and soaked. "Sir, I did *not* lie, sir."

"You just withheld the truth, that it? You know what I think of that thumb-sucker shit? I think it stinks. Now you tell me what happened."

"Sir, you already know what happened," Nathan said, fingering sweat from his temples and sideburns.

"I want to hear it from you."

"All right. I went after the thing. I did it on my own. I didn't think there was time to wait for the others."

"Bullshit."

Nathan stopped. "Sir, you wanted to hear what happened and I'm telling you, sir."

"You want me to tell you what happened?"

He shrugged. "I thought you didn't know . . . "

Bougus did his in-your-face routine, which was not as disturbing as the first time he had done it to Nathan, but it was immediately effective in raising Nathan's pulse. The sergeant's eyes were so close that the universe was reduced to a starless, coal-black night. "I'll tell you what happened. You reached down inside yourself and pulled out the demon. You went after that alien with what I call an unbridled bloodlust. That, sir, when in control, is the essence of a Marine's courage. But you had no control. You let the demon beat you. You're standing here 'cause you just got lucky."

The sergeant stood there breathing in Nathan's face. Nathan didn't know if he should look away, say something, resume his walk, or do nothing.

Bougus stepped back and ran a finger between his neck and collar, wincing over the shirt's too-small neck. "They're gonna ask you about the demon. What are you gonna tell them?"

"Sir?"

"The shrinks, boy! They ain't gonna put you in AFT if they suspect you got a loose marble!"

"Sir, what am I supposed to tell them, sir?"

"Lie."

"Sir? You said lying wouldn't get me far in the Corps."

"That's right, I did. But in this case it'll get you into Accelerated Flight Training. See, West, in this case the truth is relative."

"Sir, I'm not sure I follow, sir."

"You don't have to. Be assured of this: they will ask you what happened on Mars. They will ask you about being bumped off the Tellus Mission. They will ask you about Miss Kylen Celina."

Nathan's eyes grew wide.

"Uh-huh. You had better secure that demon. You unleash him in battle. Not before. Understand?"

He gave a solemn nod. "But sir, I won't lie. I wanted that thing dead. I wasn't thinking about working together. I just wanted it. So I went. If the shrinks can't understand that, if they can't understand that a fellow Marine—a friend—was gutted in front of me and I wanted to see a little justice served, then maybe I shouldn't be flying. Because you're right. It's the demon that gives you the balls to go out there alone. I guess somehow I gotta get control of mine." He puffed his cheeks and blew out air. "When is this psych evaluation supposed to happen?"

"It already has."

seventeen

Hawkes's SA-22 stealth fighter with retractable wing design plunged into the boiling-over atmosphere of the planet. His insertion angle had been good, the friction minimal. The heat shield shut down automatically. Alien jet streams buffeted the ship, and he suddenly found himself fighting relentlessly with the stick as a dense whiteness hugged the canopy. Columns of data scrolled down his HUD but he ignored them. He alternated his gaze between the digital gyrostabilizer screen and the LIDAR image.

"He calls this mild chop?" West asked, his tone conveying that he wholeheartedly disagreed with Sergeant Bougus's definition.

"Guess so," Hawkes replied, hearing the strain in his own voice. "Hate to fly in what he calls the 'spicy stuff.'"

"Contacts," West shouted. "One, two, three, four, five."

"Uh, make that six," Wang reported nervously.

The LIDAR beeped and presented the three-dimensional bad news. The bogeys bore an uncanny resemblance to the alien craft they had discovered on Mars. "Confirm Red Leader. A-O-A twenty-nine degrees—wait! Dispersing!"

As his fighter descended farther, breaking into the troposphere, the dense clouds dissolved into a light-blue sky that could be mistaken for Earth's. An ocean of black velvet lay below, whitecaps speckling it like stars. Sunlight fired a dazzle off the nose of his ship, blinding him momentarily. When he looked again, an immense fighter passed over him; its hull fully eclipsed the sun and its white-hot triple thrusters dropped within ten or fifteen meters from his about-to-melt-any-second canopy.

"Dammit, West! I got one that wants to land on me!"

"Get out of his wash," Shane advised.

Yet even as she finished her order, the nose of Hawkes's fighter pitched up, sending him into an inverted flat spin. Blue, black, and dots of white wiped by, and there wasn't a single alarm in his cockpit that wasn't flashing or buzzing. Although he was out of control, somehow one of his target locks had found a bogey. Still a falling top, his G-suit pressurizing, bile threatening to escape from the back of his throat, Hawkes squeezed the trigger of his laser cannon. Above the screaming protest of his thrusters he heard the explosion overhead.

But there was little time to celebrate. His spin felt like it was increasing at a rate of ten to the millionth power. He reached for the autogyro toggle, battling against the centrifugal force that, like a 250-kilogram wrestler, wanted him pinned to his flight seat. A quarter-meter out of reach . . . a tenth . . .

"Drop your gear, Hawkes!" Shane cried. "You'll slow up!"

"Reds three, four, and five. Ready harpoons," West ordered.

Hawkes's hand slapped against his chest. He couldn't save himself. In a second he knew he'd black out. At least he wouldn't feel his impact with the ocean.

Thump! Thump! Thump!

"I got the remote on his thrusters," Wang said. "Powering down."

He had a vague idea of what they were attempting, but doubted it would work. As the thrusters behind him died, he was jerked forward, back, to the right, felt the jet roll and then all of his weight pressed on his straps. He saw the ocean directly below as though he were looking down from a chopper.

Three fighters in triangular formation hovered above him. Tow lines snaked to his ship from each of the planes, two of the taut cables magnetically locked to his wings, one bound to the fuselage. They had plucked him from the sky, flipped him right side up, and now, once he refired his thrusters, could let him go on his merry way. Amazing. Hawkes chucked under his breath.

"All right!" Wang cheered. "Seals are good. We just saved the Corps a whole lot of money."

"Oh, don't worry about me," Hawkes bantered. "Just save the expensive plane."

"You're a valuable asset, too," Shane assured him. "How are you feeling?"

"Nauseous, disoriented . . . just like any other day," he told her.

Someone clapped loudly outside his fighter. The vista of the ocean froze then faded into the simulator room.

"Aw, c'mon, Sarge. We still gotta finish off those contacts," West complained.

"Fall in, people," Bougus said.

Hawkes crawled out of his cockpit, wondering just how pale his complexion really was. He lined up with rest of Marines.

"This will be your final day of Accelerated Flight Training," Bougus said, looking up from his clipboard. "Thus far we're nine for nine, with Mr. Cooper Hawkes at the top of this class. He can shoot. He just can't drive."

They laughed and clapped for him. He couldn't believe it. He was a tank getting applause. His cheeks warming, Hawkes held formation but searched for a place to hide.

"You ain't a team leader yet, Hawkes," Bougus reminded. "I don't believe I'm saying this, but one day your sorry butt may be there."

"Sir, if I may, sir. You told us we were getting at least ten days of AFT. Not seven," Wang said.

Bougus grinned crookedly. "Wartime tends to change

schedules. We got three new squads waiting for AFT. And your graduation ceremony has been postponed. The rest of today you'll spend on docking and launching procedures. Can't shoot anything unless you can get off the boat."

Hawkes slumped. He had hoped they were going to finish their atmospheric dogfight. Instead they were being forced to practice parallel parking.

The drudge work ended at 1700. Hawkes returned to the barracks, showered, shaved, then joined Stone, who was also on his way to the mess hall.

"You hear?" Stone asked excitedly.

"What?"

"Bougus wants us at the hangar at 1830."

Hawkes furrowed his brow. "For what?"

They stepped into the mess hall and got on line. Stone grabbed a tray. "For what? We must've received our orders. Maybe we're getting our planes!"

"Don't bet on it," Hawkes said, despite the fact that a chill was winding up his spine.

"Oh, why you got to sour this? They spent a lot of money on us. I'm telling you, we're going to be flying soon."

With their trays overloaded with fish sticks, French fries, corn bread, and Vestan mint leaf pudding, they sat down at a long table already occupied by West, Shane, Damphousse, and Wang.

"So, you guys hear?" Damphousse asked.

"We sure did," Stone answered.

Shane put her fork down. "We shouldn't get our hopes up."

Hawkes nodded emphatically. "They'll put us on a coaster first, giving us planes then taking them away, then, finally, we might get 'em."

"The Corps shorted us on our training, that's for sure," Wang said.

"Let's forget about it until we get there," West suggested.

They ate their meals in silence. Their lives revolved around the Corps and if they weren't talking about it, well, it seemed they had nothing else to talk about, which—Hawkes reminded himself—was not true. The Corps simply had a way of making one forget about everything else. And with the war on all other topics seemed pale in comparison.

Except one.

He sneaked a look at Shane. She chewed, swallowed, and kept blowing her bangs out of her eyes. He studied her full lips, almost doubting the fact that he had kissed them. She'd been right about him: he didn't know how to deal with women.

She could teach him.

But if he forced himself on her, he'd receive a beating just shy of paralyzing. Were boxing still a legal sport, she would be a featherweight champion.

Hawkes had had many girlfriends and had lost them all. Even In Vitro women found fault with him. He couldn't understand what was wrong. Either he moved too fast, too slow, said the right thing, the wrong thing, arrived too late, too early or—and this one had shocked him—had not worn matching socks. How could a woman dump him for that?

After dinner, he caught Shane as she was replacing her tray and tossing away her trash. He asked if he could speak with her. She looked at him a little strangely, but agreed. They ambled out of the mess hall and onto the tarmac, where Hawkes paused and looked at her.

He figured it would be a good idea to begin with an apology for what had happened on the way to Mars. Though he'd heard and seen other people do it, he wasn't sure how to form the exact expression or make the words sound right.

"What is it?" she asked, brushing her hair off her

shoulder and probably growing a little impatient with him.

"I'm sorry?" Wrong. It wasn't supposed to come out like a question.

"Are you?" she asked, raising her voice even higher than he had. "For what?"

"You know . . ." Across the tarmac, the heat haze made the shapes of the hangars fluctuate. He wished he could look at her.

"Cooper. If you're sorry, then you have to be sure." If honey had a sound, that sound was Shane's voice.

"I am," he said. "I, uh, I need . . . some help."

She circled to face him. "It's polite to look at a person when you're talking to them."

"See . . . that's . . . no one really taught me . . . I mean the school they sent me to was crummy. They didn't wanna spend a lot of money on tanks back then."

"How do you want me to help you?"

"You know . . . "

"No, I don't know."

Blood rushed to his head, and he wiped his sweaty palms on his hips. He took a few steps away from her. "I know you and I will never . . . but one day . . . I . . . I don't know how . . . "

"Are we talking about love? Sex? Or what?" she asked, shocking him with her frankness.

"I know all about the sex part," he confessed. "I'm not sterile like a lot of the others." He bit his lip and lifted his gaze to meet hers. "How do you fall in love? And how do you keep someone?"

At first she looked embarrassed by his questions, but then she seemed to ponder them, squinting into the sky. Finally, she lowered her gaze and shrugged.

"You've never been in love?" he asked.

"I don't know."

"So, I guess you've never been with someone for a long time."

"That's difficult to say."

"Why?"

"It's very complicated, Cooper."

"Can you explain it to me?"

"Not really. It's hard."

He grinned. "I know. But at least now I know one thing."

"What's that?"

"I'm not alone."

Hawkes and Shane joined West and the rest of the recruits. The Marines loitered on the vast field of tarmac outside the hangar, watching the silhouettes of planes draw twenty-five degree angles across the burnt orange tableau as they returned to the distant runway.

Most of the planes rolled in the direction of hangars on the other side of the base, but Hawkes found his gaze glued to one that was apparently headed their way. Indeed, the jet drew closer, and Hawkes identified it as an SA-43 Endo/Exo Atmospheric Attack plane, a Hammerhead like the one he'd flown the first time in the simulator. But the simulator had done little justice to the magnificent piece of machinery that gleamed before his eyes. As the shadow of the plane swept over him, he heard Bartley shout, "Assemble. Sergeant Bougus is here."

After moving into the cool shade of the hangar, Nathan came to attention with the others.

Bougus strode in and assumed his usual position before them. "Today, you have been assigned your SA-43 Endo/Exo Atmospheric Attack jets. You are now members of the fifth air wing, fifty-eighth squadron."

It took all of Hawkes's limited though intense training to keep him from jumping into the air and waving a fist. Bougus would go thermonuclear were Hawkes to exhibit that kind of behavior. Still, a few of the others reacted with half-stifled gasps. He heard Wang whisper, "Yes!"

Bougus, surely expecting excitement, let the minor outbursts go unpunished. "Your current orders are to take forty-eight hours' leave."

And that brought on a collective moan from the recruits.

"Sir, two days, sir?" Damphousse asked.

West stepped forward. "Sir, ship us out, sir!"

Shane cleared her throat. "Sir, why have we been on accelerated training if we're not going to be used, sir?"

The sergeant was three seconds away from detonation as he locked on and crossed to his target: Shane. But then his face softened and the countdown ceased. He took a deep breath before speaking. "Other than what you found last week, we have no idea what lies ahead. We still know basically nothing of the enemy. Numbers. Tactics. Weapons. We've got some hardware, but nothing's been assimilated. That is why we have been losing—and losing badly—in every battle of this war." He paused to make eye contact with each member of the squadron. "Don't be in such a hurry. Trust me. The war'll wait for you."

"Sir, what are we supposed to do for two days, sir— besides worry?" Stone asked.

"My advice? See your families. It could be for the last time. Go." He clicked his heels and executed a perfect salute.

Hawkes and the rest returned the sergeant's salute.

"Dismissed."

As Bougus marched off, Hawkes abruptly found himself with nowhere to go. He crossed to the doorway of the hangar and leaned against a warm metal support strut. He listened to West and Shane, who had paused behind him.

"You gonna see your sisters?" he asked.

"I don't think they want to see me."

"I never told my folks I was joining the Corps. I don't know if I wanna be there for that reaction."

"They'll want to see you."

"You wanna be witness to that?"

She must have agreed, for they left together, and as they did so, Hawkes realized that he envied West. Yes, the guy still had a few trace elements of Mr. Hotshot in him, but for the past week he had walked instead of strutting, spoken instead of ordering, and smiled instead of sneering. What West had that Hawkes lacked was the ability to talk comfortably with Shane. Hawkes wasn't sure if the guy was making his move on her, since West seemed preoccupied by the face on his photo tag. Then again, that woman might just be dead. West was probably, however it was done, coming to terms with her loss. Now he and Shane were going to his house. Someone had once told Hawkes that you don't bring a girl home to meet your parents unless you're really serious about her. He could never make that connection.

An SA-43 rolled slowly out of the hangar next door. The pilot appeared from the shadows, his helmet in the crook of his arm. Lettering painted below the Marine's cockpit identified him as Lt. T. C. McQueen, and Hawkes recognized the man as the Angry Angel who'd sat by himself at Asteroids. There was something else about him that Hawkes suspected. He started toward plane and pilot, playing out his hunch.

McQueen was doing his walk around, checking seals and tire pressure, opening up compartments to read the gauges within. The Marine did not acknowledge Hawkes. The pilot wasn't rude, just busy.

He watched McQueen, and as he did, he was reminded of the stark truth that from here on out the battle would be real, not simulated. If he made a mistake he would die. Simple math.

Then, wanting to bang his foolish head against the hull of McQueen's plane, he thought about his death, about *who* he would die for. He would die for a country that had treated with him hostility and prejudice all his life, for a country that had created the horrible In Vitro program in the first place. He would die for people like

Davis, Otto, Tatum, and Shell, the animals who had attempted to hang him.

In the lingering heat of twilight, Hawkes felt cold. Somewhere along the line he'd gone wrong. He had decided not to get himself booted out of the Corps and had gone along with their program. He even loved the flying. But he wasn't supposed to love any of it! All of it had been a sentence laid down by a judge who had had an aversion to the truth. The Marine Corps was a place to do his time. Heroes wound up like Pags.

Once abandoned, the old feeling of rebellion was back with vengeance. He'd find a way to get out of going. He would. "I'll never get in one of those," he told McQueen.

Without looking at him, the pilot said, "Ten of us tanks were with the Tellus colony."

I knew it. He hadn't sat alone at the bar for nothing. The other Angels hadn't wanted him around. Yet he's a fool, about to join them and risk his life . . . for what? Nothing.

"Ten tanks, huh? Only makes the aliens just as bad." Hawkes put a hand on McQueen's shoulder and pulled the pilot away from his plane. He fixed the guy with a penetrating stare. "I'm not gonna die for them."

McQueen nodded as though he understood everything. Perhaps getting the Marine to see the light was easier than Hawkes had thought.

Then the pilot removed Hawkes's hand from his shoulder. "Who *would* you die for?"

The question jarred him. He already knew who he *wouldn't* die for, but was there anyone—anything—so important to him that that person, that concept, was worth his life? He'd had no one, had always been alone in the world. Friends had come and gone. He could weigh the question all day. Maybe it didn't have an answer. Shaking, torn, he spun on his heel and stormed off.

By nightfall, the flat desert of tarmac was a distant

memory. He retreated down a dark road paralleled on both sides by clusters of oaks, pines, and sago palms. Crickets conversed about the heat of the past day, and above their din, the mighty rush of jet engines intermittently struck a painful chord. By morning, the war, the Corps, all of it, would be out of his life forever.

eighteen

The farmhouse was roughly 1,800 kilometers north of the base, nestled among the green hills of a New England town appropriately named Farmingville. The home had been in Nathan's family for three generations. The Wests took great pride in their little piece of Americana, and Nathan was sure that he or one of his brothers would carry on the tradition. Save for the trio of mini satellite dishes that had been mounted on the roof a half-dozen years prior, the place had remained unchanged for as long as he could remember. Sure, Dad would have the house painted now and again, change the flower beds, put the light-pink impatiens here, the darker pink begonias there, but he was a man who relished stability and routine.

Presently, however, there were new additions to the house, ones that made Nathan hesitate at the foot of the driveway.

"What's wrong?" Shane asked, smoothing the wrinkles out of her green uniform.

He took another look at the yellow ribbons tied to the front porch. "I guess I was kind of hoping to tell them myself. They must've talked to Kylen's father. . . . "

They were but halfway up the drive when the porch's screen door flew open. Nathan's fourteen-year-old brother John ran across the porch, disregarded the steps and jumped onto the concrete, shouting, "Nathan! Nathan! Mom! Dad! It's Nathan!"

Nathan extended his arms to hug his brother, but

he'd forgotten that John was at that age where hugs are simply not acceptable manly behavior.

Grinning ear to ear, John grabbed his hand and gave him a thumbs-up shake. "I told everybody at school how you're gonna be a pilot up there," he said, tilting his head to the sky.

A figure appeared behind the screen door and lingered there. Though the person was cast mostly in shadow, Nathan knew it was Mom. Slowly, the door opened and she slid from behind it. She crossed to the edge of the porch and stood at the top of the steps, grabbing a round wooden column for support. She had probably just come from work, as she was still clad in office attire that accented her grace and sophistication. Yet now, Nathan had trouble picturing her as anything else but a pale mother sadly seeing her boy as a man for the first time.

He released John's hand and moved toward her. He climbed the steps, and before he could say anything, she pulled his head to her shoulder. She trembled, and he thought she might cry.

The screen door opened once more. Nathan looked up and saw his father. "Mom, Dad, John. This is my friend, Shane Vansen."

Shane smiled. "It's a pleasure, Mr. and Mrs. West."

John jogged back to Shane and gave her the once-over. "You're a pilot too, aren't you?"

Shane nodded.

"Dinner's almost ready," his mother said, and doing a poor job of disguising the fact that she was choked up, she turned from him and headed back into the house.

Nathan rose onto the porch, took his father's hand and shook it. "I was gonna give you a rock I pocketed on Mars, but it never got through quarantine."

Dad's lips came together. He'd never seen the man more doleful. "Come on inside."

He stood there, not following his father but thinking twice about complying. It was safe to guess that the entire visit was going to be a gloomy, depressing reminder of just how much his parents despised his decision to join the Corps. All his life Nathan had shunned conflicts. When his parents had fought, he had run into his room and hidden beneath his bed. He was too big for that now, figuratively and literally, yet the same desire to flee persisted.

Shane came onto the porch, and though he knew she could read the tension in his family, she didn't seem moved by it. She gestured with her head toward the door.

Before they could enter, Neil, Nathan's seventeen-year-old middle brother, came out with an expression of deep concern.

"Hey, Neil. Shane, this is my brother Neil."

Neil put his back to the screen door, blocking their entrance. "The TV said we're about to begin another battle," he uttered gravely.

Nathan exchanged a dire look with Shane. They went inside, heading swiftly for the television.

In the living room, Shane, Nathan, and his brothers sat on the sofa before the 162-centimeter flat-screen TV mounted on the wall. A special news report was on. A female reporter stood before a hangar that swarmed with activity. "I'm here at the U.N. Task Force headquarters at Vandenburg, California, receiving the latest reports of the mobilization of the Russian *Kiev* starship carrier. They have joined the battle lines with the French carrier *Clemenceau* and the *U.S.S. Colin Powell.*"

Neil picked up the remote and thumbed down the sound. "I heard the alien fighters are made of an unknown metal. That we can't harm it."

"They only started reverse engineering the one we found. That's just a rumor," Nathan said, keeping his gaze on the screen. The picture switched between the too-pretty anchor in the studio and the reporter in the field, and for the moment Nathan was glad Neil had killed the sound; he could live without the banal questions posed by the anchor.

"Kylen's brother told us—"

Nathan's glare cut off Neil's sentence at the knees. He rose and started out of the room, listening to their voices behind him.

"Don't worry," Shane told Neil. "This time out we'll beat them."

"How do you know?" John asked.

"Because this time they're going up against the 127th, the Angry Angels. They'll knock the enemy into Andromeda."

But Shane didn't sound too sure of herself.

Turning down an old, welcoming hall, Nathan found the bathroom and locked himself inside. He put his face close to the mirror, trying to see if his pain was visible. He looked all right. He remembered when he and Kylen had stood before the same mirror. They had told each other how they were the perfect heights for each other, she slightly shorter than him. Yes, they had been the perfect couple.

Only a spirit stood with him now.

He left the bathroom and went into the kitchen. Dad stood at the stove, stirring his stew with a wooden spoon. Mom was at the cupboard, taking out glasses and placing them on the counter. Nathan went to the table and collapsed into a chair. "Any word?"

Dad didn't look back at him. "Kylen's father was told it had been . . . difficult to . . . identify the bodies. They don't know, Nathan."

Out of the corner of his eye, Nathan thought he saw someone move into the dark dining room that adjoined the kitchen. Probably Neil or John spying.

Mom took a plate from the cupboard. She brought it down toward the counter then suddenly smashed it to pieces. Collapsing onto her elbows, she was fraught with more pain than Nathan had ever seen in her before. But she still held it inside. Dad went to her, slid his arm over her shoulders. She wrenched away from him.

Nathan's heart raced from guilt. He had to say something and blurted out, "There was nothing I could do."

"You could have talked to us," Dad shot back.

"I knew what you would have said. And I didn't want to hear it. I enlisted because I had no choice."

Mom erupted, coming to him and beating her fist on the table. "*No . . . No . . . Now you have no choice!*"

Nathan closed his eyes and flinched, but held his seat. He didn't have the guts to look at her. "As a colonist, you never would have seen me again—so what's the difference?"

"*You'd be alive!*"

"I'd be dead!"

"Your mother means that as a colonist your life would have been about creating life, not taking it," Dad explained, his tone a notch more composed than Mom's but still nowhere near normal.

With courage and the justification to back it up, Nathan opened his eyes and regarded father. "So, now it's about saving lives. Yours, Mom's, Kylen's . . . "

"Son, you can't believe that she's still alive."

"I *have* to believe."

He hated the moment almost as much as he did the aliens. Nowhere to run. He needed to run. *Get away. Go. Leave this alone. Run. Run. Run.*

Mom took a step away, as if he had some contagious disease. "You joined the military on a chance? You're willing to die on a possibility?"

Nathan was chilled by the coincidence of her choice of words. Was there some strange fate waving its hand over them? It was true that she probably knew him better than anyone, even Kylen, but was that enough to account for what she had said?

He'd never know, but at least there was one certainty: he would—no matter what—cling to the possibility that Kylen may still be alive.

Somehow, he had to explain his reasoning to Mom. Somehow. "The tanks had me thrown off. The Corps was my only chance to get to her." Seeing their disapproving glares sent him bolting to his feet. His chair threatened to fall but didn't. "And if there's a possibility that giving my life will get her back—"

"Nathan, you're young," Dad interrupted. "You see everything as life or death."

"Dad, I've seen these things we're at war with—"

"When you're older, you'll understand."

He couldn't believe what he was hearing! Parental clichés! Rhetoric! He shouted, "These aliens massacred hundreds of—"

Mom grabbed the pocket of his shirt. *"Nothing is worth dying for!"*

About to scream back at his mother, Nathan froze as Shane materialized from the gloom of the dining room. She had trouble meeting anyone's gaze, probably feeling like an intruder.

"There's something I'd die for," she said, a hint of longing creeping into her voice. "I'd give my life for a chance to argue with my parents." She slipped back into the darkness, leaving Nathan stunned.

As Mom and Dad hung in the silence she had created, Nathan moved to the counter, dropped to one knee, and began picking up pieces of the dish. He felt Mom's hand come to rest on the back of his head.

After dinner, Nathan and Shane went to see Kylen's father, who lived a few kilometers away. Dad loaned him the XK-26, a new, sporty version of the old model family transport. Nathan still thought of the new model as a large, battery-wasting boat.

Despite the circumstances, Kylen's dad greeted them warmly at the door and invited them in for a drink. He seated them in his den and switched off the TV, saying, "Don't need any *more* bad news."

The man had changed. Notice of his only daughter's possible death had leeched away the color in his cheeks, robbed him of the desire to shave, and had made his eyes appear as though they hadn't been closed for a week. He'd lost weight, too, the beer gut hanging down perhaps only half as far as it used to. He scratched his chest through a heavily wrinkled shirt, then went off to fetch them beers.

"We won't stay long," Nathan assured Shane.

"As long as you want, I don't mind," she said. "I know this is important to you."

He thought of her overhearing his fight with his parents. "I wish you hadn't—"

"Don't be embarrassed. And I owe you an apology. I feel like a jerk. I shouldn't have said anything."

Nathan summoned all of his sincerity. "I'm glad you did. And besides. Now we're even."

Her brow lowered in puzzlement.

"You know about my past and I know about yours. That night you hit Hawkes—"

"You were up?"

He nodded. And she understood.

Kylen's dad returned with their beers and lowered himself with a groan into an easy chair in which he now probably spent most of his time. He wasn't drinking, just repeatedly staring at the remote in his hand as he ran an index finger over it. He'd just shut off the TV, yet it was obvious that the device was his only link to the knowledge of whether Kylen had lived or died. Certainly, someone from the Tellus complex would call him, but that call would most assuredly arrive *after* a list of the dead was already read on the news. Tellus mission security and confidentiality would fail. Too many people wanted to know. Corruption at Tellus would be as bad as it was in Washington.

"If you want the TV back on that's fine," Nathan said.

Kylen's dad looked relieved. "I'll keep the volume low . . . so we can talk."

Nathan swallowed. "I really only have one thing to

say, sir. I just . . . wish I had been with her when they had attacked. I know it's not my fault, but I feel like I abandoned her. I tried to stow away, but they caught me. And so she went alone. She was going to live our dream for both of us. And I was going to meet up with her . . . somehow."

"Do you remember when my wife died?" Kylen's father asked Nathan.

"I guess I was about seventeen. That was about the time I met Kylen."

"You two weren't married, but you felt something that a lot of married people don't feel. And that something was torn away from you, the same way it was when I lost my wife." He leaned forward, setting down the remote on the arm of his chair and bringing his hands together. "You *do not* get over it. And now—maybe—I've lost Kylen, too."

Shane rose. "I need to—"

"Down the hall to your left," Kylen's father said.

They watched Shane leave, then Nathan said solemnly, "I'll try to find her."

"You know what I want most from you?"

"What's that?"

Kylen's father got out of his chair, went down on his knees before Nathan, took both of Nathan's hands in his own and squeezed them until it hurt. He spoke slowly, and there was a sudden ferocity in his voice. "I want you to go out there and bring these vermin to their knees. Get them for getting her."

"We still don't know she's dead," Nathan insisted.

The old man let out a shivery sigh. "I'm starting to give up hope. So now I'm going to put my hope in you, the hope that you'll kill as many of them as you can."

Shane came from the hall and stopped, her eyes widening at the sight of Kylen's father on his knees. She looked lost, not knowing if she should enter the den or not. Then Kylen's father saw her. Pretending nothing was wrong, he returned to his chair.

"You ready?" Nathan asked her.

"Sure."

They told Kylen's father that they'd see themselves out. They left the broken man in his chair, his drawn face cast in the flickering glow of the TV.

nineteen

I can get up myself.

Probably. But it looks like you could use a hand . . . and I'm offerin' one.

Ain't easy for me to recognize a helping hand.

If that's a thank you, don't worry about it. Someday you'll pay me back.

Cooper Hawkes had made the decision to go AWOL.

But he kept second-guessing it by reminding himself of the good things about military life, about the feeling of belonging to a team.

He would never be alone in the Corps.

I don't want to die for nothing!

By marching at a steadily increasing rate, he thought he could get away from his doubts, away from the guilt. He tried as he had been for the past couple of hours to ignore the metal birds that squalled in the air. He told himself that their sounds would eventually become meaningless white noise, but he knew that was a lie. One part of him wanted to run back to his bunk and relax for the next forty-eight hours, then join the squadron. The other part, well, the other part was stronger.

Ahead, the road curved to the right, and the tree trunks and giant fronds that fenced it off were suddenly shimmering. Hawkes detected the rattle of an unconventional engine, definitely not electric. A single headlight burned through a thin mist and drew toward him. He squinted, and behind the glare he saw an old motorcycle, one that lacked anti-grav capability and still had wheels. The bike slowed and veered across the road, finally coming to a stop before him.

"She dumped you out and left you to walk, didn't she . . . "

He was built like an oil drum and had neither shaved his face nor trimmed his graying hair in the past couple of years. His black, open-faced helmet with a small spike mounted atop it made him a human bayonet, and his black leather vest did little to contain his sagging, gorilla-like chest. The digitized, three-dimensional tattoos on his bicep seemed to jump out at Hawkes. The largest one was a grim reaper with a rifle instead of a scythe, and beneath the figure were the words: A.U. #5475 CYBORG UNDERTAKERS.

Chug Chug Chug Chug . . . Hawkes could barely hear the biker over the engine. Realizing this, the beefy man reached up with stubby fingers and turned a key. The bike sputtered into silence. "I said, she dumped you out and left you to walk."

"Oh, you think I was with a woman in a car?" Hawkes asked.

"Course I do. Lemme see now"—he gave Hawkes an appraising once-over—"you're a Marine. Flyboy. You don't got to be embarrassed about it. Where you headed?" The biker lifted a thumb over his shoulder. "Hope it ain't back that way. Ain't nuthin' for ten, fifteen klicks, and even then all you're gonna find's a little store that—dammit—is closed."

Hawkes absently bit the inside of his cheek, sinking into the dismal news. "I guess I was going that way."

"Tell you what. I'm swinging past the base. You wanna lift? I don't mind helping out a fellow service man." The biker lifted his brow, and his forehead became grooved like the tires of his ride.

Before Hawkes could answer, a particularly loud rumble tore apart the night sky. A wing of SA-43s whooshed by, climbing from about a thousand kilometers toward space.

"I tried to get my own ass back in this fight, but the Army told me I'm too old. Reserves won't even take me. 'Sides, I guess they'd make me cut my hair. I thought the A.I. War was the last one we were ever gonna have. I lost a lot of buddies back then. At least we got a museum to honor their memories, but it just doesn't seem like enough. I went there once, but I . . . couldn't stay long."

"Why?"

The biker looked puzzled over Hawkes's question. Hawkes wondered about the reaction. It was an innocent question, a simple one.

"You've never been in combat, have you?" the biker asked, as though accusing Hawkes of a crime.

"I, uh . . . yeah."

Chortling, the biker unbuttoned his chin strap and folded his arms across his chest. "You're too young. You're talkin' 'bout simulated, ain't you . . . "

Hawkes looked in the direction of the base. "Maybe I will take that ride."

"I thought so," the biker said, and Hawkes wasn't sure if the big man was referring to the question of combat or the fact that Hawkes did, after all, want the lift.

The biker leaned forward. "Hop on." He kick-started the motorcycle to life.

Hawkes complied, and, over the roar, he shouted, "I was on Mars. And I saw my buddy die."

The engine ceased. The biker craned his neck back toward Hawkes. "Then you were with those Marines I heard about on the net."

"Yeah. And if you'll do me a favor, I don't exactly wanna go back to the base."

The biker let him off at a chain-link fence with a warning sign:

KEEP OUT. PROPERTY OF U.S.M.C.
VIOLATORS WILL BE PROSECUTED TO
THE FULLEST EXTENT OF THE LAW.

"Hey, you want, I'll wait for you," the biker called after him.

Hawkes paused to glance back at him. "You don't have to."

"Think I will. Out of respect . . . for them."

Hawkes scaled the fence and jumped down into the restricted area. The grounds were encircled by trees and carpeted with a thick layer of St. Augustine sod. Once past the perimeter foliage, he arrived in a vast clearing dotted with waist-high white crosses. He remembered how Shane had described the place as looking like Arlington National Cemetery, but that comparison didn't mean anything to him. He passed cross after cross, then finally arrived at the mound of dirt that was still damp and made his nose crinkle a bit with the smell of humus. Now, the deeper pitch of transports taking off accompanied the hum of insects.

Shrouded in shadows, Hawkes scanned the landscape. He was confident that he wouldn't be spotted, but if he were, he'd feel more foolish than concerned about the punishment for trespassing. They would not court-martial him for breaking into a cemetery but they'd certainly make him explain his act. That, he considered, would be punishment enough.

His gaze lowered to the mound. "Pags, I, uh, I wanted to say something when they buried you, but I didn't know what. And now that I'm here, I still don't. 'Sides, they don't let anybody say much at those things."

Teachers had told Hawkes that he needed to learn to express himself better, that he was a wonderful observer and a fast learner, but if he couldn't convey what he knew to others in both verbal and written forms, then much of his talent might be locked inside him. Simple moments had left him speechless.

Something on the vast scale of parting words to a dead friend was a universe out of reach.

But he forged on. "I guess I just wanted to say . . . you were the only guy who was ever okay to me."

While a warm Gulf breeze swept over him, he sat on the mound and beat a fist onto his thigh over his inability to convert thoughts into words. "I wish, somehow, you could just feel my insides. And know. Maybe right now you can. I doubt it." He took up a handful of dirt. "I wish I could know what you feel now. I thought, before, I knew what it would be like, but seein' you up there . . . all bloody . . . "

He looked beyond the trees and saw the dark figure of the biker. The man was on his knees, his head bowed, his helmet under an arm. Then Hawkes searched for Mars, not knowing whether the planet was visible at the hour or not. He figured he'd try anyway. It felt right to do so.

Tiny yet intense points of light glinted among the stars. There was no Mars, no moon, and no clouds, only the endless void that a hundred years prior would have been a valley, a beachhead, or coastal waters. To try to defend or conquer even a small portion of space seemed a great impossibility, a fool's errand.

Who would *you die for?*

McQueen's question was an icicle in his heart; it tormented him with chills and made him clench his teeth so hard that his head shook. "Aw, Pags, I wish I could know if anyone or anything is worth it."

He rose, wiped his hand and rear free of dirt, then shuffled back to the fence and hopped it.

"That's what it's all about," the biker said, swinging a leg over his ride. "Right back there. Ain't a lot of people walkin' around with as much honor or courage as they had."

Hawkes delayed before getting on the bike. "Why'd you join the Army in the first place?"

"Everybody jokes, says it seemed like a good idea at

the time. Course they were drunk at the time. But as for me, it wasn't that I didn't have anything better to do or that I wanted to make a career of it, or that I had a choice between service or jail, but I kept watchin' the news and seein' people die and thought I had to do something about that. See, I didn't have to have a personal reason for doing what I did. I didn't have a brother or sister or folks who were killed. I think there just comes a time in every person's life when they gotta put somethin' else first. Making sacrifices ain't a pleasant business"—he inclined his head to the sky—"but without those people, shit . . . don't wanna think about that. Now, I'm ramblin'. Where you headed?"

twenty

"We haven't been here in a long time, Nathan,"
John said, waving the flashlight around and shining it in
Nathan's eyes. "And you still haven't told us why you
wanted to come here in the first place."

Neil added his voice to John's. "And why couldn't
Shane come? I like her. She could've come."

He waited until he was seated and resting his head
against one of the tree-fort's walls before answering. "I
don't think we should forget about this place."

They looked at him, uncertain.

"What I mean is," he quickly qualified, "we should
talk about all the stuff we used to do."

"Like when that blue jay built her nest above us and
she kept swooping down and"—Neil looked at John—
"you went to take a look at her eggs and got pecked
right on the head."

John scratched his pate, remembering the old war
wound. "That wasn't as bad as the time you built that
raft and nearly drowned."

Nathan smiled over the memory of having to save his
brother. Neil hadn't been in danger; he'd just failed to
realize that all he had to do was stand. The water had
been neck-deep. "You still owe me for that one," he
reminded Neil.

"You're only going to be here for a couple of days—"
John began then broke off. "I wonder if they'd let your
family come with you. I'll bet Dad would wanna go."

Neil elbowed John, who winced. "You idiot. He's
going into space, into battle. We can't go along." Then

he foisted a pompous expression at John. "But in a year, *I'll* be old enough to enlist."

"Unh-uh. Forget that," Nathan said sternly.

"I heard Dad telling Mom they might draft me anyway," Neil said. "I might not even have to enlist. But don't they have a rule about sending brothers or something?"

Nathan shrugged. "You guys know why I joined. I didn't want to become some big hero or anything. I just—"

"We heard why," John said. "She's far away. But Shane's right here . . . "

"She's a friend. That's all. She's got a whole world of her own problems. She doesn't need any of mine."

"So, why are we up here, Nathan?" Neil's wide-eyed expression said that he hadn't accepted the vague answer Nathan had already given John, and was not about to play any more games.

Nathan took in a long breath. "I wanted to talk to you guys. I guess I wanted to tell you that I'm going to miss you."

"'Cause you might never see us again," Neil said softly. "And 'cause you might die."

John snickered. "He ain't gonna die."

"One of his friends already has," Neil spat back. "He might be next."

"Neil's right, John. But I'm giving you my word that I'll try as hard as I can not to get killed."

"You'd better," John warned. "'Cause I heard Mom telling somebody on the phone that Kylen's father was going crazy—and I don't want Dad going crazy. And I'll . . . miss you."

"Nobody's going crazy and nobody's dead," Nathan corrected. "There's just a lot of waiting going on. And it's frustrating."

"That's how we're going to feel when you leave," Neil said. "But maybe I'll join you soon. Those bastards won't have a chance against us."

He wished there was something he could say to

purge Neil of the desire to enlist. He hoped there was a rule about brothers that forbade the Corps from taking Neil. His mother might not survive the news that two of her three boys were in battle, and his father, well, Dad might wind up like Kylen's father after all.

"What's it like to fly one of those jets?" John asked. "Barry at school told me it's exactly like the VR-cade, only they don't give you any bags in case you puke."

Nathan half-grinned. "I don't wanna let you down, but I've only been in the simulator. When I get back, I'll be flying my first SA-43."

"Damn . . ." Neil said. "I almost can't imagine you flying one of those. I mean, my brother at the controls. I remember when you smacked up Mom's car taking us to soccer practice."

Lifting an index finger, Nathan explained, "That was only because I didn't—"

"You were looking at that *girl*," John said. "And that fat lady whose car you hit was yelling at you like she would never run out of breath."

"Think you'll crash your jet?" Neil asked.

Nathan scowled. "What kind of a question is that? The only way I'll be crashing is if I get shot down. And even then, the Corps has a new track-and-harpoon program to save pilots and planes."

John pursed his lips. "They must've put you through boot camp, huh?"

"Was it as bad as everyone says it is?" Neil queried.

"Two things you don't do in boot camp: get your D.I. mad at you, and get your squadron mad at you. Do either one, or both, and you'll hate it a million times more."

They continued talking about the Corps, and then, slowly, the tide went out on their conversation. John and Neil had apparently run out of questions, or at least weren't voicing them. Nathan studied John, who held his fingers in front of the flashlight and formed the shadows of monsters on the fort wall. Then he shifted his gaze to Neil, who was idly picking splinters from the floor and rolling them between his fingers. Nathan's breath became staggered as he looked upon his brothers for what Sergeant Bougus had said might be the last time. He wanted the moment to be important, meaningful, but somehow it felt almost like any other night. It had been a while since he had recognized the need to be alone with his brothers, to bond with them, and that made the evening different. But something was supposed to wash over him, a revelation, something that would carve the moment indelibly into his memory. He simply sat in the tree-fort with his brothers, wanting to say things like: "If I die, you'll take care of Mom, won't you guys . . ." But whether he died or not, Mom was too independent to be taken care of. He repressed the grim impulse to ask his brothers how they would feel if he were to die. They would barely know how to answer that question. The most he would get out of them might be a word: sad. He already knew that they loved him; he was just permitting his insecurity to get the best of him.

"Let's get down," Neil suggested, seizing Nathan's wrist and checking his watch phone. "I'm supposed to be getting a call about now."

"I'm sorry for dragging you guys up here," Nathan said, then glanced at the watch himself to check for messages. There were none. He got to his feet, careful to duck beneath the low ceiling. "And thanks for coming."

John stood erect. "It's not good-bye yet, Nathan. We still have tomorrow."

He brightened. "Yeah. What do you guys want to do?"

"You really want to know?" John asked, then turned to Neil, who nodded his consent with a smile. "We wanna see Shane in a bikini."

Nathan allowed himself a second's smile, then rolled his eyes to make sure his brothers knew that he didn't approve of their lusting after Shane. Though his own hormones had leveled off to a point of saving him from embarrassment, Nathan could still vividly remember the days of following girls through clothing stores, tracking their scent like an unabashed hound faithful to the unrelenting urges.

He was last to descend the rope ladder, and, once on the ground with his brothers, he crossed from the forest to the south forty of his parents' farm.

John noticed the lights first. He stopped, pointed to the sky, and Nathan saw the boy's Adam's apple bulge in a deep swallow.

After a glance that told him all he needed to know, Nathan broke into a sprint. "Come on! Let's find out how we're doing."

Though he had a head start, both Neil and John beat him to the house. Out of breath, he entered through the back door and burst into the kitchen, the smell of dinner still lingering in the air. He heard the TV from the living room and hustled toward the sound.

Shane sat on the edge of the sofa, her chin in her palm, her gaze intent on the screen. Bolted to positions behind her were Mom and Dad; they clung to each other, both with ashen faces and glassy eyes. Neil and John had thrown themselves onto the floor and now leaned on their elbows. Nathan took a seat beside his friend.

After consulting his electronic notebook, a middle-aged reporter—who in Nathan's opinion could best be described in a word: scared—looked off-camera for a cue. Behind him, a passageway stretched straight away, and two Navy officers exited a hatch and ran for one on the other side. "We have it? Good," the reporter said, then faced the camera. "The following, we must warn, are scenes we regret having to show you."

Images apparently recorded from an attack jet's wing-mounted camera replaced the reporter and depicted a fierce firefight above, beneath, and around an immense gray space carrier.

Alien fighters strafed the hull of the ship with salvo

after salvo of laser fire, and the few remaining Hammerhead jets that were trying to fend off the alien swarm were suddenly blasted to pieces or damaged to the point where their pilots had to eject. What was worse, the half-dozen or more floating Marines were picked off like clay targets before an expert skeet shooter.

Then, one of the carrier's main dishes took a triplet of alien bolts that cobwebbed it with energy and, after second, caused it to shatter.

A stray shot fired from an unseen plane came directly at the screen. Nathan jerked back as the image was ripped away into static.

Another signal broke in and revealed the receiving bay of a medivac shuttle. The place was a vast metallic lake bed of stretchers weighted with bleeding and burned pilots, most of whom were still unbandaged. Medics shouted and moved in clusters through the maze of wounded. The camera panned right to a row of uncovered corpses piled three-high. Two medics added a woman to the already obscene number of casualties. The reporter's voice strained over the horrific aftermath. "The space carriers *Nimitz* and *H.M.S. Montgomery* have been destroyed."

Though the new image on the screen was very grainy, the contrast high, Nathan could see the *Montgomery*, adrift in space. What little was left of her bow was pinpricked by the tiny, residual glows of internal explosions and fires. Small clouds of debris took chaotic orbits and spiraled in the carrier's wake. Twenty or thirty alien fighters still circled and spat their venom upon her, doing so at a leisurely pace, for there wasn't a single Hammerhead present to stop them. The carrier began to list, and as it did, the signal began to break up.

The reporter's face returned. "From here on the *U.S.S. Yorktown*, the 127th airborne, known as 'The Angry Angels,' are engaging the enemy—and meeting heavy resistance."

Another wing-mounted camera took in the terrible yet captivating action as the pilot stole along the belly of the cruiser, trying to get a target lock on an alien fighter that was a mere jet's length ahead of her. Accompanying the image was her voice through the link:

"Copy you, Mac. Don't think my lock's working. I'm right on this bug and getting nothing!"

"They jammin' us or what?" the man speculated.

Stunned over recognizing the female pilot's voice, Nathan turned to Shane. "That's Collins from the bar."

Shane wouldn't look at him. "And I'm actually rooting for her now."

John's jaw hung slack. "You know her?"

Nathan nodded, then pointed to the screen.

Now, the same battle was seen from another angle, this one taken from the safer distance of a Japanese frigate, the nose of which was seen in the foreground. The *Yorktown* was a jogged metallic rectangle amid a haze of falling glitter. "The enemy have refused terms of surrender," the reporter voiced-over. Then he appeared, and the passageway was now clogged with smoke. "There are electric flashes"—behind him, artificial lightning erupted from behind a half-open hatch—"and you can hear the metal buckling in the bow of the carrier." He looked away as he pressed his index finger on the small receiver clipped to his ear. "Peter, are we still linked with the feed?"

Nathan could indeed hear the groaning protest of the hull, a sound that left him shaken and cold.

The smoke around the reporter became so thick that he was barely seen. Facing the audience, he assured, "I'll try to stay on as long—" A sudden flash behind the man made him look back as the picture wiped into snow.

Mom gasped.

A slightly disheveled news anchor was caught off guard as he suddenly realized he was on camera. He wheeled his chair closer to the desk, lifted and clapped papers to straighten them, then hemmed. "Uh, it seems we've temporarily lost our link with Mark Briggs aboard the *Yorktown*. We'll return to him as soon as possible. In the meantime, let's go to Mimi Levanto, who's standing by at Space Station Goddard, for her report on the efforts there."

"We'll return to the *Yorktown*?" Nathan asked sarcastically, then stood. "The carrier's gone!" He couldn't bear any more. He stomped out of the room and toward the front door.

It was a beautiful night, paid homage to by the croaking frogs who knew nothing of war and death. The sky that had recently been speckled with battle now denied the fact that Marines had lost their lives. He heard the screen door close, but didn't look back. He figured it was Shane.

"Nathan . . ."

Finding his blue star, Nathan fixed on it. He clenched his fists. "How did any of this happen? I'll tell you how. It started with senators and governors. Then again, it started with tanks. She wouldn't be there, and I wouldn't be about to die. Look at what's happened."

Shane seemed to consider what he had said for a long moment, then crossed in front of him. "When we go back, I want you to remember one thing. Cooper didn't take her away from you."

He bowed his head, ashamed that she now knew that he had more than one reason for hating the tank. In fact, she knew a lot more than he cared for her to know. But he had invited her and should have realized that it would all come out.

The screen door banged shut. Dad moved to the edge of the porch. "It's over."

Nathan lifted his gaze to Shane, who, like him, didn't know how to react. There was just shock, numbness.

His watch phone abruptly beeped simultaneously with Shane's. A tinny voice followed:

"Attention all pilots of the Marine Corps Aviators

Cavalry. You are to report immediately to base for active duty."

Mom, who had come up next to Dad, put a hand over her mouth.

"Repeat ... MCAC pilots are to be suited and ready to roll by 0600. Walk arounds must be complete by 0615, and launch lines will commence by 0630. Thumb your compliance codes now."

Nathan and Shane hit buttons on their phones that would send a signal back to the base stating that they were on their way.

The moment that he had been carefully folding away since coming home had now been dumped on him as though from a bloated, dark cloud. He was like a statue in front of his house, his family, his friend, wishing he could refuse the beckoning stars of war.

twenty-one

Nathan had not slept on the flight back to Loxley. He had closed his eyes and found himself behind the stick of Collins's fighter, struggling frantically like she had to get a lock on the alien craft. Then the ship had braked, causing him to fly over it. The sickening sound of his thrusters being ravaged by laser fire had made him jerk violently and open his eyes.

Once he and Shane had arrived at the base, they had gone to their barracks for showers, discovering they had been the last, save for Hawkes, to return. Nathan had taken a granola bar offered to him by Low, then had headed alone to the hangars.

Now he was in the dimly lit shelter for his Hammerhead. He strolled along her belly, running fingers over her gray, polymeric skin. "You were right, Neil. This definitely isn't Mom's car, and I almost can't imagine myself flying her."

Arriving beneath the nose of the plane, Nathan stepped out of its shadow and stared at the black lettering stenciled in heat-resistant paint below the canopy:

5TH AIR WING 58TH SQUADRON USMC

On the opposite side of the canopy:

LT. NATHAN WEST

The jet was *his*. And he would soon entrust his life to the strength of its hull, the calculations of its computer mind, and the response of its thruster-driven heart. He moved to the wing, ducked under it, and wandered to the rear of the craft. Then he walked back to the nose. He had completed four walk arounds already, but something still felt wrong. He inspected the canopy, then the nose of the plane. Then he knew.

Hunting around, Nathan found a service ladder and rolled it to his jet. He went to a wall of black metal cabinets, each labeled with its contents. Finding the one he wanted, he opened it and gathered his supplies. He mounted the ladder and sat on the second-to-last rung. Once the cans were open, he dipped his brush and began to paint.

It took him all of twenty minutes, and when he was done, he stood back to inspect his artwork.

A blue star composed of a simple circle and cross glimmered above the words: BEYOND AND BACK.

"Nathan!"

Shane had just come through the side door and was running toward him. Unsure of why she was present and fearing the worst, he braced himself.

"Nathan," she repeated, arriving out of breath below him. "Our orders are in. We have to report to the orientation room."

After hurriedly gathering up the paint and brushes, then stowing them and the ladder, he went back to Shane, who had been staring at his blue star. "Ready?" he said.

It took a moment for his question to register, then she nodded.

Sunrise over the base was nothing to be admired; it was simply a clock marking the minutes until launch. They loped across the tarmac, headed for the main complex, and it dawned on Nathan that he'd forgotten something. He'd been so excited to get orders—any orders—that he'd never asked Shane about the details. Then again, he hoped they weren't going to repair another tracking drone. "Any idea where we're headed?"

"Damphousse heard we're going right to the line."

Sirens blared behind them and grew louder. Suddenly, an olive-drab van cut in front of them.

"Dammit! He missed me by a molecule," Shane screamed.

"Hey, you ass—" Nathan backed off his epithet as he noted the red cross painted over a square white field on the back of the van. Another van roared past them, and both pulled up to the base hospital that adjoined the main complex.

They sprinted up to the vans and paused to see what was happening. The hospital's doors slid automatically open and eight or nine medics hastened to the now-open rear doors of each of the vans. Survivors on stretchers were hauled out along with the dead, who were in black body bags.

Nathan recognized a uniform.

So did Shane. "The 127th," she uttered weakly.

The elite force, some burned, some comatose, some with shattered limbs, were carried into the hospital. Nathan counted more dead than living.

Out of breath, Shane placed her palm over her heart. "Ohmygod. They were the best . . . "

The moment was like a crystal ball that conjured up too vivid a picture. Nathan found himself shooting a look to the sentry gate. How much would they question him if he were to attempt to leave? He shuttered the thought away. "Come on."

Shane grabbed his arm. A last pilot was being unloaded from one of the vans. She led Nathan closer. Though bubbling burns covered one side of the Marine's face and neck, he was still conscious. It was the Angel they had noticed their first day on the base, the one who had sat alone in the bar. They were near enough to see his patch: T. C. MCQUEEN.

A shadow appeared next to Nathan's. Hawkes now stood next to him. The tank's slicked-back hair and sweaty face could be attributed to the morning heat, but the feature that betrayed him was the pallid hue of his complexion. Then a look floated between Hawkes and McQueen, a look that Nathan could not interpret. The Angel disappeared into the hospital. The tank muttered something unintelligible before he started off for the complex.

"Have you figured out what's going on between them?" Shane asked.

Nathan's face tightened in puzzlement. "What do you mean?"

"McQueen's an In Vitro."

Nathan looked to Hawkes. "I guess he just saw his future, too."

They entered the orientation room to find the other eighteen pilots of the fifty-eighth squadron already slouching in their seats and chatting nervously with each other. Shane steered them to the chairs next to Hawkes. Why did she have to put them practically on top of the tank, Nathan wondered.

"Hey, Nathan," Damphousse called. "You ready for the line?"

He looked back to flash her a wink and a thumbs-up.

"I still won't be ready," Wang complained. "Even when we're in the middle of the furball."

"You'd better be ready if you're gonna be my wing man," Carter threatened.

Lieutenant Colonel Fouts appeared from a side door. He paused a moment to exchange a few words with Sergeant Bougus, then crossed to front and center.

The sergeant cleared his throat. "AAAH-TEN-TION!"

Nathan and the rest sprang to their feet.

The lieutenant colonel quickly waved them down. "Be seated."

Despite the large number of human beings in the room, beings who breathed, blinked, scratched, swallowed, fidgeted, and occasionally coughed, the room was remarkably silent. Nathan sat attentively, ready to hang on the colonel's every word.

"The information you are about to receive is classified level red."

Shane drew back in her chair, and Nathan found his brow lifting in surprise as the others stirred, but for the most part, repressed their reactions.

The lieutenant colonel narrowed his gaze. "I need not remind you of the consequences of divulging class red information."

Nathan threw Hawkes a sidelong stare that said: "You hear that? He's talking to you!" But before Hawkes noticed the look, Shane gently touched Nathan's chin and directed his attention forward.

"Fifty-eighth, because of you we've caught a break. A major break. Within the wreckage of the alien recon vehicle recovered during your H.I.S.T. was an encoded transmission detailing the enemy's projected battle plans."

"I thought the ship alone was a find," Shane whispered.

"Subsequently, all enemy movements have been anticipated. Fearing the captured information may be deceptive, we have not shown our hand. Until now."

Even though they had found the ship by accident, and even though they weren't the ones to discover the transmission, Nathan now felt like he was an intimate and vital part of the war effort. He wasn't some nameless pilot about to be blown away. He was Nathan West, proud member of the group whose find might turn the tide of the war. Everyone who had been on Mars already deserved a medal. His invigorated confidence made him want to immediately climb into his cockpit and, as Bougus had said, go "tear-assing across the cosmos, huntin' for heaven."

He glanced at Shane, who wasn't focused on the lieutenant colonel. She furtively studied Hawkes. What was that interesting about the tank? Nathan looked for himself. Hawkes shook his head negatively, slapped his arms across his chest, then huffed.

"What's wrong?" Shane asked him.

"This ain't right," he replied curtly.

Damphousse stuck her head between Shane and Hawkes to shush them.

Standing behind a small holo projector, Fouts threw a switch, bringing to life a three-dimensional map of their sector of the Milky Way galaxy. Nathan had seen many holos as a colonist in training but none this detailed or elaborate. Instead of being tiny, nearly indistinguishable points of light, the planets in each system actually contained colored surface features, and, if one stared at them long enough, one could see that they spun on their axes and followed their orbits around the sun in real time.

The lieutenant colonel stepped to the right side of the map, then pointed to an object in the far, lower portion. Nathan already knew what the object was. "The Earth is here," Fouts confirmed. He strode 11.6 light-years to the opposite end of the map. "In seventy-one hours, the enemy intends to attack with extreme intent, directing two-thirds of its forces to the Groombridge thirty-four star system naval base." He pointed to Groombridge thirty-four, a binary star system with four planets orbiting the smaller star, three orbiting the larger. A data bar below the system supplied the absolute magnitude, distance, spectral type, and apparent visual magnitude for each star as seen from Earth. "This is known as point G." Fouts shifted to the center of the holo. "The Earth forces—the greatest mobilization of military might since the twentieth century—will surprise attack from behind enemy positions at two points." He indicated a sector near Barnard's Star. "Point F, here, and,"—he singled out another, near Wolf 359—"point H, here. The Marines will participate with the Eighth Air Wing. This will be possible due to a fortuitous projected wormhole opening in the Galileo regions."

Shane tilted her head toward Nathan and whispered, "This will work."

Indeed, Nathan had already bought ninety-nine percent of the plan. Yet there was a dangerous one percent that kept him tense, and the feeling was fueled by Hawkes. Every word out of the lieutenant colonel's mouth was met by the tank's disapproving stare and occasional snorts. What did Hawkes know that the world's military did not?

"From captured information we have ascertained the following: their planes are faster, with a better rate of climb. But ours are more maneuverable and better armed. It evens out."

Shane proffered her palm with a smile. Amidst murmurs of approval throughout the room, Nathan high-fived her. She tried the same with Hawkes, who ignored her.

The energy in the room was infectious, finding its way into Fouts's voice. "Surprise has been their best weapon. Now . . . it is *ours.*"

"It's too easy," Hawkes blurted out, then fidgeted as every gaze found him.

Nathan sighed. "Here we go . . ." But in truth he was anxious to hear why the tank had misgivings.

"Sir, if the plans weren't planted, then they would at least assume that we have them. They'd change their objectives."

"No doubt their intelligence reported that we would be unable to decipher the transmission, and, in fact, it has taken fifty Charno Quantum computers interlinked on four continents to decode the enemy's complex language. And, as mentioned, their movements have since been in accord with the captured plans."

Hawkes unfolded his arms and slid up in his seat. "What if they assumed we would eventually be able to decipher the transmission? And what if they didn't change their plans in an attempt to lure us away, then surround and finish us?"

"We can second-guess them and ourselves to death," Nathan told the tank. "What we have to do is respond to the facts."

Fouts nodded. "I can assure you, Lieutenant"—he squinted at the tank's name patch—"Hawkes, that thousands of computer simulations have been run, every possible enemy move played out."

"I hope you're right," Hawkes said gravely.

By now, Nathan's patience was threadbare and had him tapping his foot in anticipation of their orders. He decided he wasn't going to wait for Fouts. "Sir, are we deploying to point F or H, sir?"

The lieutenant colonel hesitated, and suddenly he looked a lot like Governor Overmeyer, the harbinger of doom.

No, his news can't be that bad . . . or can it . . .

"The fifty-eighth squadron will operate in a support capacity at point A."

"Point A," Damphousse repeated enthusiastically, believing that point A was a position of extreme importance.

Obviously she hadn't heard the words *support capacity.*

Turning back to the map, Fouts singled out point A. "Here. Rear left flank."

Rear left flank! Give. Give. Give. Take. Take. Take. You're ready, son. You're combat ready. We have a nice bunk for you to hide under, a nice bunk right here in the rear left flank!

With his vision clouded by anger, Nathan failed to see a superior officer at the head of the room. Instead, he saw a governor, a senator, and a puppet all wrapped into one uniformed man. "Why bother telling us the plan if we weren't going to be a part of it?"

Piqued by Nathan's tone, Fouts's retort was delivered in a voice equally acidic. "You are part of it: rear left flank."

In the space of a heartbeat Nathan was on his feet.

"Sir, request permission to transfer to Eighth Air Wing."

From the corner of his eye, he could see Shane's expression of shock.

Then she rose and it was plain that she hadn't been shocked over his insubordination but over the fact that his request was a good idea. "Sir, request permission to transfer to Eighth Air Wing."

"Requests denied."

Cornered, Nathan figured he had better try the soft approach with Fouts. Arguing—he should have known—would get him nowhere. "Sir, with all due respect, we have a right to follow through—"

"Sit down, Lieutenants!"

Nathan bowed his head and shrank back in inevitable defeat. He wanted to throttle Damphousse for her misinformation. Who had told her they were going right to the line? Indeed, when he was done with Damphousse, he'd wring that person's neck.

After giving himself a moment to settle, Fouts said, "The fifty-eighth squadron is to report to the naval space carrier *Saratoga*, across the Jupiter Line, by 0840 tomorrow. You'll meet Commodore Eichner on board. Dismissed."

twenty-two

Nine of the squadron's twenty SA-43
Hammerheads were perched on the apron outside a row
of hangars. Suited and ready, Nathan shielded his eyes
from the dazzles being fired off the open canopies as he
approached his plane. He grimaced slightly over the
stench of fuel that hung in the air.

Sergeant Bougus was doing his own personal walk
around of each plane, checking a laser cannon mount
here, a wing seam there. His act was more ritual than
necessity. "This ain't gonna be no pep talk," he said as
everyone gathered. "And you may all no longer work for
a livin', but I'm still givin' you orders. Fall in."

Nathan assumed his position and locked his heels as
he had many times before. But this time he stood below
one of the most powerful military aircraft ever
designed, about to climb aboard the beast and rocket
off to—

A lousy support mission.

He should be nervous and thrilled. Yes, he was awed
by the presence of the planes and the mighty image that
he and the rest of the squadron conveyed; however, he
couldn't help gritting his teeth and swearing under his
breath.

"I'm looking at your faces and I'm seeing some pilots
who look mighty pissed off," Bougus began. "Raise your
hand if you're pissed."

As Nathan indicated he was, he looked down the line.
Yes, everyone was definitely inflamed over their orders.

The sergeant gestured for hands down then began his

routine pacing. He paused before Damphousse. "What does *gung ho* mean, lieutenant?"

"Sir, it means working together, sir."

"Does anybody know where this conversation is leading?"

"Sir, yes, sir," Wang said. "You are going to tell us that even though we are rear left flank, we are still an important part of the war effort, sir."

"No, I'm not, you shitbird!" He rushed to Wang. "You people got screwed! I recommended that they send you poor bastards to the line because you people are squared away. Other squadrons could learn from you people. But you got screwed."

"Sir, we feel bad enough already, sir," Bartley said. "Maybe we *do* need a pep talk."

Bougus paused, either considering Bartley's suggestion or ticking off mental seconds until he would detonate. "What you need is a swift kick into reality. This war gets bad enough, your candyass support position *will* be front line. Stuff *that* in your skivvies while you're feeling sorry for yourself."

"Sir. We trained, we got planes. Why won't they let us fight, sir?" Stone asked.

"Look at me. What do you see?"

"Sir?"

"WHAT DO YOU SEE?"

"Sir, a senior drill instructor, sir."

"BULLSHIT. I'm a broken down old man who's forced to turn thumb-suckers into ass-kickers. I ain't *ever* going to no front line. I might as well be tongue-cleaning toilets!"

"Sir, that's not true, sir," Nathan said, then realized he had just called the sergeant a liar.

But the expected chide didn't come. On the contrary, the sergeant nodded. "'Course that ain't true! I woulda swallowed laser fire a long time ago." He came to attention. "Let me tell who you're lookin' at. I am the fifth generation of Marine Corps drill instructors in my family.

One of my ancestors was training grunts to be sent to Vietnam. I am part of a proud tradition. I am past, present, and future, alive before your eyes. Look at each other. You are the same."

Nathan loosened his jaw, feeling his anger beginning to evaporate. Now he felt stupid for being upset in the first place. Every person did, indeed, have a job to do, and it was his job to support the attack, just as it was Bougus's job to make him feel like an idiot for being angry . . .

"Sir, would you like to hear our war cry?" Shane asked, then smiled at Nathan.

Bougus put a hand to his ear. "Whattaya got?"

Nine pilots screamed at the top of their lungs, producing an ear-splitting, bestial chorus that stunned and caught the attention of a line of new recruits marching by.

"Hoo-yah! That *is* a war cry! Now. Mount your horses."

The takeoff crews were already swarming around their planes as Nathan put on his padded skullcap, then helmet. A crewman slapped the hook-on ladder to his jet and Nathan ascended it. At the top, he took in the view of Hawkes's jet parked two down from his. The tank had painted snarling shark's teeth and the words: PAGS'S PAYBACK on the nose of his Hammerhead.

With the cockpit fitting Nathan like a second skin, he ran through his pre-flight check list: lap and shoulder belt; leg restraints; O_2, computer, and comlink cables plugged to his suit; pre-flight thruster sequence engaged; canopy toggle flipped to lower. Since he was at the end of the apron, Nathan would be first to take off. He flashed the plane captain a thumbs-up and the tall man waved him out toward a service road that led to the runway. Nathan eased back the thruster control. His engines whined in response and the jet lurched forward. He looked down to Sergeant Bougus. Nathan and the rest were finally leaving the nest, and that fact was reflected in Bougus's wistful expression. Nathan proudly returned the man's salute then started off.

Reaching the runway, he braked and called the tower for clearance to launch. Permission was granted, and he opened up the thrusters. The simulator had done a poor job of re-creating the engines' incredible muscular bellows. The tarmac, hangars, and perimeter fences were soon long streaks of color, and, with a pulse that threatened to break into near light-speed, Nathan eased back his stick and left the ground. Multiple sonic booms reverberated in his thruster wash as he soared into a sky as blue as the Tellusian sun.

See ya! And don't worry, Neil. I'll keep an eye on the cars ahead of me.

He thumbed on the NAV system, which already had his course pre-programmed, then eased back and flipped a toggle to let the autopilot steer him toward the ionosphere.

Wipe that stupid grin off your face, Nathan, you have a job to do.

But look at me! I'm flying. I'm a Marine.

Skipchatter between the pilots and the tower confirmed that all twenty birds of the fifty-eighth were off the ground. Nathan fixed his gaze ahead, and was glad he did, for at that moment his Hammerhead passed from day into starry night. The NAV system console beeped, signaling the crossover. With Earth curving back away from him, Nathan disengaged the autopilot and banked right until he was locked into the formation course. He engaged the HUD and saw the other four Hammerheads of his wing; they were closing in on him, ready to form a deadly arrow with Nathan as its laser-sighted tip. All four wings of the squadron would assume a formation that put Nathan's wing next to Shane's in the front, with Mordock's and Crispan's wings in the left and right flanks, respectively.

"Gold Leader, this is G-Four," Wang identified. "Systems nominal. Formation looking good. Link good."

"G-Three in," Damphousse said. "Cool, clean, and very mean."

"G-Two's a go," Carter added.

"G-One, on my mark." Low said.

"Gold Wing. Gold Leader reporting links and locks one hundred percent. Steady as we go," Nathan said. "Red Leader, wing report?"

"Bartley's having trouble with her link," Shane informed him. "She's breaking up but she thinks she knows why. Other than that, we're right and tight. White and Blue wings report no problems."

Nathan adjusted his heads-up display to zoom in on their destination. A distorted video image of the carrier *Saratoga* appeared, but the signal wasn't any better than some of the footage of the news reports he had watched back home. A zillion-dollar system gave him a thirty-cent picture.

"Red Leader, have target destination IDed in display," Nathan said.

"Gold Leader, confirm *Saratoga* position at 32.5 megastatute kilometers."

Nathan was about to reply when his heads-up display flickered, then vanished into a shower of static. He turned a dial, trying to boost the system's signal. "Just a mick, I'm getting interference on the LIDAR."

It was ridiculous to do so, but Nathan made a visual scan of the space around him and his wing. The void looked innocent enough; there wasn't anything present that might cause the interference. Solar flares? Maybe. More likely his equipment wasn't living up to its engineer's expectations.

With a great charge of interference that made him cower, the heads-up display abruptly locked onto a UFO zooming past at close range. Nathan shot a look over his shoulder. Nothing. "Check six . . . I had a contact on the HUD." Switching to another LIDAR frequency, he added, "Musta been an asteroid or—"

Bang. There it was.

And an asteroid it wasn't.

An alien reconnaissance craft cruised through local space; it was exactly like the one he had encountered on Mars save for the fact that this one was ready to do business. The heads-up now did a fine job of reproducing the wings and dorsal fin of the ominous-looking ship.

Bougus hadn't been kidding about the line coming to rear left flank.

Nathan tried to keep the hysteria out of his voice. And failed. "*Red Leader. Confirm bandit—a recon vehicle—on the LIDAR.*"

He could only imagine the look on Shane's face and the faces of the rest of the squadron.

After letting his gloved finger trace the recon ship's trajectory, he checked a data bar. "Ten o'clock, thirty-five degrees south, ninety-six megameters."

"I can't see 'em! I can't see 'em," Wang shouted. "LIDAR's blank."

"Wrong freq, Wang."

"I'm picking up something," Damphousse sang darkly.

"Confirm! Confirm!" Hawkes cried. LIDAR channel four! Contact, ten o'clock."

We should engage. Now.

No, wait. What's our strategy? Assume diamond formations and surround?

Nathan took a deep breath and called for Shane. "Red Leader, we're—"

"Gold Leader," Shane interrupted, "alter intercept angle thirty degrees. Blue Wing, White Wing, watch six. HACK!"

He banked left then dropped into a full-throttle dive, watching as his wing followed, their movements a little sloppy but generally mirroring his. Once the NAV system indicated that he'd reached the new angle, he cut speed by one quarter and leveled off to probe his HUD. Nothing. Nothing.

Patience . . . there you are.

"Got 'em, Red Leader," he informed. "Twelve o'clock high."

"I don't think he's picked us up," Hawkes said.

"We got him, is all that matters," Carter opined.

"Confirm at twelve high." Shane's voice was steady but had a definite edge. "Let's light the pipes and head downtown."

"Copy, Red Leader. Blue and White Wings going high and we're coming under and up to surround. Gold Wing . . . ready?"

"On your mark," Damphousse said.

Nathan checked what was at the moment his favorite digital readout:

WEAPONS SYSTEMS: UNARMED

He tapped one, two, three, and the fourth button.

PROXIMITY GUNS: ARMED AND READY.

But they weren't what he really needed.

LASER CANNONS PRIMING . . . PLEASE WAIT.

Come on, come on, come on . . .

CHARGE COMPLETE.

"MARK!"

Nathan maxed his thrusters. The Hammerhead rocked him into his seat and screamed toward the alien craft at what felt like a runaway velocity. His HUD showed his and Shane's wings veering away from Blue and White Wings.

Then, framed by his long canopy, he glimpsed the alien ship as it rolled into an inverted dive in an attempt to evade Gold and Red Wings.

"He jinked!" Shane cried. "SCRAM! SCRAM!"

Both wings broke formation, and suddenly there were nine Hammerheads crisscrossing from multiple angles above and below Nathan. He saw Shane release a volley of bolts that the alien miraculously corkscrewed through unscathed.

Though he hated to admit it, the time had come for a crack shot. "Hawkes! Get in the fight!"

"Tracking! Can't get a lock!" the tank complained nervously.

"Eyeball it! Take the shot!" Nathan ordered, then turned his Hammerhead on a wing and streaked toward the fleeing alien.

"Negative! R-Four and G-Three in my fire line."

"R-Four, G-Three, break off pursuit!" Shane commanded angrily.

As the two Hammerheads that were blocking Hawkes's fighter peeled right and left, Nathan saw one of his own target locks float over the image of the alien and freeze. "I gotta lock! Firing!"

He thumbed the trigger. A pair of bolts erupted from his cannons followed by a repercussive tremor that passed through the craft. One of his bolts grazed Hawkes's right wing and was thrown off target while the alien nosedived to avoid the other.

"Coop! Damage report," Shane requested.

"Thanks a lot, West! I had the shot! Why'd you have to—"

"Damage report!" Shane repeated.

"Right wing scorched. Systems still nominal," the tank said, sounding a little calmer. "My HUD's blank. Contact gone."

"It must be jamming our LIDAR. Went below us like a fish on a line," Nathan said.

"Then, hey, Shane. Let's go fishin'," Hawkes suggested. "You can stay on shore, West. Maybe take in some target practice."

Nathan tensed. "I had target lock. I didn't—"

"No time to argue," Shane cut him off. "And no time to fish. We don't have the fuel. Return to designated course. I'll call Spacecom and report ACM with the enemy."

The four wings regrouped and the squadron resumed its original formation.

It took another five minutes for Nathan to fully catch his breath. Finally, he was calm enough to notice the view. Despite the fact that it was still 200 million kilometers away, Jupiter loomed in the distance. Knowing the planet was ten times the size of Earth was one thing, but seeing that truth up-close was going to be something extraordinary.

With a long ride ahead, and trying to wrest off the lingering frustration of losing the fighter and guilt of nearly hitting Hawkes, Nathan thought about getting a little shut-eye. But why did he have to be on board a jet every time he wanted to sleep? The thin mattress of his bunk back in the barracks was looking better and better. He activated the autopilot, closed his eyes, and listened to the hum of his thrusters and the hiss of his oxygen.

It was a lovely wake-up call consisting of the demonic little buzzing of his proximity beacon followed by someone whose voice—and especially humor—he could do without.

"Thar she blows," Hawkes announced.

The supercarrier *Saratoga* was a floating polymeric metropolis reminiscent of the old naval aircraft carriers Nathan had seen on history discs. The vessel contained a sixty-thousand-square-meter flight deck that was heavily trafficked, and Nathan estimated the girth of the carrier at a hundred meters. Blue, red, and white flashes came randomly from along the flanks of the ship, and the tiny running lights of fighters and transports illuminated their comings and goings. It was unnerving to know that somewhere down on that flight deck Nathan was supposed to find a parking space. He'd have better luck at a shopping mall during the holidays.

They were contacted by the carrier's tower and their NAV systems were, thankfully, fed coordinates for their approach. As Nathan hovered a moment before beginning his vertical descent, he passed into a strange and beautiful glow. Below him was the metallic deck, but now to his left and above were the swirling orange, white, and black gasses of Jupiter. He was disappointed that the great red spot was presently on the far side of the planet, but the *Saratoga*'s orbit would eventually take it over the storm.

All of the landing practice in the simulator was put to good use. He hit the deck gently and silently, cut retros, then was directed by two members of the deck crew to a platform that would drop him into the lower deck. Once in position, he powered down, felt a jerk, then was swallowed by the carrier.

In the cavernous lower deck, the arm of a jet crane swung in front of him and locked into place. Nathan fingered the DETACH button on his cockpit control panel. His pit was lifted away from the rest of his jet and placed on a flatbed. Soon, five other pilots joined him, two beside, three facing. Wang, Damphousse, and Shane all beamed.

The flatbed was guided automatically past a string of flashing red lights mounted to the ceiling and into an air lock. While waiting for pressurization, Nathan finished shutting down his remaining systems, detached his suit cables and removed his helmet. The lock's opposite doors slid apart. Nathan opened his canopy with the others and jumped down. He moved out of the lock and into an immense tunnel, the ceiling of which was ribbed with clusters of many-sized duct work. Halls intersected the tunnel at five or six points, and the twenty or thirty members of the ship's support crew assigned to the area were in a state of frenzy, darting down halls and reaching for wall links to shout orders. Flight mechanics and pilots also double-timed toward prep bays.

As the rest of the squadron assembled behind him, Nathan turned to Shane. "What's going on here? They seem pretty hairy."

"We probably landed in the middle of a drill," she hazarded.

Hawkes seized a passing mechanic by the arm. "Hey, what's going—"

The woman glared at him and tore herself away.

"AHHH-TEN-TION," Wang shouted.

Commodore Eichner had just come from around a corner. He strode toward Nathan and the other pilots, stopped and brought a hand up to his graying temple in salute. "Five-eight. Follow me to the orientation room."

"Sir, what's going on?" Shane asked.

"Spacecom checked out your report of the enemy recon vehicle. Radio telescopes have since found not only no trace of enemy troops in the Groombridge system, but rather a force amassing outside our solar system."

Hawkes beat his fist loudly into his palm. "The enemy plans *were* a setup." Then he leered at Nathan.

The commodore pursed his lips and swallowed. "At this point, no one needs their plans to know which direction they're heading."

twenty-three

"We don't wanna hear any I-told-you-so's outta you," Mr. Hotshot said as they hurried through the corridor.

It was convenient that Commodore Eichner was far enough ahead to be out of earshot, but even if he weren't, Hawkes's reply would have been the same. "This war's bein' run by a buncha brainwipes."

I can assure you, Lieutenant Hawkes, that thousands of computer simulations have been run, every possible enemy move played out.

And they call tanks stupid . . .

"They probably did their best," Shane said. "And I guess we have to do ours."

Hawkes didn't look at her as he retorted, "The Marines are looking for a few good suckers. And they've found one."

"Shuddup, Hawkes," Mr. Badshot grunted.

"Sir, yes, sir," he spat back.

The dawning argument fell off into the rhythmic pounding of their boots. Hawkes wanted to say more; he wanted to ram the fact that he was right down each pilot's throat, then go back to the base and do the same to Lieutenant Colonel Fouts. Pentagon desk drones had no *feel* for war. Hawkes had been on Mars. He'd seen an alien recon ship. He'd seen one of the things in action. And that experience had given him a vibe. Barely able to explain it himself, he just *knew* that the aliens had been baiting them.

So he had been right. And everyone was doomed. And he didn't even have to be present.

Why did he have to meet that damned biker? Why did Pags have to help him in the first place? Hawkes could have dropped out of the Corps and served the rest of his term in jail. He'd made the decision not to go AWOL after his forty-eight hours of leave, had even rushed back to the base when summoned on his watch phone. Had he known then that the odds would be this stacked against him, he would have surely run.

Eichner left them at the orientation room door and hurried off, saying he'd return in a few minutes. Hawkes followed the rest into the cramped quarters. The place was bathed in an eerie red light and had enough chairs to accommodate thirty or forty pilots. In the middle of the room sat a long table weighted down with steel and plastic equipment crates that would prevent the back half of the room from seeing anything. Hawkes wandered to the right, slumped into a chair and slid his helmet under it. He glanced up absently into a clear LCD board that reflected computer-generated images of the *Saratoga* in Jovian orbit and the approaching alien armada. He groaned disgustedly, then looked around.

Shane had found a small desk in the corner. She sat with her head bowed, the back of her hand over her mouth. Was she praying? Crying? Hawkes wanted to go to her, tell her he hadn't meant what he had said, and somehow comfort her. But he couldn't. The words, the damned words . . . as always, they were beyond him, and even if he had them, the tone, well, that was impossible. Why was anger so easy to communicate, and other feelings so difficult?

He looked to West . . . and there was his answer. Mr. Hotshot sat holding his photo tags, dreaming of Ms. Tellus. Didn't the idiot know she was probably dead? A mean thought, yes, but it *was* wartime. Hawkes thought he should go remind West of the fact. The Marine looked to have suddenly forgotten everything that was going on around them, and if West's head wasn't in the right place then Hawkes didn't want to be flying anywhere near him. One grazing had already been enough, enough to make him wonder if West would have taken the risky shot if it had been Shane's fighter on the alien's tail. It had probably been easy for West to put a tank's life in jeopardy. West was cocky. And stupid.

Yeah, as stupid as I am for coming back.

You know why you're here. You made the decision.

"I don't wanna listen to that," Damphousse said softly, referring to the clipped comlink transmissions between the advanced scout ships and the *Saratoga's* bridge. She took a seat beside him. "It's getting me jittery."

Hawkes glanced back to Shane, who hadn't moved. "Do you pray?" he asked Damphousse.

"I do now," she said in a shivering voice.

"I mean all the time . . . daily."

"Not daily. Maybe weekly, I guess. It's not like I have a schedule or anything."

"Why?"

"Why don't I have a—"

"No," he said, then faced her. "Why do you pray?"

She seemed startled. "Uh, I guess for two reasons. Maybe to ask God for something or to thank Him for what I have."

"I don't pray," he told her. "I'm not sure if God is a god for tanks. Maybe he's just for everyone else. I mean, who is my God, right? Some geneticist?"

"Have you ever tried?"

He shook his head.

She took his hands in hers. "Close your eyes."

"You're not gonna say anything, are you? I don't want you to."

"I won't. You think about what you want, what will help you most now. And about all you have, about giving thanks for it. Just reach out, reach out into space. Let go . . . "

Hawkes closed his eyes and tried to see God. A speckled darkness cloaked him, then he broke free from it and floated toward a sun so hot that it had burned away all of its color. In the shimmering whiteness, he strained to hear a voice but there was stillness. He called to God and tried to think of a way to say what he wanted, what he needed. How would he thank the supreme being?

He opened his eyes and shuddered free of the vision. Damphousse's eyes were still closed. "I can't do it," he confessed. "I just . . . I can't."

She came out of her prayer and studied him as though she understood. Could she really? "It's all right. It just takes time . . . "

During the next fifteen minutes, Hawkes and the rest of the pilots sat in the grip of the comlink transmissions. No one spoke. The voices they heard were often frantic, often astonished, wholly depressing.

Finally, the door opened and Eichner entered. Everyone else snapped to attention, but Hawkes took his time. The commodore crossed in front of the group, his face about as long as an astronomical unit. Perhaps he was going to cry. . . . He paused, and Hawkes shot a look to Shane: what's he doing?

The door swung open once more. McQueen hobbled inside. The burns on his face only made his intense eyes flare brighter. He struggled to the center of the room, where he reached under the table and, strangely enraged, dumped it over onto its side, sending crates crashing to the floor and Marines jumping back to clear the way. He winced as he lowered himself into a chair, then waved everyone around him. "I want to be able to look in your eyes."

McQueen was hard-core, taking none and giving his all. Hawkes just wished he knew why. What inspired the tank to fight? If Hawkes knew that it might help him understand. Hawkes had only one reason for coming back. Maybe it was enough. But he needed to be sure.

Once surrounded by the pilots, McQueen took a moment to gather his thoughts, then began. "Courage.

Honor. Dedication. Sacrifice." He voiced each word slowly, in a tone that was fiercely honest. "Those are the words they used to get ya here. But now, the only word that means a damn to you is life. Yours. Your buddy's."

Hawkes wasn't the only one nodding.

"The one certainty in war is that in an hour, maybe two, you'll either be alive . . . or dead."

Tell me why! Tell me why I should buy into your certainty!

"For the next hour, here's your best chance of staying alive." McQueen's lip twisted and his head shook subtly as if he were battling off a seizure. "The Trojan Asteroid belt trails Jupiter's orbit. Our objective is to hide in the debris. This may be as difficult as engaging the enemy. You're gonna have to react to the pitch and yaw of the asteroids in order to keep out of sight and shielded from whatever kind of LIDAR the aliens are using. Intelligence says they'll fly right by."

"Sir, I don't understand, sir. We're just going to hide from them?" Low asked.

"Marines hide? I don't think so. Once they're by you, ambush 'em."

"Sir, I don't know how many planes they have, but I'm positive—as I'm sure you are—that it's a helluva lot more than we do, sir," Shane said grimly. "I don't know how to put this, but . . . do we stand any kind of a chance?"

McQueen leaned forward, resting an elbow on a knee. "No one's asking you to wax their tails. Your goal is to stall them. Our forces at Groombridge have doubled back and are right now passing through the Kali wormhole. If we successfully delay the enemy we'll have reinforcements appearing from behind them and out of the sun—and that's when we teach 'em something every human knows: payback's a bitch."

Hawkes tossed a look at the door. If he didn't leave soon, jump in his cockpit and get out there, he might stay behind. During Accelerated Flight Training, he'd been subjected to over a dozen ejections and their accompanying freefalls. And always, during the seconds before blowing the canopy, he had panicked and considered not doing it. Then he had played a game with himself, counting the number one over and over through the remaining ten seconds, as though they were all the number one and there was no time to be scared in a second. Click, he'd throw the switch and be airborne.

Now he had to get out there, blanket his thoughts with one long second, forget about being a tank, about whether he might die for something or nothing. He had to do his job remembering he was not alone.

"I know you're all anxious to get prepped. Just give me another minute. I guess I'm here 'cause I've been in a knife fight with 'em. Listen up. They come at you in groups. Check your six. And they have a low angle of attack, so keep your nose level. That could be tough. The planes you've been issued have an upgripe in the retro thrusters."

"Sir, the NAV system tends to compensate for that if you pull up three degrees and hit the brakes at eighty-five percent, sir," Shane said.

McQueen nodded. "And that three to eighty-five ratio can be adjusted accordingly, but you're gonna have to do it manually. There's just no time to play with the control chips. Like I said, it's gonna be tough."

A few of the Marines started for the door.

"And one more thing—"

The pilots stopped.

"It's okay to be scared. See you in an hour."

Hawkes stayed in the orientation room until everyone was gone. He proffered a hand to McQueen.

"I don't need any help," the veteran said.

"This ain't help," Hawkes answered.

"What is it then?"

Hawkes shrugged. "I don't know."

McQueen began to rise, his face contorting in pain. Then he resignedly took Hawkes's hand. "Thought you were never gonna fly."

"Changed my mind."

"How come?"

"Guess I'm stupid."

Reaching the doorway, McQueen paused. "Going out there in a hunk of metal, outnumbered and inexperienced, I guess you are stupid . . . or brave. It's always hard to tell." He tottered into the corridor.

Hawkes regarded the LCD board. The alien armada had both grown and advanced significantly. In the center of the screen, three tiny scout ships fled toward the *Saratoga* under the heavy fire of a dozen pursuing alien planes.

Shifting abruptly away, Hawkes fetched his helmet and rushed out of the room for the preparation bays. After taking one turn, then another, he realized he was lost. He stopped a passing medic and asked her for directions. She told him to head down the hall, make a left, then another.

When he reached the main tunnel of the lower flight deck, he ran right into a spotlight. A young news reporter seized his sleeve at the elbow and jerked him beside her. "And here is Lieutenant Hawkes," she said, reading his name patch, then looking back up at the cameraman. "The lieutenant has been gracious enough to speak with us during this dire hour." She thrust her microphone into his face. "What are our plans to defeat the enemy, lieutenant?"

Hawkes squinted and choked up. The lens of the camera was like the muzzle of a large weapon.

"C'mon, lieutenant. It's doubtful the enemy is monitoring this feed. The entire world wants to know what's going on. What can you tell them?"

"I'm, uh, I don't think I'm supposed to say anything."

"But think about the billions hanging on your every move. If you were one of them, wouldn't you want to know?"

"I guess so but—"

"Don't you think your family back home deserves to know what's happening to you?"

Hawkes stepped forward, reaching to—

"Hey, don't touch the lens!" the cameraman shouted.

Suddenly, two MPs charged up and strong-armed the reporter and cameraman. "Guess you didn't read your visitor's pass. This area is a NO MEDIA ZONE!" the taller MP barked.

The other MP flashed an apologetic look at Hawkes. "Sorry, lieutenant," she said.

As the reporter and her accomplice were ushered away, Hawkes smoothed out his sleeve, then resumed his course.

Weaving into the prep bays, he found himself elbowed and shouldered by the scores of flight crew personnel readying the many cockpits. Charging lines were already being removed from the first dozen pits, and Blue and White Wings were seated and buckling in. A small, one-person rover rolled by with a replacement canopy. Another rover tailed it, carrying a dozen long cylindrical laser cannon batteries. The driver of the rover wore an EVA suit and steered her vehicle into the air lock.

Hawkes stepped deeper into the chaos, searching for the mobile bed that contained his cockpit. He spotted Damphousse, Wang, and Low, who were below their bed and double-checking each other's suits and helmets. He moved on before they saw him, wanting to avoid the good lucks and other words of encouragement that would, at the moment, make him feel awkward. Besides, he was trying to count that single second over and over. He caught sight of his cockpit two beds down on the right. He marched toward it.

Ahead, two mechanics finished a conversation, and as they left, West appeared from behind them. He was headed straight for Hawkes.

What do you want? You gonna say something to me? Wish me luck? Right. All I have to say to you is try not to shoot me . . .

He didn't look at West as they passed, and perhaps Mr. Hotshot had done the same. Hawkes took the ladder up to his bed, noting that he was the first pilot to arrive, then paused to don his helmet.

"Hawkes?"

Recognizing the voice, he stiffened as he looked back. West was the only person in the prep bay not moving. What was that expression on his face? Mr. Hotshot was serious, maybe a little sad. Hawkes wanted to believe that when they got into the middle of the furball, West would be there. Was that what the Marine wanted to tell him? Maybe, but it didn't appear as if he would say anything else.

Hawkes slowly nodded. West left.

"Sir," a wiry crewman called, popping up from the other side of his pit. "You're all set, but I noticed you have a piece of unauthorized equipment aboard. Regulation 527 section B—I know it 'cause I had to look it up—states that any officer—"

"Do you always obey your superior officers?"

"Sir, without question, sir."

"Good. I order you *not* to report your find."

"But—"

"Get outta here."

The boy departed in a huff, head shaking. If nothing else, it would be interesting to see if Hawkes had turned the kid into a rule-breaker like himself. All the crewman had to do was obey his order of silence. If questioned, he could simply state he'd been directed not to speak. And it wasn't as if Hawkes's unauthorized equipment was a thermonuclear device. The crewman had just been too nosy.

Helmet sealed, he lowered himself into his seat. The other pilots arrived and slid into their cockpits. As his canopy servos hummed, lowering the shield, Hawkes tossed a glance to the bed ahead of his.

Shane was strapped in, her face all duty as she eyed her instrument panels. Then she looked at the pilot across from her, who had to be West, and lifted a thumbs-up.

A Klaxon signaled the opening of the air lock. Shane's bed rumbled forward and soon was gone. Hawkes continued to count his eternal second, and then it was his turn. Beyond the lock, his cockpit was reattached to his Hammerhead, then the jet was lifted onto the flight deck. While the wing leaders waited for signals from the plane captain and bridge, Hawkes stared toward the edge of the solar system where a vast band of darkness eclipsed the stars.

twenty-four

This is what you wanted, Shane. It all comes *down to this. What would Kim, Lauren, and everyone else think if they saw you now?*

They'd probably think I'm insane.

Mommy? Daddy? I might be coming home soon . . .

"What the hell's the delay?" Nathan asked, cutting into the static of her link.

She adjusted the link's sensitivity and replied, "Cut the skipchatter unless you got something important to say."

"Sorry, Sarge."

Shane swallowed, checked her thruster console. Fuel full, thrusters idling at .01 percent.

"Gold Wing you are cleared for launch."

"Copy, tower," Nathan replied. "Gold Leader launching."

Shane felt the flight deck vibrate under her jet as the thruster tubes of Nathan's Hammerhead flared bright blue. Then, with an incredible sudden burst, he missiled off into space. The other four jets of his wing chased close behind him, finally gathering into a string that turned as if under the direction of one mind. Shane knew that her own wing would look as impressive and powerful; she just couldn't believe she was a part of it. Six months prior she had been standing in a living room on a planet that seemed a lifetime away, screaming at the top of her lungs at her sisters. Five months prior she'd been thinking about going back to school and had even gone to the U.S.D. campus for an application, one she had never filled out. Four months prior she had quit her job at *Virgosoft* because they had kept pressuring her into taking a management position. Three months prior she had been working in a Mexican restaurant in Old Town San Diego and had served a table of Marines. They hadn't said anything to persuade her. She had just looked at them . . . and known.

"Red Wing, you are cleared for launch."

"Copy, tower. Red Leader go."

When she had launched from Loxley she had groaned over how the jet had slammed her against her seat. Now, with only the tiny particles of hydrogen to slow the craft, particles that offered no discernible resistance, she slingshoted off the *Saratoga* at twice the speed, grinning instead of groaning. The supercarrier shrank to a gray pea floating before a massive orange.

All right, all right, all right. Check your data bars. Get that HUD and LIDAR on line. Good. Count 'em off, one, two, three, and there's Hawkes pulling up the rear.

"Gold Wing. ETA to Trojan: forty-nine seconds," Nathan said.

At that, the asteroid field swept into view on Shane's HUD. She could look through the image at the actual jagged chunks of icy rock, but their representations on the HUD told her much more than her eyes. The pitching and yawing planetoids were instantly measured and their trajectories plotted by her NAV system. She took note of her own wing's ETA and reported it to them.

"Gold Wing. Scatter," Nathan ordered.

Like five specks of blue glitter tossed in the air, the jets of Nathan's wing dived into the cosmic refuse and vanished.

Shane edged her stick forward. "Red Wing. Insert in two . . . one . . . go." She hurtled toward a gap between two great rocks that each had to be half the size of the *Saratoga*. With her NAV system beeping busily, plotting intercept course after intercept course, she made it past the rocks and found herself plowing through a cloud of small, fist-sized stones which struck her Hammerhead in a deafening roll of reverberating caroms. "Red Wing! Break off from leader and assume cover."

The hull of her jet had been built to withstand small asteroid showers but she hadn't planned on testing its design. The cloud thinned, and then only an occasional chunk streaked by. She braked hard as she neared a massive rock mottled with ice. A data bar listed its diameter at .0879 kilometers. It would do. She clicked on her retrorocket system and felt the little blasts of power from her ship's nose, tail, and wings as she guided her stick, mirroring the erratic course of the asteroid.

"Gold Leader to Red. My wing's in position."

Shane checked her HUD. Everyone but Hawkes had found a hiding place. Hawkes's thrusters were idling and he drifted aimlessly. "We're almost there ourselves, Nathan." Then she switched her link to the wing's independent channel. "Come on, Cooper. Hurry up!"

"Don't rush me!" he fired back. "I'm looking for the right one."

"Blue Wing making insertion," Mordock said.

Shane watched her HUD as the five jets of Blue Wing began their descent. Mordock's jet threaded deftly into the complex maze, but the fourth pilot in his wing was straying dangerously close to a long, jagged rock that resembled the blade of a dagger. Shane dialed to Blue Wing's channel. "B-Four! Watch your NAV. Nine o'clock! Nine o'clock!"

"Get out of there, Lindquist!"

"There's something wrong with my—I can't—AHHH-HHHHHHHHHH!"

The errant Hammerhead careened head-on into the asteroid, and as it did, Shane saw the backside of the stone as it became haloed in light and twinkling, polymeric shards of hull. *Ohmygod.*

"We lost Lindquist! We lost Lindquist!"

"Lindy, acknowledge! Lindy!"

"Shuddup! She's gone!" Mordock screamed.

"No," another pilot argued, "she might've ejected!"

"Negative," Shane said. "There's no beacon, and there was no e-seq signal on my HUD."

"I don't give a shit about what you got, Vansen. Get on your own channel."

"I don't wanna hear nothin' outta your mouth, Perry," Mordock interjected. "Got me?"

Mordock's hysterical personnel were his own problem now. Shane switched to Red channel, which still kept her in contact with each wing leader. "Nathan?"

"I was listening," he said. "Forget about it. Just keep hidden. And keep watching."

"Wing Leaders. Hold positions. You should be picking up the enemy attack force on LIDAR," Commodore Eichner informed.

Three alien hiveships grew ominously into view on Shane's HUD. Each blue-gray vessel was shaped like a pair of massive isosceles pyramids glued at their bases, their tops sheared off at forty-five-degree angles. A long seam divided the upper and lower pyramids, and it was from this gap that a flurry of alien fighters spewed into space.

"*Saratoga* . . . this is Gold Leader. I'm tied on."

"Copy, Gold Leader," communications officer Nelson replied. "Correct for course—"

Shane frowned and adjusted her link. "Nathan, what happened?"

"It's not our link. It's him. Wait. I think I know why. Check your LIDAR."

The enemy armada was moving off its predicted course. If they continued, they would avert the asteroid field.

"*Saratoga*. LIDAR shows the enemy to be—"

"Affirmative, Gold Leader. Will advise," Nelson replied unemotionally.

"ADVISE? They're moving away!"

"Nathan, sit tight," Shane said. "Command knows what they're doing."

"The hell they do! We're sitting here for nothing! Gold Wing. Prepare to move!"

"No, Nathan!"

"Gold Wing . . . hold position," Nelson ordered.

Shane heard Commodore Eichner, who must have been near Nelson, ask, "Could they know we're here?"

"No, they'd attack," McQueen answered.

"Nathan?" she called.

He swore through a sigh. "Holding."

The problem posed a single question that command needed to answer: How could the enemy's course be diverted?

Then Shane had part of the solution. "Something's gotta bring them our way."

twenty-five

The asteroid dipped suddenly, exposing Hawkes's Hammerhead. Frantically, he released his stick and hit retros to drop. The edge of his wing brushed ever-so-slightly against the icy surface of the stone, and he corrected course to achieve at least a two-meter gap. Hiding had been, thus far, an exercise in reflexes, and an exercise that now might prove futile.

Marine intelligence had screwed up again. Surprised? Hawkes wasn't. Pilots knew more about the war than generals. Pilots like Shane. She'd been right. Something would have to bring the enemy their way. Hawkes reached into the hip pocket of his flight suit.

"Commodore. We can't sit here. We gotta act!" Shane protested.

"Negative. This is not a suicide mission. That's an order! Repeat. Hold your position."

Hawkes took a brief look at the gold micro-CD before sliding it into his unauthorized disc drive. He hit PLAY and smiled knowingly.

The opening guitar barrage of The Ramones' "Blitzkrieg Bop" blared through the link.

The officers back on the *Saratoga's* bridge were probably looking at one another, puzzled. They hadn't been present to see Pags's performance of the song. They'd been too busy making feeble plans.

A light flashed on his link's console. Someone was trying to communicate with him on another channel. He dismissed the request, hit full thrusters and pictured himself burning rubber away from his asteroid, singing, "HEY, HO, LET'S GO!" with The Ramones.

He put the long field of rocks mined with Hammerheads below him, and the three hiveships scrolled into the center of his HUD. Hawkes switched link channels so that he could hear both the music and skipchatter. "Fifty-eighth. I'm baitin' them past you."

"I'm coming to help you out," West said.

"Negative, Gold Leader," Shane countered. "Hold your position! He'll bring 'em past. Wait 'til we all can go."

Hawkes's LIDAR picked up so many contacts that its *blipping* rolled into a single tone that said get the hell out of the area. The HUD revealed a black tsunami of planes that was about to come crashing down on him.

Hey, ho, let's go!

He banked hard, riding a wall of space as if he were a bobsledder taking a seventy-five-degree turn. By flying under the first attack wave he was able to roll around behind them. The HUD told him that the wave was still too far from the asteroid field, and not only that, they hadn't spotted him. Only one way to truly draw their attention.

Squeezing every ounce of speed out of the Hammerhead, Hawkes armed all weapons systems and maxed the volume on his micro-CD player. "I'm goin' in! Fangs out!"

Rocketing above the rear squadrons of alien craft, he directed his plane at the lead wing. Target locks floated and—

Guns! Guns! Guns!

Hawkes strafed the craft, gritting his teeth and narrowing his gaze on the HUD. The dorsal wing of the first fighter disintegrated and it went spiraling out of formation. Another enemy plane attempted to avoid Hawkes's fire and banked left—directly into its comrade. The sharp wings of both ships became entangled, and the two rolled end over end to finally separate. Hawkes got a lock on one and put an abrupt end to that pilot's wild ride. Then he jinxed hard right and rolled away, scanning the HUD.

Come on, sucker. Come on. I know you want payback as badly as I.

The wing leader wheeled around and leveled off in pursuit of Hawkes. The rest of its squadron dispersed to follow.

Hawkes knew he had to bring them very close for the ambush to happen. If he could just hold out long enough . . .

Lieutenant Colonel Fouts had said that the Hammerhead was more maneuverable than the enemy's fighters. Hawkes needed for Fouts to be right. He spotted a particularly large asteroid on the fringe of the field and tapped two buttons on his NAV system's console.

WARNING: DEVIATION COURSE NOT LAID IN. AUTO-OVERRIDE DISENGAGED.

Another look at the HUD was cause for minor celebration. "Wing leaders, they're locked in!" he reported excitedly. "Approaching position."

"Wait for it," Shane ordered.

PROXIMITY ALERT. FAILURE TO DEVIATE FROM PRESENT COURSE WILL RESULT IN COLLISION.

The NAV system wasn't happy about flying head-on at an asteroid without assisting the pilot.

TRACKING . . . TRACKING . . . LIDAR JAM INEFFECTIVE. ENEMY CRAFT FIRING . . .

And Hawkes wasn't thrilled about the eruption of alien laser fire.

With both hands on the stick, he watched as the asteroid filled his canopy like a great hand of gray stone and opaque ice, ready to close its fingers around him. He made out tiny fissures in the rock and soft, rolling patterns in the ice as he taught the aliens his version of follow-the-leader.

PROXIMITY ALERT. COLLISION IMMINENT.

But that was what the NAV computer thought, and *it*

wasn't flying the ship. Hawkes had the choice to dive or climb. A data bar reported the dimensions of the asteroid and his course toward it.

Someone was screaming in his link, but, as though in one of his rages, he heard only the racing rhythm of his heart.

Picking the shortest path of evasion, he held his breath, thought of backing off the thrusters, then thought to hell with it. He steered down, turning his fighter into a roller coaster thundering over tracks engineered by a psychopath. Above, the surface of the asteroid wiped by. Ahead, open space waved him home. A concentrated flash originated from behind him. *Got one.*

But then a look to his HUD indicated that at least six more jets still vied for a piece of him. He pulled up, leveling beneath the asteroid field. Both sides of his canopy lit up under weapons' fire that came so close it would have fogged his glass in an atmosphere. He cut left into a roll—

—but a bolt struck the Hammerhead where the canopy's seam met the hull. Talons of energy pried into the ship and played across his console. He came out of his roll, hit forward retros, then pulled back.

No response from the jet. His stick was dead.

The NAV system control panel flickered, went dark for a moment, then flickered again.

"My control's froze," he screamed into his link.

TRACKING SEVEN CONTACTS. LIDAR JAM INEFFECTIVE. SUB-CHANNELS JAMMED BY ENEMY.

He beat a fist on the NAV panel, which continued to short-out.

TRACKING THIRTEEN CONTACTS. LIDAR JAM INEFFECTIVE. SUB-CHANNELS JAMMED BY ENEMY.

Cocking his head, Hawkes gaped at the triangular formations of black claws. His breath quickened. Then he lost it. "I'm dead."

"KILL RIGHT THRUSTERS, YOU STUPID TANK!"

The cool, reserved veteran never sounded more emotional. Obeying McQueen, Hawkes was slammed back into his seat as he shot far ahead of his pursuers and discovered that control was once again his.

But what did the right thrusters have to do with the NAV system? That console was steadily illuminated now, and a data bar stated: SHORT BYPASSED. RIGHT THRUSTER CONTROL DISENGAGED. Hawkes realized that he must have been hit in the tail, and it was *that* bolt which had temporarily off-lined his NAV.

"Downtown!" Shane yelled, and Hawkes saw her fighter jinx left and out of the asteroid field.

At the moment, with more than a dozen of the enemy still on his rear, Hawkes decided to once again test the bugs' driving skills . . . and bravery. He adjusted the micro-CD player to repeat the "Blitzkrieg Bop," banked sharply right, then pointed *Pags's Payback* at the aliens. With drums pounding, vocals resounding, and targets locked, he let his rage consume him as he cackled and released his first salvo.

twenty-six

"I want you to team up. Golds One and Two . . .
Go. Golds Three and Four . . . Go," Nathan commanded,
then watched as his wing broke off in pairs, Carter and
Low to the right, Wang and Damphousse to the left.

What Nathan feared almost as much as the alien laser
fire was flying into one of the craft. His NAV system
made vector corrections, but a hit like the one Hawkes
had taken would send Nathan out of control into the
dozens of individual dogfights. To call the battle a furball was an understatement. He would make it a point
to tell Sergeant Bougus to invent a new word.

"Three on our six," Damphousse accounted shakily.
"Carter? Low? Can you help us shake 'em."

"I'm going to roll back for a shot," Wang said.

"Hold off a mike," Low told him, "I'm locked and . . .
FIRING!"

"Holy . . . Good shot, Low!"

"Thanks, but there's—Wang! LOOKOUT!"

"Cutting . . . away . . . and"—Wang hissed—"THERE."
Laser fire blazed from his ship and struck one, two,
three alien fighters which melted off Nathan's HUD.
"HOO-YAH!" the young Marine yelped.

"You been taking lessons from Coop?" Damphousse
asked Wang.

"Speaking of him," Carter said. "He just buzzed about
twelve of 'em and took out at least half. But check your
HUDS. They're running him ragged."

Shane's fighter sliced across Nathan's path, and he
turned his head to watch her zero in on three enemy

planes. "They do fly in gangs," she murmured, then followed up her words with a pyrotechnic eruption from her guns that sent one of the fighters tumbling and shedding glowing splinters of its hull. The remaining two ships veered off to avoid Shane's cannons and the debris of the destroyed jet.

"This is R-Three," Hawkes identified. "I'm defensive. Little help!"

Nathan's NAV system traced the signal and displayed the tank's ship on the HUD. Bucking and rolling, Hawkes was unable to evade the seven, no, now eight ships in diamond formation that hunted him. A round of alien fire glanced a forward wing on his fighter's nose.

"Hang on, Hawkes," he said, then executed a rolling climb to put him over the tank's coordinates. Once above the fray, Nathan brought himself around to descend at a forty-five-degree angle upon the alien wings' six. There wasn't much distance between the lead fighter and Hawkes. Nathan opted to intercept that craft first. His Hammerhead vibrated as he increased velocity and swooped, target locks swirling, swirling, but failing to lock.

Dammit!

His mouth went dry as he decided to strafe the jet anyway, but his volley of bolts either fell short or merely grazed it. Nathan soared over the craft then nudged his stick to climb.

Engines flared as the alien fighter lifted away from its wing in pursuit.

Nathan pulled himself into an inverted loop, and while upside down he nervously checked his HUD. The alien was a wasp buzzing intently about his neck. As they pulled out of the loop, the enemy plane shot after him, sewing up the gap to half a ship's length. The NAV system console beeped.

PROXIMITY ALERT. COURSE—

There were more words on the screen, but Nathan

didn't waste time reading them. The view through his canopy was inevitably clear:

Hawkes's Hammerhead strung along two remaining aliens and all three were on a collision course with Nathan.

He gasped, two-handed the stick and slammed it toward the instrument panels. "HAWKES! HIT THE DECK!"

Nathan revved his thrusters and simultaneously nosedived with Hawkes. Their fighters passed within ten meters of each other, and the long shadows of the tank's plane cast Nathan's cockpit in gloom. Warnings spilled across the NAV system's screen as Nathan flicked his glance between it and the inverted SA-43 overhead.

Behind them, the alien plane that had been on Nathan's tail collided with the other two jets, sending an expanding ball of metallic smithereens in all directions. The thruster tubes of Nathan's ship were struck by some of the wreckage, jolting the craft repeatedly before the fragments were either melted or floated away.

Nathan threw back his head. "Yeeeeeeahhhhhh!"

A war cry from Shane echoed his.

"Not so fast," Hawkes said. "Bandit is locked on you, Shane. Check six!"

Nathan's LIDAR sounded an alarm.

"You see it, West?"

"Yeah," Nathan answered. "I'm on it."

"In your trail," Hawkes replied.

"Your NAV system up for it?"

Hawkes snickered. "We'll find out."

"MARK!"

Nathan arced wide under the belly of the battle. Blue and White Wings had joined forces and furiously engaged a score of alien craft that were attempting to run a pinwheel formation around them. Hammerheads spat glowing venom at the aliens, tearing their ring to shreds.

"Nice counter, Mordock!" Nathan complemented the other wing leader.

"Can't talk to you now, West," Mordock said, his transmission breaking up. "I'm hit. HOTAS control gone. Bypass ineffective."

"Get the hell out of there!" Nathan cried.

Two contacts neared Mordock's ship, then it disappeared soundlessly from Nathan's HUD.

"I've got her course plotted," Hawkes broke in. "ETA: thirteen seconds . . . twelve . . . eleven . . . "

Shane was beginning to panic. "Can't jink him!"

"You're running at eighty-five," Nathan said, feeling his hands begin to shake as he read her velocity from his HUD. "Max those thrusters!"

"They are!" she argued. "This is all I'm getting! He's firing!"

"Evade," Nathan shouted. "Brake and yaw!"

"We got about five seconds to do something, West," Hawkes observed bleakly. "And I don't know about you, but this bug's got my target locks jammed solid."

"Pull up alongside me," Nathan ordered. "We'll run an X-pattern in front of him . . . draw him away."

"Copy."

"Go!"

Nathan and Hawkes came up on the alien's tail like madmen, howling in their links and laying down wild fire. They burst in front of the ship, cutting across the alien's path in scissors-fashion. It was up to the alien which target he'd choose to follow.

But the son of a bitch kept on Shane's six.

Nathan banked wide and came up once again on his quarry.

Hawkes's Hammerhead was high and astern, but it was rising and falling as if riding on tall waves. "West, my NAV's freaking again. I can't get to her."

"Hold position. I have an idea."

With that, Nathan swept forward, skimming over the alien and Shane, then yo-yoed inside behind Shane, putting the bug on his six. He thumbed a button on his thruster control, then tapped in two numbers to jettison .08 percent of thruster coolant, hoping to confuse or slow the alien. He broke rapidly away.

The alien knifed through the liquid blob and continued doggedly after Shane.

"Gotta go for a shot, West," Hawkes said.

Nathan circled and put the alien in front of him. A fraction of a degree mistake would send his fire toward Shane. Gooseflesh fanned across his shoulders as he thought of how he'd nearly killed Hawkes by making a similar shot. "She's in my line . . . if I engage I could hit her!"

"Just do it, Nathan!" Shane pleaded.

Nathan reached inside himself, wanting to pull out his demon. He couldn't. She was too close. She would die in front of him. He had to shoot. No. The cockpit was suddenly too small. His eyes were watering now.

There was nowhere to run.

A spate of laser fire suddenly reached out for Shane's craft, promising to cripple or destroy it.

Noooooo!

But then each bolt was systematically picked off before it struck Shane while a volley of fire rained down from above and tore the alien ship in half.

Nathan rocked sideways to avoid the glistening hulk which tumbled away from him.

"HOO-YAH! POPPED 'IM GOOD, NATHAN!"

Frowning, then double checking his weapons console, Nathan answered, "I didn't fire!"

"Who got the kill?" Hawkes asked.

"Uh, why don't you guys check your three," Shane suggested.

Nathan felt an adrenaline rush as he watched four immense supercarriers advance in box formation from behind the alien hiveships. In the minutes that followed, a fleet of Hammerheads wove tight patterns through the asteroid field and emerged with laser cannons pumping enough fire to sweep clear the remaining alien jets. The supercarriers bombarded the hiveships in a spectacular hail of fire that brought daylight to the heavens. Outnumbered, the hiveships recalled the fighters launching from their bays and fled toward the dark side of the Jovian moon Ganymede.

Falling into a wedge pattern with Hawkes and Shane, Nathan leaned back and took in a long breath that he'd put on hold since leaving the *Saratoga*.

Communication officer Nelson's voice came over the link. "Fifty-eight . . . this is command. Damage is nominal. Enemy in retreat. Return to base. Objective achieved."

The supercarriers continued to target the enemy, only now it wasn't a battle but a distant fireworks show of celebration. Nathan joined the rest of the fighting fifty-eighth, who cheered in the link as they headed home.

Mom, Dad, everyone. I made it. I'm all right.

twenty-seven

The United States Marine Corps Space Aviator recruit depot, Loxley, Alabama, radiated in more than just the sunlight of a perfect afternoon. The eyes of everyone in the fifty-eighth squadron shone with a brilliance that Nathan knew was seen by every applauding Marine and civilian seated in the bleachers. He spotted Mom, Dad, Neil, and John, and surprisingly, Kylen's father, who winked and waved a fist. Nathan wanted to lift the gleaming medal hanging from his neck to make sure they saw it, but certainly they did, and besides, he was at attention.

Behind the line of Marines facing the audience was a stage erected on the tarmac. American and Earth flags served as backdrops, and beneath these was a podium at which Spencer Chartwell addressed the audience. "Welcome. I don't usually attend these sort of things, but the extraordinary work of these brave young men and women demanded my presence. Today is a special day for all of us. Because of the valiant efforts of the Marine Corps fifty-eighth squadron, the many peoples of Earth breathe a single sigh of relief. And now, at their graduation ceremony, we honor them."

Nathan saw Shane's eyes swell with tears, then he looked quickly away and held his head rigid.

"I believe the great twentieth century leader Winston Churchill would agree: 'Never in the field of conflict has so much been owed by so many to so few.'"

The audience applauded, and Kylen's father got those

around him to their feet. It took nearly a minute for the clapping to subside.

"We of Earth are proud and grateful. Celebrate well, although I suppose the break in the storm is momentary. The thunder shall return. The lightning will certainly strike again."

Nathan would completely enjoy his respite from the war, for the truth in Chartwell's words was disturbingly plain. At least when the thunder and lightning did return, the Marines would be ready for it, and the proof flew overhead.

New and old members of the Angry Angels swooped out of the sun and roared across the sky. As the squadron passed over the crowd, they executed a single, perfectly choreographed barrel roll in recognition of the fifty-eighth.

Sergeant Bougus came down the line of Marines, pausing to acknowledge each with the snap of his white-gloved hand to his forehead. Members of the crowd stood and saluted the squadron. Bougus arrived in front of Nathan. The sergeant gave a slight nod after his salute, a nod that presumably meant Nathan had done all right.

By nightfall, the carnival atmosphere had moved to the apron outside an empty hangar, where a bar had been set up and two Marines with synthesizers played popular songs. Some pilots danced with their spouses or friends, while others sat at tables chatting and drinking with their families. Nathan saw one old man roll up his sleeve for his grandson to reveal his eagle, Earth, and anchor tattoo, which he boasted he'd had done on the Mars colony.

Mom, Dad, and his brothers soon went back to the hotel for a swim, and they took Kylen's father with them. The man did not want to be too far from his television. Feeling a little lost, Nathan wandered over to the bar, where Wang and Damphousse stood listening to Low tell her animated and perhaps slightly exaggerated account of combat.

"And then I cut left retros and he's right there, the idiot, and I have him locked. One, two, he's gone," she said, spilling her drink on her wrist, not out of intoxication but excitement. "Oops."

"At least you control your plane better than that glass," Nathan chided with a grin.

"Here," Shane said, coming from behind him and handing him a drink. "We're gonna have a toast."

Hawkes, who'd been sitting alone at the other end of the bar, responded to Shane's nod and joined them. Glasses were lifted.

"Here's—" Shane began, then broke off as McQueen stepped up.

Nathan and the others straightened in the veteran's presence, and Nathan, like everyone else, did so not out of military protocol but out of deep-felt respect.

McQueen allowed himself the trace of a grin. "Congratulations." He shook hands with the group, finishing with Shane.

"Sir. I . . . your advice, those words in the orientation room . . . they kept us alive," Shane said. "And we appreciate your saying them."

"Save it. You'll have all the chances in the world to thank me. I've just been assigned as your squadron commander."

Brows lifted in pleasant surprise, and Nathan found himself chilled over the prospect until—

"And if you people ever pull anything like what you did under *my* command, the only metal you'll be wearing are cuffs in the stockade." He moved toward the end of the bar, gestured to the bartender for a drink, then faced the group, ready to join the toast.

Wang regarded McQueen with a shrug. "At least he doesn't yell."

Shane raised her glass, her gaze trained on the veteran. "Here's . . . to being alive for one more hour."

Nathan clinked glasses with the rest, then watched as Hawkes and McQueen subtly raised their glasses to each other. Moving to the bar, Nathan took a sip of his champagne, then set down the drink.

He had been happy, truly happy, for most of the day. But now he couldn't help but notice his photo tags tangled with the medal on his chest. Had he already forgotten that the reason he'd joined the Corps was the possibility of seeing Kylen again? For a short time maybe he had. He untangled the tags and lifted her picture. Shane slid a hand onto his shoulder, and he offered her a wan smile of thanks before moving away.

"Where are you going?"

"I forgot something."

epilogue

Nathan lay prone on his cot in the dark bar-racks. A small flashlight rested at his elbow, illuminating his journal. He rubbed the flat end of a pencil tip over a blank page, revealing the imprint of words he had written to Kylen. He remembered most of them, but he wanted to be sure. When he was done, he copied the letter onto another page and pocketed the journal.

After hiking to the far north end of the base, he looked back at the victory party, now just a blanket of tiny lights and muffled sounds. Then he considered the glimmering stars, stars thankfully at rest. He gripped his photo tags in one hand, the medal in the other, and thought of the end of his letter.

Elsewhere . . . stars are born. Other systems, much larger, much older, continue to breathe.

He imagined a brilliant flow of yellow and red gas drifting before distant stars. The gas dissolved into the image of a spiral galaxy, a beautiful celestial flower in full bloom.

The solar system dies of crib death . . . if that's what it takes, then okay.

A comet trailing a brilliant ice blue tail streaked toward a dimming Earth.

If I must wait that long, then all right. Because when I think of this . . . nothing is more desirable than the hope of watching that last day when the sun flickers out, with you beside me. We'll sit alone on a dark chunk of ice at the top of the world and . . .

Reeling from a burst of loss and longing, Nathan tore

the medal from his neck and pitched it with all his might at the bright blue star that was to have been his home.

He watched the medal fall light-years short of Kylen, but that didn't matter. He whispered his promise:

"The stars above, below, and between us will never shine brighter . . . as we drift away . . . into space."

Peter Telep has written for the television shows *In The Heat of The Night* and *The Legend of Prince Valiant.* He is the recipient of the John W. Steinbeck Award for fiction, has been a winner in the *Writer's Digest* magazine contest in both the fiction and script categories, and holds a B.A. in English from the University of Central Florida. His other novels, *Squire* and *Squire's Blood,* are also available from HarperPrism, as will be the forthcoming *Squire's Honor.* Mr. Telep lives in Orlando, Florida, with his wife Nancy.